THE
12TH
CLEANSING

THE
12TH
CLEANSING

A COLD CASE REIGNITED
BY A SERIAL KILLER'S RETURN

N. JOSEPH GLASS

Copyright © 2025 by N. Joseph Glass

First paperback edition 2025
ISBN 978-1-80541-804-7 (Paperback)
ISBN 978-1-80541-805-4 (eBook)

glassauthor.com

Day 1

WALKER MICHAELS

Gruesome scenes never got easier to look at the more he saw them. In each new body Detective Walker Michaels examined, the face of the first victim stared at him, begging for justice. It shone clear and vivid as a memory burned into his brain, haunting his nightmares. As horrific as that was, at least his eyes no longer transposed his daughter's face onto the victim. She had escaped this lunatic's rampage.

A four-year gap led him to conclude this was over—a cold case with no more victims being the best outcome he could reach. Now the evidence shone clearly under the sunshine waking the park's emerald-green grass. The Moralist was back.

Detective Michaels' head hung from a limp neck. The wilted shoulders under his navy-blue suit jacket couldn't bear the weight of another dead teenage girl. He closed his eyes to the four years he wasted rebuilding his career, himself, from the ashes of the consuming fire of that notorious serial killer case. Any phoenix he thought he raised disintegrated inside him like a tissue to a flame. Another young lady had been robbed of life under his watch. The task ahead of informing her parents slid into the background of a deep sigh.

"Whatcha think, Boss. Gotta be him, *right*?"

Brandon Jones, Walker Michaels' newest partner, always asked the obvious questions. In Michaels' experience, that fit the job description of Junior Detective—at least on the Marietta City police force. The senior detective wondered if he had annoyed his superiors this much before he had earned his stripes.

"Mm… Same M.O."

Running his fingers through his salt-and-pepper hair, he squinted at his partner studying the body. From thin crooked post to thin crooked post, a warm breeze rustled a distorted circle of yellow police tape encircling the body. Its flapping split the dawn's silence like static. As far as Michaels knew, this was the first murder victim the rookie detective had ever seen. Some vomited. Remembering the harassment he had endured over twenty years back, he never gave a newbie any flak for it.

"He'd been doing, *what*? Three or four of these a year for three years. Looks like he's back after a four-year hiatus, *right*?"

Ignoring the history lesson on his own case, Michaels squatted beside the body. The air reeked of the lemony scent dripping from the white blossoms adorning the forty-foot Southern Magnolia. The morning sun did its best to slice through its thick-leaved branches, blanketing the vic in heavy shadow. About sixteen, he reckoned, and laid out in the usual manner. As with all the others, the Moralist had turned this young woman into an exhibition. Laying naked and face up in the grass, she had a fig leaf sewn over her genitalia, her arms extended in a crucifix posture.

"*Doing these?*" The senior detective twisted his neck to look up at Jones. "He slaughtered these young women, desecrated their bodies, and put them on display."

"I meant no disrespect, Boss. Just trying to put it all together. I know nobody knows this case like you. It's the only one you never solved, *right?*"

"Would you quit calling me 'Boss' already," he barked in a raspy voice. "I ain't nobody's boss, least of all yours."

"Sorry, B— um…"

"Michaels will do. Or hadn't you noticed *everyone* at the station using last names, *Detective?*"

With gloved hands and sharp eyes, Michaels examined the body. As expected, he found no bruises or signs of struggle. Every detail screamed at him, taunting him. His cold case had reheated, and his nemesis had returned to the hunt. As he stood, his knees protested the movement with crackles that warned of early-onset arthritis. Worse in the colder months, it was one of the only good things about a Georgia summer. He ran the back of his hand over his sweaty brow.

"I want you to study the body and the scene. Take all the time you need. Write notes, ask questions. You need to learn from this, and, who knows? You might even make yourself useful to the investigation."

The younger man with the rolled-up sleeves had a unique way about him. After circling the girl's body half a dozen times, he squatted, stood, hunched over her, and prostrated himself. To look in her ears, Jones moved the hair off her shoulder with his pen the way they did in too many cop shows. And they always put that contaminated pen back in their pocket. Something about the young lady's neck caused Michaels to hold back an insulting comment, but it wasn't the lack of bruising he had noted earlier.

Officer Willoughby approached and offered Michaels a coffee from the Starbucks across the park, which he readily accepted—black with two sugars. Awakened by his phone at 5:38, he had dressed and rushed out too hurriedly to get his morning jolt, leaving the memory of his wife in the empty bed. After slurping a sip of the scalding pick-me-up, Michaels asked the girl's name. The Moralist always left a calling card.

"Sandy Rawlings." Willoughby handed him the note.

Sandy Rawlings is another victim of the immorality plaguing our society. It is prolific, saturating our media and corrupting young minds. This child of God has been cleansed and absolved of her sins.

Pinching the cardstock paper between his fingers, Michaels said, "Word for word."

"Didn't identify you by name this time."

"Only did that once. And not on the note with the body... This, this is him."

"I was afraid of that even before I got here... from the way the witness described the scene. I hoped to be wrong, then I found the note."

From a scowl, Michaels grumbled, "I assume the forensic photographer got pictures of the scene *before you touched* anything."

"Of course. And, I guess we should have left the note for you detectives. We just wanted to know if it was really him."

"You should have, yes." Michaels pushed an almost empty cup into the officer's hand and showed him his back.

"The M.E. will do the detail work, Jones. When you're done CSI-ing, I want you to question the man who found her."

"*Me?*"

"Would you rather take the lead when we visit Miss Rawlings' parents?"

ALLEN RAWLINGS

A llen Rawlings sat in the armchair watching his wife burrowing a channel into the carpet. Jesus swung on the cross around her neck with each step. Neither had slept nor eaten, and Sonya didn't even sit. Every passing hour intensified Allen's prayers.

Late last night, the police had told Allen there was nothing they could do and not to worry. The lady cop's reassurances that teenage girls sometimes stayed out all night and to call back if they hadn't heard from her in forty-eight hours did little to settle him and only seemed to make Sonya more agitated. They had fought when Allen insisted on going to look for Sandra. More than his wife's pleading and sobbing, when Allen realized he had no idea where his daughter was, he dropped his key fob. His phone calls woke anyone who might have had a clue where Sandra might have gone.

An ominous alert dinged from the phone in his hand. The *Ring* doorbell app announced someone approaching the house. Sonya ignored it or perhaps hadn't heard it over her mumbled prayers. Allen's heart plunged into his stomach when he saw an older man in a dark blue suit and a younger one in a green shirt and silver tie coming up the walkway. These were not Mormons or Jehovah's Witnesses. He didn't have the ardor for a scriptural argument in him this morning anyway. Uniformed officers might have brought hope. These two came for something entirely different.

"Sonya, go check that Connor's still sleeping or has his headphones on, would you? Don't call him, just see he's as isolated and oblivious as usual."

She furled her brow at him as she often did and offered no reply. As she doddered up the stairs, Allen walked to the door before the plain-clothes detectives could ring the bell. From the cross above the door, his Lord and Savior cast a solemn gaze. A promise to watch over those who passed under him until they returned home.

Both men raised eyebrows at the door swinging into the house to reveal Allen standing there, downcast and disheveled. When they asked if he was Mister Rawlings, Allen nodded and stepped aside. Like a rehearsed scene in a Shakespearian tragedy, each acted their part with an unspoken acceptance of what this was. The somber gentlemen entered, half-nodding to Allen as they passed.

He studied the square of parquet flooring as they stepped inside, then asked them to remove their shoes, knowing how Sonya would react to seeing them polluting the beige carpet they had installed five or six months ago. The men obliged, though the younger one removed his loafers with a grimace. They said nothing as they followed Allen's gesture to sit on the sofa.

"Mister Rawlings, is anyone else at home? Your wife, perhaps?"

Nodding, he said, "She'll be right down. I didn't want my son here for this."

They didn't reply, but the older man, clearly worn-out and weathered, gave him a knowing look. When Sonya returned, her face showed no surprise at finding these men in her living room. The senior stood and said, "Ma'am."

"Thank you for removing your shoes," she said matter-of-factly. "It's why you'd never tell this carpet is already two years old. Would you gentlemen like some coffee?"

Trapping his junior partner in a half-nod, the older man said, "No, thank you."

"This is about Sandy, isn't it? You've started looking, I take it." She sat in the chair Allen had vacated, and he stood beside her, clasping her hand. In her other, she pinched the crucifix at her chest. "We told that cop on the phone our Sandy doesn't stay out past curfew and is no runaway. She's not like those other girls. We raised her right."

"I'm sure you did, ma'am. And yes, we're here with news of your daughter…" He cleared his throat of its obvious lump.

The words stabbed like a sword, confirming what Allen had already concluded. His eyes glossed over when he saw some of the tension flee his wife's shoulders, knowing her naïve misunderstanding gave her a measure of hope these men were about to crush.

"There has been an incident. Early this morning, a jogger in Bishop park noticed something unusual under a magnolia tree and went to take a closer look…"

The detective, who had not introduced himself, paused. Allen understood the technique. Starting with 'Your daughter is dead' would be too shattering a blow. As if it could help, they would slowly get there in a futile effort to break the news gently.

"He found the body of a young woman, a teenager…"

Allen studied the face he had spent twenty-one years of marriage trying to read and found it expectant and ill-prepared for the coming devastation.

"We confirmed her identity when her personal items were found not far from the body… I'm afraid that young lady was your daughter… I'm terribly sorry for your loss."

As if unfazed by the overwhelming revelation, Sonya's face remained blank. "I see."

Squeezing her hand, Allen stared at her. The realization had not yet clouded her eyes. To let his wife hear the words, he turned to the older man and asked, "She… was murdered?" He also needed to solidify this nightmare that changed their lives forever. Unless he, too, was stubbornly grasping a thread of Sonya's irrational hope.

"I'm afraid so, sir. We'll have more detail from the coroner, but we believe she died between the hours of midnight and 4 AM."

"What… happened? Did she suffer?" Allen spoke through tears and a mess of mucus dripping from his nose. He thoughtlessly ran the backside of his hand under his nostrils.

"We don't believe so. She was found lying in a park. Her clothes were folded neatly beside her. She had been—"

"It wasn't her." With her hands freed, Sonya intertwined her fingers between her bouncing knees and leaned forward in her seat. "I have no idea who you men are… coming in here and saying such awful things. *Get out*," she yelled. Rising to her feet, she repeated, "Get out. Now! Get out of my house." Like a burst water balloon, the tear ducts sprang loose, and she bellowed a guttural groan.

Both men rose to their feet and the older one reached a hand toward Sonya's shoulder. Allen pulled his wife into an embrace and joined her in open sobbing.

After granting the couple's grief its needed space, the senior detective said, "We will need to talk but realize this isn't the time. Detective Jones will stay here to answer any questions you have and can also help you find a way to tell

Sandy's brother… when you're ready." He handed Mister Rawlings a business card. "I'm Detective Walker Michaels. That's my cell number. You can call me any time, day or night."

"*Michaels*? Aren't you…" Allen pinched his eyes shut for a moment as Sonya continued dampening his shoulder. "No. Not that. It wasn't him. My little girl… and he… He, he can't be back." His cracked voice barely squeaked out the last syllable, and he dry-swallowed. "It can't be."

"We believe it was… Mister and Missus Rawlings, I will come back a bit later. After you've had a little time, we'll have some questions."

SONYA RAWLINGS

Sonya washed the dishes her husband and Detective Jones had left beside the sink—not in it, where they were supposed to go. In a hand reddened by the water's blistering heat, she pinched a yellow sponge and circled it over the flat plate. Breaching the window's repression, her empty gaze focused on the trampoline in the narrow yard of their one-and-a-half-acre lot. A memory of seven-year-old Sandy relentlessly practicing landing on her little bottom and bouncing back into a stand replayed in her mind. Connor laughed and taunted his big sister. That was before his first phone and tablet stole his attention from his family.

It seemed pointless now for Allen to have forbidden a video game console from entering the house only to give the boy two devices with thousands of games and apps at his fingertips. For Connor's twelfth birthday, his father gave him his first PlayStation. Allen had started traveling more for work by then. Their children were raised in a different world, thirty years being an incalculable chasm in technology designed to "babysit" for busy parents. A stay-at-home mom, Sonya never wanted those distractions.

Supposedly doing his homeschooling, Connor still hadn't come down. He had not seen the strange men in the home or met the one who stayed for reasons Sonya couldn't guess. How her son would react to this devastation wove into her grief. A distraction that offered no consolation.

"Honey." The voice filtered through the cascade from the tap and the clank of the *good* silverware Sonya neatly arranged in the drying rack. Pausing with dishcloth in hand, she turned, but not to Allen. Pulling open the flatware drawer, she confirmed what she knew well. There were plenty of clean *everyday* forks and spoons. The no-slam drawers in the kitchen they installed when they bought the house robbed her of an emphatic complaint her lips would never offer.

"Honey, Detective Jones would like to speak with us."

"Why is he even here? They come here… that man with him… and tell us… I mean, they devastate our family, our lives." Words yielded to the lump lodged in Sonya's throat. She closed her eyes and took a breath. "All he's done is eat breakfast and drink our coffee. And we had to wait on him like he's some sort of house guest or something."

Allen stepped forward and laid his hands on his wife's shoulders. "He wants to help us speak with Connor. He says the way we tell him about his sister can make a difference in how he handles the news."

"*News*?" She brushed his hands away and took a half-step back. "Our daughter is... and you call it news?"

"I didn't mean... I think it's a good idea to hear him out. Can you stop all this wallowing for a second to imagine how this will affect Connor? Jones has training. It's one of the reasons he's still here. And he offered to speak with Connor, too, if that could help. I have no idea how to tell him his sister—"

"This is a family matter—*our* family. It feels like... like, I can't even cry with that man in our home."

Confronting how she had been holding back her tears unleashed them in a torrent. Her legs lost the will to support her, and Sonya fell into her husband's embrace. The forgotten feeling of Allen's hand consolingly rubbing her back lacked any calming effect. He handed her a tissue, and she quickly needed another.

"Mom... is everything okay? Who's that man in the living room?"

CONNOR RAWLINGS

something was terribly wrong. Connor could not recall the last time he had seen his mother cry like that—if ever. Emotional and irritatingly affectionate, sure, but never a wreck, fallen apart and blathering like this. Dad said nothing. He looked at Connor with an unfamiliar glaze in his eye, something Connor didn't understand. After blowing her nose, Mom used her palm to flatten the wrinkles in her dress.

Only when Connor noticed his mother had on the same dress she wore to church yesterday did it hit him. According to the clock, his sister should have gone to school. Connor knew she hadn't. "Where's Sandy?"

* * *

Eyes closed, leaning back in his Secret Lab gaming chair, Connor let the music drown out the world. Noise-cancelling headphones had sheltered him from reality, from his family, when things were bad, which was most of the time. This had surpassed every day before, and he sought that isolation more than ever. "Your sister didn't come home last night." That was how they started. "There has been an... *incident*," they called it.

"Why don't adults talk to teenagers as real people, not like kids," he mentally grumbled. They never said the words. Two simple words. "She's dead." That was all they had to say. "Your sister skipped curfew last night and now she's dead." No, they said 'incident' as if that made it better, made Sandy not dead or something. His mind fought the onslaught of the pounding drums of the music Dad would freak out over him listening to. Vivid mental images of the conversation ploughed through his thoughts despite his best efforts to defeat them.

Something touched his shoulder, and his body jerked forward from its lean. A scrunched, blood-red face turned to complain to whichever parent violated the agreed upon knock-before-entering rule in place since he turned twelve.

That detective had breached Connor's private sanctum.

He didn't look much older than twenty-something until he gestured to silence the music and remove the headphones the way his dad would—like an old man. Eying the Atlanta Braves commemorative baseball bat leaning against the wall by the closet door, Connor's impulses raged inside him. He stood and pulled the headphones from his ears. The music blared from the center of the cushioned pads and the tall guy in Connor's room widened his eyes. The lyrics *"Please tell Lucifer he can't have this one. Her spirit is too strong"* thrusted through the air between them.

"*Crack the Skye*," the man said. "Appropriate enough, I guess."

Connor shrugged then pulled his eyes up from the floor. "*You* know Mastodon?" He pressed pause on the Spotify widget on his phone's screen.

"That album was inspired by the death of the drummer's sister. Her name was Skye."

No words came. Connor didn't know if he needed any.

"And the *solution*—" the cop used air quotes "—the song ends on?" When Connor didn't reply, the man continued, "I can see the pain. You can make it all go away."

"Dailer's sister, Skye, committed… My sister was killed. Oh, sorry. I mean she died in an *incident*." Connor used his own sarcastic air quotes over his sharp tone.

The stranger in his room dropped his shoulders and focused his eyes. "Look, there's no playbook for this sorta thing. Your parents are hurt, blindsided by this tragedy. I know you are, too. Understand they have no idea how to act or what to say, let alone how to tell their son his sister was murdered."

"So, it was murder then? Not some fight with her boyfriend that got outta hand?"

"Boyfriend? We'll want more four-one-one on that... when you're ready."

After rolling his eyes, Connor said, "He's back, isn't he? The Moralist killed my sister."

"Why'd you say that?"

"I just googled it. He's the only one I've ever heard of killing teenage girls. And he was never caught. Plus, Sandy's boyfriend. Her date last night. That sicko psycho was a stalker. Kills 'em when they finally give it up."

The detective played the part by pulling a small, black-covered notebook and a pen from his back pants pocket. "Let me get this straight. You're saying you knew she was seeing this boy... and planned to have sex with him last night, *right*?"

"I thought she'd lost it a while ago, you know. Almost seventeen. I think I was wrong... by how nervous she was. Isn't that when the Moralist strikes?"

"Some time after, yeah. Though he's even struck at least once before the deed was done."

"Cleansing them and saving their soul or something. Sandy didn't need no soul saving. She was..." His voice cracked and he paused, turning his head from the cop to the window. After a second or maybe a few, he turned back to face the man taking notes. "She was selfish and conceited but wasn't nobody's slut."

An extended palm asked permission to sit, and Connor nodded. The man sat on the edge of the unmade bed.

"Would you like to talk about her? Sandy, I mean?"

Connor sat in his chair. "You a cop or a shrink?"

"Detective, actually. And I will nail the bastard who did this to your sister. If I can help in any other way, I'll do that too."

Connor sniffled and ran the backside of his hand under his nose. "You said when I'm ready. I'm not. Go talk to my parents, though they won't have much to say besides how wonderful Sandy is. Um, was. She's with God now, Dad'll tell you. They're oblivious. Oh, don't mention the boyfriend in front of my dad. He'll go ballistic."

After slapping both of his thighs, the detective stood and sighed. "You're right. When you're ready." Stepping into the hall, he turned back to face Connor. "Ever get into Periphery?"

"Some, sure."

"Give *It's Only Smiles* a listen. Singer's sister died, and he pours his feelings into that one. I think it's a better fit even than *Crack the Skye*."

It surprised Connor when the cop closed the door, returning him to the seclusion that, for the first time, filled the room with emptiness. His thumb swiped over the keyboard in the Spotify search field. Pulling the headphones over his ears, he let the music take him elsewhere. A song about a dead sister kept him in the moment. What didn't he know about Sandy?

WALKER
MICHAELS

I t had been at least two years since Woody retired. Detective Michaels had only been to see the new medical examiner once. That case was open-and-shut as the murder weapon had been found in the suspect's car, lying on the passenger seat. The guy didn't even try to hide the blood-drenched hammer from the officer who pulled him over for a busted taillight.

For the life of him, Walker Michaels couldn't recall the new M.E.'s name as he pushed the double swinging doors to the autopsy room. The dreadful image of the corpse that used to be young Sandy Rawlings greeted him, toes first. Michaels couldn't stop his eyes from crawling up her legs to stare at the leaf, the telltale mark of the Moralist.

A wave of gratitude swept through him for his own daughter Bonnie having married young, just after graduating from Kennesaw State University. She was a teenager and single when the killings started, the demented cleansing ceremonies of the Moralist. Every ring of his cellphone back then came with a morbid fear of finding the next desecrated and lifeless body of a young girl not a stranger.

Now he looked upon Sandra Rawlings, a life extinguished before finishing high school. He knew the cause of death, the methods used, and how she supposedly didn't suffer through the ritual. The Moralist kept his victims alive. Woody had Michaels repeatedly assure the families of those poor girls they were not truly conscious as he performed female genital mutilation. He shook his head at the memory as he knew he had said it to lift a trace of pain from the parents' immense grief.

That mental picture stabbed his heart, so he purged it from his mind, unable to comprehend a young woman being even semiconscious as she was being butchered. Although unverified, he was grateful Woody had put his conclusion on his reports and the parents were told a less horrifying version of their daughters' last moments. Perhaps it would help ease the Rawlings' agony as well. "Did she suffer?" Sandy's father had asked.

"Detective Michaels."

Finally able to pull his gaze from the body, Michaels looked the man in his unfamiliar face. It lacked the calming effect of Woody's compassionate eyes. "Sorry, yes. Doctor...?"

"Young. You can call me Travis."

They didn't shake hands, as the appropriately named youthful medical examiner's were already gloved and ready to work. As if to find Woody Clayton standing there as touched by the death as himself, Michaels studied the room. All he found was Travis Young's clinical stare.

"Just call me Michaels. No one calls me Walker. Too many Chuck Norris jokes there." When the blank stare scrunched into a puzzled look, he added, "You know, Walker, Texas Ranger?"

"Oh, from Talladega Nights. Classic."

All Michaels could do was wag his head at this kid. "So, what have you got so far?"

"Not much. I'm just getting started. But I've reviewed Doctor Clayton's notes on the Moralist slayings, and, at a perfunctory stage, this looks like his modus operandi."

"That much was—" Michaels pretended to clear his throat. "Thanks for the preliminary. How soon before you have something? Time of death would be great to know sooner than later; beyond the four-hour window we got at the scene."

"I can tell you already, we're likely closer to the end of that window. Maybe 3 AM, ish. You see, we were able to handle the body. I didn't have much difficulty getting her arms to her sides." He motioned to the corpse on display. "I'm not sure if you know this, but rigor mortis sets in more quickly in summer's heat. Of course, it was the middle of the night, so not as hot. I'd say three to four is most likely. When did she go missing?"

"We don't have the details yet, only when she left home and when she was supposed to be back."

"Well, I'm about to get started on this one. I'll have some more—"

"*This one*... is Sandy. She's a young lady whose life, whose future, was snuffed out in a most gruesome way." A well-timed ring of his cell yanked Michaels' fierce eyes off the inexperienced M.E. "I'd appreciate getting your results as soon as you have them, Doc."

"Of course, Detective."

*   *   *

The wood laminate desk looked and felt like government budgeted furniture but was miles ahead of the metal one he had sat behind for years. Just looking at that old gray monstrosity was enough to make anyone depressed. Even when they didn't have a murder case on the board. The chair, though relatively new, left much to be desired for comfort. If Michaels could call it a consolation, this case would have his butt out of the Ikea-style mesh chair often. In that light, he'd have preferred the sore cheeks and stiff thigh muscles of more mundane days.

Between serial killer victims, homicides didn't come in abundance in his jurisdiction—one of many reasons he had refused offers to serve as sergeant of a Fulton County precinct. The Atlanta folks had their hands full.

It sat on the desk, taunting him. The manila folder held a fraction of the bulk it would soon contain. To officially start his investigation, Detective Michaels hauled his weary self from the chair and pulled the folder from his uncluttered desktop. Sluggish steps contradicted the urgency churning in his gut, fueling the urge to catch this guy once and for all. As the Action Board drew closer, he considered the need to finish the case he should have closed years ago. Before the Moralist could slay another teenage girl.

Thoughtlessly, his neck turned to cast his gaze at Seargent Carter's office. As if she were sitting there, judging his failure, he grimaced at the empty chair. It would have been better, he reckoned, if she had blamed him then. The city wanted a fall guy to keep the papers—Michaels knew most news was consumed digitally but always said *papers*—from telling the people a serial killer was still on the loose in Marietta. If his sergeant had gone to bat for him, he couldn't know. Roneesha Carter shot straight as an arrow, but their entanglement over the case gave the idea room to grow.

In the center of the dry-erase board, Michaels held the cropped photo of Sandra Rawlings—just her lifeless face until they had a better picture from her parents—and set a round magnetic tack over her chestnut bangs. Above the picture he wrote 'Sandy' in red marker. Now he needed to think.

Every clue would connect back to her at the hub until the board became a spiderweb of interconnecting lines leading to and from evidence, suspects, locations, witnesses, and any other detail, no matter how irrelevant it seemed. Over the course of his three-plus-year investigation of the Moralist, the board had become so crowded he had taped additional pictures and notes over the surrounding wall. Knowing his nights of halfway decent sleep were over, Michaels sighed deeply at the sight of the almost empty Action Board.

Below Sandy's photo he wrote: *Allen (Father)*; below that, *Sonya (Mother)*; then, *Connor (Brother, 14/15)*. Below those names he drew three lines, placeholders for other family and close acquaintances. Yes, it was a serial killer case, but he never ruled out the usual suspects.

A slap on the back startled him and the last line went askew. The quickly rising rage settled when Jones pushed a cup of Starbucks coffee toward him.

"Black, two sugars, *right*? Figured you'd need it."

"You figured right. I think the uniforms make coffee from toilet water. Thanks." Grabbing the cup, he sipped liberally.

"Your famous Action Board. I was wondering when I'd get to see it in... *action*. Been slow since I came up."

Michaels scowled as he swallowed the hot drink, sweetened just enough to lessen its bitter bite. "Are you complaining we've had no killings? Had that *itch* for a murder case, hmm?"

"What? No. I mean, this is homicide, right? I didn't want anyone killed, but… I mean, it's why we're here, right? Now we get—I mean… we've *got to* do our jobs."

"You're a quick learn, at least." Michaels slapped the folder into his partner's chest. "How would you lay out the board?"

Junior Detective Brandon Jones grasped the sand-colored folder and flipped through it. "I guess I'd put—"

"No, just do it… It's dry erase." He handed Jones the blue and red markers and stepped back to enjoy his coffee, pleased his partner remembered to order him the bold roast.

"Sumatra?" He pulled another sip. "No, Espresso roast."

Jones smirked. "Good palate, Detective. They had Verona today."

Keeping his mouth shut, for now, Michaels leaned on his desk, the closest to the Action Board, to observe the newbie work. For a detective, the logical layout of a board could make or break the case, and someone needed to take the reins when he finally walked away. Younger detectives preferred to work on their computers, tablets, and even on their tiny cellphone screens. Technology may have made some things easier, but in Michaels' experience, a wide view of a full Action Board solved cases.

Not this one. Not yet.

As Jones studied the files in the folder and began scribbling on the board, Michaels wondered skeptically if they could stop the Moralist before another young life was lost. Until he finally caught him, there would be more victims.

SONYA RAWLINGS

Her husband had said he needed to go out. To clear his head. Although she had protested her dutiful share, Sonya sat in his chair and let the solace wash over her. That young detective with poor taste in what he likely thought was a well-matched shirt and tie combination had finally left them to grieve as a family. In the armchair's contemplation, Sonya realized that meant her cleaning the kitchen, Allen out or locked in his office, and Connor upstairs, isolated under his headphones as usual.

Staring at the family portrait above the fireplace mantle, she thought he had taken it well. Of course, how a brother faced learning his sister was never coming home couldn't compare to a mother losing her baby girl. She figured no grief could be as powerful. Sandy's hair had a more reddish hue in that photo from last Christmas.

The tears had stopped. What did that mean?

That thought summoned a fresh flow, and this time, for the first time since Sandy didn't come home for curfew and the detectives came, she let it all out. Guttural screams chased the silence from the living room, and she mindlessly pulled the end of her dress to her face and groaned into the soft cotton fabric.

"*Mom?*"

Startled by the call of her name, Sonya dropped her hands and tugged the hem of her dress over her knees. Her son handed her a box of tissues and said nothing more. The scene's immodesty reddened her cheeks.

"Sorry." She moved to the sofa and patted the cushion beside her. "Come. Sit with me."

For some minutes they sat, absorbed in the quietness of the moment. It felt to Sonya almost like a normal day. Allen could have been at work and Sandy at school—the silence cared not and came to keep Sonya company either way. Today would have been Sandy's first day back at school. With Allen at work and Connor in his room, Sonya would have been alone.

The teenage years put Sandy and Connor in their rooms most of the time when they were home, usually glued to some screen with earbuds or headphones insulating them from their parents. To her, it felt like they were drifting apart. Allen wasn't around enough to notice, and Sonya no longer tired of his business trips.

She dared not tell him this was not the first time Sandy had missed a curfew. Her skin prickled at the thought of her daughter's murder investigation revealing the boyfriend no one had told Sandy's father existed. Always the more stringent of the two, he had forbidden dating until she turned seventeen. Sonya figured a few months made little difference, so, while Sandy thought she had everyone fooled, her mother allowed it so long as the curfew violations didn't keep her out past midnight. Whenever her father was there, Sandy came home on time.

Except for last night.

"Where's Dad? Did he go to work?"

Connor's voice brought Sonya back to the sofa, into the moment she couldn't believe her life had become. "What?"

"Don't tell me Dad went to work. I swear, that job is more important—"

"No, sweetheart. He did some things in his office here to clear his day and stay home with us."

"Then where is he? Why isn't he here?" The words were sharp enough to cut glass.

"He took a walk, is all." Sonya took her son's hand. "Look, this is...well... We all, I think... we will all handle this differently—and that's okay. Our faith will get us through this. Until it does, there is no right or wrong way to grasp what happened... or to grieve."

"No, Ma, there *is* a wrong way—leaving your family!"

Connor ripped his hand from hers, jumped up, and stormed up the stairs. Sonya started to her feet then sat back down. That empty chair stole her mind. She'd sat in it to hear the older of the two strangers say her daughter had been found dead in a park. While he didn't say the words, she understood Allen's conclusion, as confirmed by the detective. Their daughter was killed. Why did it mean that deranged serial killer did it? Something about the detective's name…

Curiosity pulled Sonya to her feet, and she scampered into the kitchen and took a seat at the small desk opposite the sink and stove. Though he was seldom at home, Allen had an entire room as his home office. After considerable discussion, she had been granted the concession of this small workspace when Allen had her kitchen installed.

When she lifted the laptop's lid, the screen threw pale light on her. Her face unlocked the computer using what Allen called *Face ID*. In the Safari browser, which he told her to use instead of Chrome, she began searching for archived articles about the Moralist case.

After a frustrating twenty or more minutes, she found an article on the Marietta Weekly's website from three and a half years ago. It said the case would remain open and encouraged people, especially teenage girls and their parents, to remain vigilant. The killings appeared to have stopped, but the Moralist was still at large. While she grasped that term, it made little sense to her.

Sonya wondered if they had become complacent as parents. Back then, Sandy had been too young to be considered at risk, as Allen kept saying to reassure a worried mother. Besides, at that age, their daughter never went anywhere unaccompanied. Now, however, Sandy had reached the teenage years of that maniac's prey and had a boyfriend.

Did this mean she had lost her virginity or was about to take her dating to that level? Was that why that deranged lunatic killed her baby, to cleanse her and absolve her of her sins? Taking a deep breath under closed eyes, Sonya's mind raced over all the things she should have done differently. How many ways she could have prevented this. Protected her little girl.

That photo called her back to the living room. Everyone looked so happy in their holiday sweaters. It was the last family portrait they would ever take. The commotion of the neighbor's children coming home from school overtook her. Closing her eyes, she imagined Sandy running in from her first day back at school. Sonya's eyes popped open when she visualized her husband's face upon learning she knew their daughter had a boyfriend.

Allen entered the house like a hurricane through the front door. Out of breath and seething, he said nothing to the back of Sonya's head. The walk had failed in its goal of calming him. When she turned to ask if he was okay, he wore the face her mind had feared seeing.

BRANDON JONES

t looked good to him. A logical layout of notes and details branched out from the dead girl in the center. He had done his homework, read over old cases and studied pictures of the original Moralist Action Board. Expectantly, Jones waited for the pat-on-the-back every junior detective yearned to receive from their senior partner. As he stood from his lean, Michaels exhaled an "Mm" that did little to stoke the ego.

"Did I get it wrong? Uh, we don't have much yet... Waiting for pictures from the family and the full forensics and autopsy reports."

The maddening pause stretched out like an hour waiting in line at the tag office. Cobb county allowed car registrations to be renewed online, but Jones still lived in Paulding.

Tapping a finger on the girl's picture, Michaels broke the silence. "We need a better photo, one that shows the life she had, the life taken from her by this monster." With a heavy sigh, the experienced detective reclaimed his lean on the desk behind him.

"So, is this a good start?" Jones gestured toward the board behind him. "We need the boyfriend's name. I got nothing more than that they went to the same school. He goes under suspects, *right*?"

When his senior partner said nothing, Jones felt a quietness surround him, drowning out the noises of ringing phones, chattering officers and detectives, and the beeping of a garbage truck reversing outside.

"I wasn't sure about the parents. I know in a normal murder..." Jones shuddered. Thunderous sounds crashing outside rushed into the conversation as clanking and shattering glass smashed into the back of the truck in the alley. They always emptied the recycling dumpster on Mondays. "In a typical murder case, we'd have the parents and close family members as suspects and be looking at the father, especially, *right*?"

"This ain't no typical case, is it?" Michaels studied his black shoes as if the polished shine held answers Jones didn't yet know.

"No. I know when we've got a serial killer, and especially with one where the vics don't seem connected, we rule the usual suspects out."

"Hmm. The victims do have connections. Their age and... *development* into becoming sexually active. Some knew each other, had gone to the same school. But you're correct. There's nothing more linking the young ladies." The approval drew a smile on Jones' lips. "But you're also wrong—well, not entirely wrong—about one thing. We don't rule anyone out as a suspect, no matter how unlikely."

"Gotcha, Boss. Um, Michaels, sir. Who were the leading suspects in the Moralist case? I couldn't find that list in the file."

Michaels cast a somber look at his young partner. "Cause if you did, you'd see a list of crossed out names. When we found the first body, we naturally treated it as an isolated murder, tried to grasp the sick motivations behind the mutilation."

"The first vic didn't come with a greeting card, *right*?"

"*Come with*? No. We found the first note with the second victim. That's when we understood what we were dealing with. Never figured the monster would go on so long, kill so many." Like an old dog on a muggy August afternoon, Michaels wagged his head.

"So, on the first vic, you must have had the standard suspects list, then, *right*?"

"The father looked good for it. We questioned the boyfriend. I thought maybe he pushed her into it. Even if it wasn't rape, we thought he forced himself on her. Maybe she resisted or threatened to report it as rape... We considered every angle. In the end, we concluded it was consensual. The girl had confided in her best friend about the encounter—encounters with the boyfriend."

"That's why the Moralist chose her, considering her a slut or something."

"He considers them victims. Not of his heinous acts. Of the immoral society they live in." Michaels took a seat at his desk and opened the case folder. "Needless to say, our suspect list went out the window when we realized we had a serial killer preying on young women in Marietta. Close family members dropped off that list real quick."

"But you want to keep them on in, in this case. You think we should look at the father and boyfriend?"

"He's a religious man. Stern with his daughter. Did you pick up on the tension between him and the wife?"

"Yeah. And the boy, Connor, gave me the same impression."

Michaels furled his brow. "You spoke with him?"

"The Rawlings didn't do so well breaking the news. I offered to help. Isn't that why you left me there, sir?"

"Quit it with the *sirs* and *bosses*. I left you there to help the parents, to guide them in how to speak to the boy and answer any questions they had. At this stage, we need to tread carefully with them. I have a—" He cleared his throat forcefully. "I've got a daughter, and I can't imagine…"

"And I tried. They had no questions, the parents. Well, the father, he did ask me one thing. He asked why you were on the case when you failed to stop the Moralist years ago."

Looking ready for a fiery comeback, Michaels pursed his lips but dipped his head instead. "I wondered the same." After an elongated pause, he said, "Tell me what you got on the boyfriend."

ALLEN RAWLINGS

A llen stepped off the parquet entryway onto the beige carpet, and Sonya called out, "Shoes." Grumbling, he tried to pull his foot out of his sneaker by stepping on the heel with the other shoe. He grunted as he bent down to untie the laces and free his feet, and left the footwear tossed on the floor. When he slammed the front door, one of the sneakers ricocheted off the base board and rolled onto the carpet.

Sonya's silence halted his stomping toward the living room. He stared blankly at her as she walked to the kitchen, away from him.

"*Well*?" He stretched the word into a question.

As she dragged herself from the kitchen to the living room, his wife turned a blank face toward him, the aftermath of tears distorting her usually bright eyes. Her hand clutched a fresh box of tissues.

"Aren't you going to ask me where I've been?" he said. She plopped onto the sofa and said nothing. "That cop, Michaels, isn't going to do a da—" Closing his mouth, he exhaled through flared nostrils. "He's not going to find the guy who did this."

"And you think *you* can catch the killer?" A familiar nothingness on her face hid her feelings. "Can we just try to face what's happened, be here for each... for Connor? Let the police do their job."

"Let the—" Allen pressed his lips and stiffened his shoulders. "Last night they told us everything would be fine. That Sandra just stayed out, as young ladies do. 'Don't worry,' that woman told us. And don't get me started on Walker Michaels."

"His sergeant, the D.A., and the mayor all praised him for his tireless work and said they had done and would continue doing all they could on the Moralist case."

Allen stared at his wife for a moment. "You remember that? You, you barely ever watch the news and didn't follow that story. Sandra was too young, you said. You didn't even worry about it at the time."

"*You* said she was too young. I googled it just now, or whatever the new computer uses for searching. Detective Michaels received commendations."

"For failing. Now look what's happened to—" Allen choked on the lump swelling in his throat. "I had to do something."

"Where did you go?" A calmness overtook Sonya's countenance, and she looked more like herself. Allen saw a face almost identical to the one he married twenty-two years ago, wrinkles only branching from her eyes when she squinted. "What did you do that the cops can't?"

"Or won't." With every muscle tightening, Allen sat on his chair beside the sofa. "They'll handle this differently, thinking it's a serial killer murder. The usual suspects, people closer to Sandra, will be overlooked."

"All those British cop shows you watch…" She sighed. "Don't you think it was him? The way they found her? The…" Sonya blew her nose.

Shifting in his seat, Allen exhaled deeply. "Of course. It looks just like it. But it's been a few years since the last one. Why her? Why now? We can't rule out the people closest to Sandra. To us. Close family, friends, schoolmates. What if someone wanted to harm our daughter and throw the cops off?"

"Wait… Are you saying it may have been someone else? That someone may have had something *personal* against our daughter? Why? Why would anyone…" Tears gathered in her eyes.

"I… I don't know. I think we should pursue all possibilities. Like Richie."

"What does my brother have to do with anything? What are you even saying?"

"I'm saying anyone. Everyone. The cops won't handle this, so I will."

When Allen reached for her hand, Sonya pulled away. "Let the police do the police work. Now is not the time for vengeance. 'Vengeance is mine: I will repay, saith the Lord.' Now is the time for our family to be together, to help Connor. You've been away so—"

"No." Allen stood, pointing a finger at his wife so close she flinched. "Don't start that. Not now. You know how hard I work to provide for this family. You're the one who wanted to stay home to raise the kids, gave up your career to do it. What was I supposed to do, supporting this family on one income?"

"You wanted it as much as me. You told me it was the best way to raise God-fearing children. You even pushed for homeschooling." Sonya leaned back, away from the shaky finger in her face. "But work isn't the only thing. You spend too much time at the church. I, I can't do this now. We've discussed this plenty."

"I'm a deacon there, they count on me. You know that."

"We count on you here, too. Don't we count *to you*?" Sonya buried her face in her palms and sobbed.

Allen moved beside her and rubbed his hand over her back. "Of course you do. Everything I do is for you and the kids. Even the work at the church. It helps build a stronger community, a safe place for our family."

"Safe?" Sonya whimpered through the tears. She did not raise her head. "Things have changed now. Connor needs you here. I need you here."

Pulling her into an embrace, Allen said, "You're right, honey. I'm sorry. We'll get through this together. But I can't move on until the person responsible pays for what he's done. I just can't sit by and do nothing."

WALKER
MICHAELS

T he Action Board would soon be crowded, but not
with anything Michaels found flipping through the
current case folder. A thin young officer in uniform
called his name and Walker turned to see what he had been
expecting with equal eagerness and dread. The hand trolley
straightened, and the three cardboard boxes swayed and
leaned forward. The officer palm-slapped the lid of the top
box to steady the tower of previous case notes he'd carted
up from the archive. Dust clouded off the cover with the
dull thud.

"Thank you." Michaels pulled himself from the lean he
had sunken into on his desk. Those three boxes held three
years of his life in a corrugated prison. Years that distanced
him from his daughter and witnessed the passing of his wife.
Of all the memories that rushed in on him at this moment,
why did he have to revisit that one?

"Three years of evidence, reports, and notes." Jones whistled. "You know this is all digitized, *right*? We can easily sort it all and organize it on our computers. I can show you how."

As he lifted the lid of the top box, Michaels replied, "What? Don't want to risk those soft hands getting a paper cut?" He breathed out half a chuckle.

With fingers splayed, Jones examined the back of his hands, then his soft, pinkish palms. "I'm just trying to help, is all. We can go through this more quickly on the computer."

"Quick often misses things, *son*." Michaels delivered the derogatory moniker through a smirk. "I need my board to see the whole picture. Computer screens ain't near big enough."

"I'm not questioning your methods. I know you got close last time. You almost had the guy once, right?"

Lifting a box from the pile, Michaels nodded to Jones to put the second one on his desk. As he pulled folders and evidence bags, he said, "Hmm. Not sure I'd say close."

"But you got to the scene while he was still there. You almost caught him that time."

"I've got my doubts that was him. We might have just scared some random passerby... Or a fan."

"A fan?"

"I don't know what's the scarier thought, that someone could butcher young ladies like that, thinking they're doing the Lord's work, or that folks idolize 'em for it."

"How'd you get there so quick? To that last vic, I mean." Following his partner's lead, Jones began piling folders from his box onto his desk.

"I hoped the Moralist slipped up. I thought we might've gotten him, too. I happened to be close to the Silver Comet Trail when someone called in saying they saw a man carrying a large object wrapped in black plastic. He said he thought it was a body." Michaels stopped organizing the evidence bags by ID tag and straightened his back. "The M.E. had said there were traces of polyethylene and speculated he carried the bodies wrapped in plastic tarps or perhaps industrial trash bags."

"And he had time to… um, exhibit the body before you got there?"

"That's the bit that hung in my craw, you know?" After a deep sigh, Detective Michaels crossed his arms. "I didn't think he could have. Even if the FGM was done prior to moving the body, which we concluded was the case, he had little time to unwrap her, lay her out, and leave the note with her clothes and belongings. And then to disappear by the time I got there? I was minutes from the scene when the call came in."

"What luck. I mean… but you didn't get him."

Shrugging, Michaels said, "Most likely, that witness rushed the timing. He said he called when he got back to his car. Even a few minutes would have given the Moralist time."

"I remember reading that the circumcisions, FGM, had to be performed elsewhere. The bodies were deposited at the scene afterward and then meticulously arranged on display."

"That was the last one... the last Moralist killing."

"Maybe it *was* him, then. I mean, the last thing he'd want to do was place the body, *right*? I bet he left the clothes and the note, then went back for the vic. By time you got there, he must've just positioned the body. I bet he got spooked by being so close to getting caught, he quit."

After taking that in, Michaels wagged his head. "People like that, their minds don't work like normal people's do. It's why they're so hard to predict, the most difficult to catch. The clever ones, anyway. He didn't quit for fear of getting caught. Something else made him stop. Besides, I don't think the guy at the scene was him."

"If you didn't catch that guy, how can you be sure?"

"Cause if it was, it'd mean I missed my one chance." Michaels' shoulders faltered. "But now we gotta face the fact he's back... What made him stop for four years? And why'd he decide to start up again now?"

"You think those answers are in these boxes?"

Michaels returned to sorting the evidence bags. "No. We need to speak with the family. And soon. We gave them the day to grieve, but we need to know this girl, her family, her friends. Her comings and goings. We need a complete profile

of her young life. I want to know who Sandy Rawlings was."
After a deep sigh, he added, "Why *her*?"

"I say we start with the boyfriend. Even if he's not a suspect, he's the one… Well, it's sorta his fault, *right*?"

"What do you mean? Because he deflowered the virgin?"

Jones snickered. "*Deflowered*? How old are you? But yeah, I mean, that's when the Moralist kills. When the girls give it up. That's when he needs to cleanse their souls. So, we start with the boyfriend."

"Hmm. You're not entirely off." He appeased his junior partner with half a smile. "We need to know the timing of their encounter, or encounters. And since we know the Moralist studies his victims, knows their patterns and observes their behavior to see if they become what he considers immoral, that boy, whoever he is, has been observed as well."

"He never kills the boys though." Jones paused pensively. "I wonder why."

"He's an old-fashioned moralist, Jones. Those kind hold men and women to different standards."

The junior detective tapped a finger on his chin. "Or maybe… He thinks he's cleansing these girls, *right*? Saving their souls. In his twisted view, he's helping them. Could be he judges the boys as part of the immoral society he writes about in his notes, unworthy of salvation."

"Detective, I hadn't thought of that."

"Then why not kill them? I mean, if he's judged them... and they're the ones defiling the girls."

Like a deer in headlights, Michaels stared at Jones. "Take the list of the boyfriends from each of the previous victims and crosscheck that against all missing persons reports over the same three-year period."

CONNOR RAWLINGS

After being gone most of the day, his father still wasn't *present* in any real sense of the word. After a disagreement with his mother, Connor's dad spent an hour or more in his office. As always, he locked himself in there. Most of the time he spent at home was either in there or in front of the Braves game.

The whole house reeked of chamomile tea. First in a string of people to visit, the Millers arrived before dinner. After a quick greeting and listening to the obligatory, 'We're so sorry,' Connor asked to be excused. The request's denial came in a stern look from his father. Wearing a softer expression, his mother patted the sofa beside her. Before Connor could sit, Mary Miller plopped beside his mom. At least that meant she stopped hugging him. A tall lady and a rock climber, her hugs hurt.

Having been dragged to some people's home when a church member lost someone, Connor didn't know how this was better than leaving the family to grieve alone. He had no use for these people when his sister hadn't just been killed. He didn't need them here now. From the look of it, his mom didn't need it either. When Mary threw her arms around her, it only made her cry.

Sitting in Dad's chair, Peter Miller again asked if Allen was almost finished. When he knocked on the office door, his friend and fellow church deacon told him he'd be out in a minute. From experience, Connor knew how long his father's minutes could be. When he finally emerged, Peter grabbed him in a man hug and slapped his back with a pop.

At the woman's insistence, Connor put his nose in a bunch of white roses. Mary proudly said they were from her garden. "Don't worry, I stripped off all the thorns," she said. The only scent Connor could smell came from the chamomile. The irony of having four half-full teacups on the coffee table gave him something else to think about for a second. After endless condolences broken only by moments of uncomfortable silence, Mary Miller stunned everyone.

"If it was the Moralist... If he came back... We know why he did what he did. I can't believe Sandy—"

"What?" Connor's mother turned as white as a ghost, her mouth agape.

His father had a more volatile reaction. Up from his chair, trembling like Sandy's Chihuahua, he pointed a finger at the woman. Whenever that finger point came his way, Connor knew he was in huge trouble.

"How dare you imply such a thing about my daughter!"

Outwardly flustered, Mary sunk into the sofa cushion.

Her husband rose from beside her. "Allen, that's not what she meant. You know that. We loved Sandy, everyone did. She was so popular at the church and always volunteered with the youth ministry."

"Yes, of course…" Mary's words came out stuttered under the fiery gaze raining down on her. "I never meant to imply anything different. Only that the Moralist thought he was cleansing those girls. He was saving their souls. We all know Sandy was a good girl. She was lovely, developing into such a beautiful young woman."

"Her name is *Sandra*."

When Connor's dad stormed off toward his office, Peter followed. While the words were hard to make out, the heat in them was evidenced clearly in the volume of the muffled voices.

"Connor, dear, would you please take these to the kitchen?"

If the request came from his mother, it would have been bad enough. Who did this woman think she was, ordering him around like that? When his mother gave him a look, he complied. Though they spoke softly, Connor could hear every word leaking into the kitchen.

"I'm so sorry, Sonya. You know I didn't mean…"

"It's fine. This is, well, it's such a difficult time. No one knows how to act or what to say. All day, since they came, those detectives…" His mother blew her nose. "Allen and I have practically been at each other's throats. Any little thing sets him—sets *us* off."

The quick correction furrowed Connor's brow, and he shook his head.

"She was such a lovely girl. A young woman, really. Wasn't she? She developed early and looked at least nineteen, don't you think?"

What she might have meant by that comment, Connor could only guess. He never considered his sister mature. More like thirteen. She still had her dolls. He couldn't imagine anyone thinking she was older. *Nineteen*? He could hardly believe she was almost seventeen.

After a long pause, his mother said, "A few at the church said how much she reminded them of me. Maybe when I was younger, but…"

Although another silence visited the living room, Connor knew his mom had started crying again. When he peeked his head in, Mary had her in an embrace.

"It's okay, Connor," Mary said when she noticed him.

That made his head spin. Nothing about this day, this situation, his sister's death, or these people invading their home was okay. The volume from his dad's office had reduced.

Either they'd calmed down or killed each other. Connor knew they were close friends but also knew that didn't matter.

When his mother turned and noticed him, she composed herself, stood, and straightened her dress. "I'll clean the tea setting." Entering the kitchen, she laid a hand on Connor's shoulder and went straight to the sink. As she waited for the hot water, Mary slid in beside her.

"Let me do that." She rolled up her sleeves.

August in Georgia was hot, and the humidity was insane. Yet the Millers both wore long sleeves. Peter claimed the linen was light and kept the sun off his skin, which made it cooler than wearing short sleeves. Connor didn't buy it. Hanging out in the summer, he and his friends often went shirtless. His dad drank Peter's juice but mostly wore short sleeve linen shirts. And the last few times he'd seen Mary, she was in a tank top, so she was more normal than her husband.

"Oh, Mary, no. The soap might sting. Are you okay? What happened?"

As if she needed a second to understand the question, Mary stared at Connor's mother. "Oh, it's nothing. Remember that song from when we were kids... 'Every rose has its thorn.' It's true." She rolled down her sleeves and started washing the teacups. "I insist. Let me do this for you. Go, sit with your son."

A deafening roar like a car crash came from his dad's office.

ALLEN
RAWLINGS

P eter made every excuse in the book for his wife's uncalled-for words. Though he'd cut her off before she could state it, Allen understood the implication. Everyone in Marietta knew about the Moralist. Knew why he killed. Knew about the immorality motive and the cleansings. A good father, he believed he had raised his daughter right. Taught her Christian morals and virtues. Protected her from the wayward world.

"My Sandra didn't need cleansing."

"Mary didn't mean to imply that. You know how I, how much *we* both love your family. You're good parents. But... we live in a wicked world."

Lifting his eyes to the crucifix above the office door, Allen exhaled through flared nostrils. Too heavy to maintain the gaze, his head dipped.

"He was supposed to protect her."

Once the sobbing started, Allen could not contain it. Peter put an arm around his shoulder as the minutes absorbed the moment. Sobriety returned, and Allen again considered why anyone would have killed his little girl.

"She wasn't like that," he insisted. "Didn't even have a boyfriend."

"You were young once. More so today, kids don't need to date to get involved—"

Allen's chest heaved. "So, my daughter slept around. Is that what you're telling me? You're telling me someone killed her because she was what… some… street slut?"

"No, I…" Peter backed into the wall behind him.

Getting right in his face, Allen yelled indignation at his friend. "She kept her curfew. She knew she wasn't to date— or spend time with boys—until she was seventeen. And her mother knew the rules. When I was away, she enforced them. Sandra was a good girl."

"You're a great dad, Allen. Taught her well. And you trusted Sonya to do the same when you were away." That pinched Allen's brow. His eyes drilled into Peter, who continued, "You've helped so many parents at church with their kids. We have some of the finest, most upstanding youths in the county."

Still seething, Allen replied, "Yet you and Mary come here and accuse Sandra of deserving to be cleansed. Like she was some… *whore*. One of those girls prancing around half-naked, sexing any willing boy to come along."

"Mary, um, we didn't mean that. We know she was a good girl. All Mary was saying is that Sandy became a young woman—practically overnight. A girl in a woman's body. Like Sonya, when we were younger."

"Sandra's not like her mother. Not in that way. She didn't lead any boy down a corrupt path. Don't give me any of that Proverbs chapter five 'lips like a honeycomb' crap. My daughter was no immoral woman seducing young men."

Taking him by the arms, Peter looked into his eyes. "We both know the world is a very different place from when Solomon wrote that wise Proverb. Today it's the boys who corrupt wholesome young ladies, teenagers or even younger, into moral decay. The girls are the victims."

"My Sandra *was* a victim. But not of the immoral world. Of some delusional murderer… who killed her for no reason. Why would anyone kill my baby girl? Who would do such a thing? *Why*?"

"She's been called to the Lord. Have faith, Allen. Remember, when there's one set of footprints on the sand, Jesus is carrying you."

Again, Allen's eyes climbed to focus on his Lord and Savior hanging above the door. Protector of the faithful, where was He last night when Sandra needed him? Pushing Peter off him, Allen searched for a release. Lifting the printer off his desk, the cables yanked free as he tugged. Allen threw it with all his might. It and the wooden crucifix with the dead man on it crashed to the floor in pieces.

"Get out. Now!"

When Allen pulled the office door open, Sonya's wide eyes fell upon him. Looking past him, she examined the other man in the office. Her shoulders relaxed. Peter excused himself and stepped around them. Sucking in and expelling deep breaths, Allen stared through his wife. Her eyes trembled as she studied his.

"How dare they. They come here, at a moment like this, and, and… and tell me my daughter was one of those loose girls."

"They never said that."

Turning from her as she began picking up the fragmented pieces of Jesus and the printer, Allen slammed a fist on his desk. "They implied she deserved…" His voice cracked and tears flooded his eyes.

As she wrapped her arms around him and pressed into his back, Sonya said, "They didn't mean that. She was a victim. Everyone knows that."

A victim. But an alternate meaning of 'victim' now rang like church bells in Allen's skull. He pulled away from his wife's arms but kept her behind him.

"Did she ever violate curfew before last night?"

Day 2

BRANDON JONES

In the months since being assigned together, Michaels always made Brandon drive. Considering himself a good driver and having more recently completed the pursuit driving course Michaels must have taken decades ago, Jones didn't mind. His partner said it gave him time to think, which meant they usually drove in absolute silence. On their first day together, Jones learned quickly how much Senior Detective Grumpy Pants didn't tolerate small talk in the car.

It startled Jones when Michaels broke his self-imposed muteness. "How'd you know about the boyfriend?"

"Connor told me. Seems the father didn't know about him, though."

"Hmm. He's a real religious—Eyes on the road!"

Nearly giving himself whiplash, Jones jerked his neck to obey. He'd never seen such a look of fright as his now sheet-white superior showed him.

"Dammit, Jones. Try not to get us killed while we investigate this murder, would you."

"Sorry, Boss." Jones could have slapped himself for using *boss* again. It was just a second. The car hadn't swerved, and there was no oncoming traffic, but he thought it best to keep his eyes forward until the vehicle stopped.

After a deep breath, Michaels continued. "Allen Rawlings is very active in his church, one of those big nondenominational ones. He's one of six deacons for a flock of about seven hundred. No wonder they call 'em mega churches."

"I thought he was in sales. Big pharma, *right*?"

"Account management. A fancy term for salesman. He's not the pastor and deacons don't get paid. Churches like that are real good at getting people to work for free."

"And he doesn't know about his daughter's boyfriend. Is theirs one of those super strict ones, like the people who ring my doorbell and wake me up on Saturday mornings?"

"*Those* folks are good people. I'm not sure about Rawlings' faith, but I think he'd not be so happy about his little girl being sexually active at sixteen."

"And she died because of it."

"*No*, Jones. She died because some sick maniac is out there killing young women."

The next several intersections on Mars Hill Road passed without words filling the now heated space in the air-conditioned vehicle. Jones reverted to his partner's no-chatter in the car rule until Michaels broke it again.

"Tell me about your chat with the brother yesterday. And two hands on the wheel, ten and two o'clock."

"Actually, they say nine and three is better."

"And they've been saying two are better than one for ages, so…"

Jones lifted his elbow from the armrest and gripped the wheel with both hands. "I didn't speak for long with Connor. Nice kid, but for sure gonna be messed up over his sister. I think there may be some issues with the parents' marriage, but that's more a feeling."

"Hmm. You think they're divided religiously, or about how to raise the kids?"

"He did say not to tell *the father* about the boyfriend. I think the mother knew. That complicates things, *right*? If this weren't a serial killer case, I'd be looking mighty close at Allen Rawlings for the murder."

"Good instincts, Detective. And you're right, this is not that sorta case. But the family situation might tell us more about who Sandy was, and what led to her death."

"I told Connor we'll nail the guy."

"You what?" Michaels' harsh tone and added volume could have shattered the windshield. "We never promise to close a case or catch the perp, do you hear? *Never*!"

"I was trying to make him feel better, is all. Let him know he'll get closure."

"*Closure*?" Michaels cackled. "That's a three-dollar word for people pretending their tragedy don't affect them no more, all that is."

"I wanted him to know he'd be alright."

"His sister was just murdered. His life'll never be the same and his parents won't ever be what they were for him before this. If we don't catch this guy, all you've done is fuel his hurt with anger. Anger toward the law, the system… toward us."

*   *   *

As they pulled into the subdivision, Jones couldn't help but admire the houses. His apartment offered him more space than he needed and no shortage of pretty women at the pool all summer, but these homes were the size of some of the smaller buildings in his complex. Four or five bedrooms and three baths, he assumed. As he rounded the corner onto the Rawlings' cul-de-sac, he noticed the wooden sides hiding behind the stone and brick fronts and thought it was a cheap trick to lower the building cost at the expense of a higher quality home. Typical, he thought, for recent years' Atlanta suburb construction. Matchstick houses, some called them.

He slowed the car as three little children ran across the street. Eight years old, or so, they never looked both ways at that age. The lawns had all browned. No amount of money or water could fend off the abuse of summer's heat. Water restrictions were in place again this year and even the wealthier subdivisions had to comply as drinking water trumped green grass.

As Jones turned into the driveway, he narrowly missed the silver BMW i3 racing backward down its slope. Allen Rawlings didn't stop or even slow at the sight of the detectives arriving at his home. The two looked at each other and Michaels shrugged before opening the door and leading the way up the walk. The *Ring* doorbell must have alerted the family to their presence, yet Michaels pressed his thumb into it. Curtains over the glass panels outlining the custom wooden door hid the home's interior from their view.

A rather put-together version of Sonya Rawlings opened the door. Jones eyed her up and down as she filled out the summer dress quite nicely. He could see where her daughter got her looks, and her figure.

"Missus Rawlings, sorry to come unannounced. Is this a bad time? Were you headed out?"

A puzzled look swept across her face before she replied, "Oh, no, it's quite alright. You just missed my husband."

"That's for sure," Jones blurted.

Ignoring him, she said, "Please come in. I was just going to make myself a drink. Would you gentlemen care for something?" She paused for them to remove their shoes before leading them through the living room and into the spotless kitchen. "I can prepare an espresso, or regular coffee, if you prefer. I was going for something… a little stronger, myself."

When she motioned toward the kitchen table, the detectives sat on the far side facing her. At the granite-topped island, she prepared a mixed drink and dropped an orange slice into the long-stemmed wineglass.

"Aperol Spritz," she said as she turned to face them. "I had it in Milan and learned to make them. I even let Sandy have some—only in the house, of course. It's just three parts Prosecco, two parts Aperol, and one part soda water. Three, two, one, so easy. Can I tempt you detectives?"

"You certainly are." Jones' kidney stung from Michaels embedding his elbow in his side. "*What*? It looks like a refreshing summer drink."

"Thank you, ma'am, but we're on duty."

"Two espressos then, it's no bother. And please, call me Sonya. *Not* Sonia. It's like how Connor sometimes calls me Ma. *Sahn-ya*."

She sipped her icy drink and set the wine glass on the counter. The espresso machine looked like it belonged in a chic coffee house on Marietta Square. It hissed and steamed as Mrs. Rawlings pulled the shots.

Connor came storming into the kitchen. "Mom, what are you doing? Why are you making these cops coffee?" As if seeing his mother for the first time, he added, "And why are you wearing *that*?"

SONYA
RAWLINGS

"**C**onnor, just in time. I should think you ought to be in this conversation too." Turning to the men seated at her kitchen table, she said, "Isn't that right, detectives?"

When her son yanked her arm to make her face him, waves of coffee eddied up to the brims of the two demitasse cups. "Ma, why are you dressed like you're going out, in *that*, and waiting on these guys? Making them *espresso*?" The pitch in his voice rose on the last word. He eyed the sweating wineglass on the counter. "You're *drinking*?"

"You almost made me spill their espressos." Sonya stepped gingerly over to the men and set the dainty porcelain cups on the table. They sat on saucers holding tiny spoons, and she asked Connor to get the sugar. The porcelain clanked as he slammed it down on the glass tabletop. Appalled by the rude behavior in front of guests, his mother shot him a stern look.

"Thank you," the older of the men said.

She had read up on him earlier. "You're welcome, Detective Michaels." Sonya noticed the younger man's eyes examining her and flashed him a furtive smile. "Detective Jones, would you like anything else?"

"Ma, stop it," her son barked.

Detective Jones raised a hand. "It's okay, Connor. Remember what I told you yesterday? Everyone copes and deals with tragedy in their own way."

"If the Moralist saw her, she'd be next."

The pop of her palm reddening her boy's face startled her almost as much as it seemed to shock him. He darted off. The stomps of his feet on the stairs roiled into the kitchen, followed by a thud from his bedroom door.

Sonya covered her face with both hands. "I, I don't... I've never done that before. Never raised a hand to either of my children."

She found herself in the warm embrace of strong, young arms. "It's okay. As I told your son, we all have different coping mechanisms. He'll be fine. Just give him, and yourself, time."

"Jones, let's step outside. Give Missus Rawlings a minute."

"Sonya," she whimpered.

Closing the sliding dining room doors behind them did little to muffle their voices. It became readily apparent that the senior was displeased with his young partner. He chewed the man out for behaving inappropriately. First for his earlier chat with Connor and now for the flirtatious interaction with "the grieving mother." When Jones said he couldn't help himself, that he'd always been attracted to "cougars," she couldn't forbid the smile from her lips. It was much better than that crude acronym some used for mothers like her. One of Connor's friends used it once. When she told Allen, he had to explain its meaning. The kid was forever banished from the house.

"Don't let your espressos get cold." When she spoke to the closed doors, they parted. The men slipped through and sat back at the table. The older one added two little spoonfuls of sugar and stirred his coffee for at least a minute. "You know, in Italy, for more than one espresso they say espressi."

"I wasn't aware of that, ma'am." He sipped the drink that must have been lukewarm and disgustingly sweet. "I apologize again for our unscheduled visit and my colleague's, um, inexperience. I understand your husband saw Sandy this morning."

"I was ready, *on time*, but..." Sonya's eyes found the ceiling and the courage to remain dry.

"I understand. I can't imagine how difficult that would be."

"He wouldn't let me go. Said I couldn't handle it."

"Maybe it's for the best. We only needed a positive ID. If this is a bad time..."

"No. I'm glad you came now. We can talk... more *openly* without... So, what can I do for you gentlemen?"

"We would like some photographs of the family, if, if that's okay with you." She nodded. "And we have some questions. Then we'd like to see Sandy's room—with your permission, of course."

"Anything you need. I can send you some pictures from my phone." She looked at the younger one. He nodded and held his phone for her to bring hers near to exchange contacts. For a reason he seemed to know, and she didn't, their phones were not compatible. They swapped and each entered their contact information in the other's.

Detective Michaels stared at her, but not in the way Jones did.

"Would you like to see Sandy's room first or start with the questions?"

"A few questions, if you don't mind, ma'am."

Inside, she did mind. Inside, she was screaming. Strange men in her house came to ask about private matters. To uncover secrets about her daughter. To search through her things. Nothing about this was okay. She fidgeted in her seat. Children were supposed to outlive their parents. Like a switch flipped in her mind, in the part that tried to rationalize emotion, the roles reversed.

"Please, all the *ma'ams* and *Missus Rawlings* makes me feel so old. I prefer Sonya. I'll text Connor to come back down."

"No, wait ma—Sonya. We'd like to speak with you first, if you don't mind."

"You can stop being so polite, Detective Michaels. I want to help you find the monster that…" Her voice lost its strength, and she contained her tears under a series of rapid blinks. Composed, she sat across from the men who had told her that her daughter had been killed, a half empty glass of spritz in her hand.

"We need the name of your daughter's boyfriend and need to know a little about him and their relationship."

Recoiling, she said, "My Sandy wasn't one of those loose girls, if that's what you're implying."

"Sonya," Jones said forcefully. "We know she had a boyfriend and aren't judging. You know why the Moralist, um, well, you know, right? We need to know all we can about this boy."

"Josh." She exhaled the word. "They were friends, mostly. And then feelings started… as they do at that age. It was all quite wholesome."

"Do you have his last name or phone number?" When she shook her head, Jones said, "We have her phone. I'm sure we can find him. What can you tell us about the relationship? How often they saw each other and where they went, etcetera."

Robotically, Sonya answered the rest of their questions, stiffening each time she had to endure their implications that her little girl was sexually active. Looking down at herself in that sundress, she knew her daughter must have attracted a lustful eye or two. If some of the good men at the church felt the pull of temptation, the boys at school no doubt saw her baby girl as an object for their shameless desires. She winced.

When the barrage of questions ended, Sonya asked if Allen would be told about the boyfriend. Jones, who said to call him Brandon, assured her they would not tell him directly, but that it would be relevant to the case, so he would likely learn it. She laid her palms flat on the glass table, closed her eyes, and sighed. Michaels, who did not tell her to call him Walker, added that her husband knew the Moralist's motivations, so he must have assumed by now Sandy had been with a boy.

"That psycho can get it wrong. Maybe he thought since she had been spending time with a boy, she was like those other girls. I read up on it this morning, from back when you worked on the case the first time, Detective Michaels. He doesn't... *touch* the girls. I mean, he didn't..." The sentence dissolved in her throat.

"He didn't." Brandon stood and patted Sonya's shoulder. "Take a moment, as much as you need. I'll go call Connor to join us."

The kinder of the two men left her in the company of the man who failed to stop the deranged serial killer. Failed to protect her daughter.

"Missus, um, Sonya. I cannot imagine how hard this is for you, and I'm terribly sorry for your loss. I have a daughter, and I, I can't imagine... Your cooperation is extremely helpful, so thank you. Before your son comes down, may I suggest..." He paused and looked upon her with gentler softness than his eyes had held when he told her Sandy had been killed. "We have people who can help. Unless you have someone you'd prefer to talk to."

When she sniffled, he jumped up to fetch her a box of tissues from the counter. Sonya stood to take one and blew her nose. "It doesn't take a detective to guess I'd have a therapist. Look around me, at this house, this family. Look at me now, in this dress... And I'm drinking a spritz before two in the afternoon."

Two rougher hands grasped her wrists now, dryer and more weatherworn. "As I mentioned before, you have my cell. You can call me any time, day or night."

"You don't suspect any of us, do you? Allen?"

"Why do you ask?"

"You always suspect the father... or close family... first."

"Our investigation's a little more complicated than that. And we approach this differently, as serial killers aren't normally close to their victims..." Sonya nodded. "We do, however, need to consider all angles. Tell me, besides the car Allen left in, do you have any other vehicles?"

Sonya sat at the table and the detective took the seat beside her. "I have my Prius; it's in the garage."

"Anything larger, like a van or SUV?"

"No. We do our part for the environment... Of course, Allen drives the church van sometimes, with a big diesel engine. But it's needed to help some members come to Sunday services."

"He has access to a van?"

"It's almost a bus. I voted against the new church logo. The bright green on white, and the way they drew the holy cross. It looks like a Holiday Inn sign. That's what the van looks like; one of those hotel shuttles at the airport. The old one was more dignified but was too small once the church expanded."

"What was the old one? What happened to it?"

"We still have it. 'Waste not, want not.' Eight years in the new church, we haven't sold the old one yet. It's parked there, I think, at the old chapel. It's become too much of a rusty eyesore to park at our beautiful new church."

"And Mister Rawlings has access to it?"

"All deacons do, I guess. And the pastor, of course. And Brian... he's the youth minister. As far as I can recall, the last time it was used was for one of his youth trips. They went to Ruby Falls. Connor didn't want to go, but Sandy did. She was quite fond of Brian until—"

When the words got stuck in her throat, she felt that same leathery hand rest upon hers. Brandon rejoined the room with Connor in tow, and Sonya pulled her hand from under the detective's.

"Let's all sit," Michaels suggested. "We have some questions for you, Connor."

ALLEN
RAWLINGS

Running the air conditioning put a strain on the i3's battery. It was too hot to sit in the car without it. The meter indicated he'd make it home, or at least to a charging point. He had arrived here too early but couldn't stay in that house another minute. Cobb County schools ended at 3:45, but today Marietta High School would let out early. News of Sandra's death spread, despite the cops' assurances they would try to keep it under wraps. Within a day, his, Sonya's, and Connor's phones were overrun by non-stop vibrations and maddening alerts.

Shortly after the bell rang, which snapped him from his stupor, a flood of teenagers abandoned the school like the exodus from Egypt. Every girl he saw was a target, and they knew it. They had all been too young when the Moralist preyed on their town for over three years. Now they were among the immoral, the ones he would go after. Which one would be next?

The car announced a call from Mom and Dad. Last night Dad took the news with about the same reaction as when they told him Sandra's dog had died. Thirty seconds on the phone being his record, he had put Allen's mother on. Her wailing was so overdramatic and deafening, Allen had to hang up. When he didn't accept the call, his mother sent a text which Allen read from the dashboard screen.

Tell us when the funeral will be. We should be able to make it. Love you.

M.H.S. wasn't the only high school in the area. Two new ones had recently been built as the county kept growing. As Atlanta mushroomed into the southeast's capital of big business, the surrounding counties built new homes, subdivisions, and apartment buildings to keep up with the onslaught of northerners coming for the new jobs. The traffic seemed to thicken daily, the roads not expanding as quickly as the population. *That's government,* Allen thought as he watched droves of new teenage drivers file into cars and take to the road. How shortsighted to welcome thousands of new taxpayers into the county without spending a dime of their tax dollars on improving transportation.

And now government employees had the job of finding his girl's killer.

Sandra must have been sweet on one of those boys. Though he'd forbidden her to date until she turned seventeen in December, he couldn't forbid her from having feelings. He remembered being in high school, dating Sonya, and her fall into sin. Only by the grace of God had Allen been pulled out and led to a higher calling. That useless detective said they found his daughter laid out in the manner of a Moralist victim. He couldn't imagine how that could have been true. After four years... he knew his daughter was safe. Only, she wasn't. And now she was dead.

No, he could not leave this to that same inept detective.

Allen didn't recall switching off the car or getting out or walking toward the sea of students filling the parking lot. While many left, hundreds remained and stood under the afternoon sun, the humidity dripping over their skin. School had only started yesterday, and this year would bring melancholy and fright no one could have anticipated. Two years behind his sister, Connor would have been a freshman here if he hadn't opted for homeschool soon after he began sixth grade and couldn't handle the middle school bullying.

Pushing through the crowds, Allen learned this was a vigil for his daughter. Thirty-some-odd hours or so since her death, and her friends and schoolmates had already organized this. Social media, he figured. A worrisome realization rushed in on him, considering his daughter's popularity greatly exceeded his wildest imagination. Several students gave him strange looks as he asked about Sandra and who her friends were until one of them recognized him.

"Mister Rawlings. I'm, I'm so sorry. We all loved her." The boy turned to the young lady beside him. "This is Sandy's dad. He's a deacon at my church. He let my mom use his address to get me into this school."

"I'm sorry, son, your name escapes me."

The boy shook Allen's hand. "You helped my mom a couple years back. Charlotte Sellers. I'm Russ, well, Russel. We hit some hard times when my dad split, and you really helped carry us through. Mom really appreciated it; she still talks about you."

"That's what we do at Crossroads Holy Ministry. We help one another, as Jesus taught us to do. Tell me, son, were you and my daughter close?"

"Not really, sir. We'd say *hey* and such, but not much more than that. I think we spoke more after Sunday school as kids than we ever did here. I'm in the chess club and she's, well, she *was* too cool for that crowd."

"I see. Can you tell me who her close friends were? I assume they'd be here, not among the ones who took off at the bell."

"I didn't really—"

"Josh is here," the girl said. "Saw him a minute ago, back there." She turned and pointed a chewed-off black fingernail into the crowd. Allen noticed the—he thought they called it gothic—look about the young lady. She and Russel seemed like an unlikely pairing.

"This Joshua was a friend of Sandra's?"

"I haven't heard anyone call her that since she was a kid."

"Yeah, but like you said, you barely said more than *hey*, just like with all the pretty girls." She stuck her pierced tongue out at Russel and retracted it as she turned to Allen. "Sure, mister, you could say they were close. He's got a worn R.E.M. T-shirt on and faded jeans. Pretty-boy type with thick brown hair. Can't miss him."

Shaking his head at the odd couple, Allen pressed on through the crowd. It looked more like what they called a mosh pit at a concert than a vigil, and the young women needed more clothing. He couldn't understand how parents let their children out of the house like that. These were kids, very developed kids, and he knew adult eyes didn't discriminate against the tender age. The last argument he had with Sandra played in his mind. She had brought home some clothes her mother allowed her to buy, and he had ripped them apart, made her clean up the mess, and deducted the cost from her allowance.

Had he spoken to her since? As if God would rewrite the past to ease his conscience, he offered a silent prayer asking that not to have been her last memory of him.

When he looked up, a boy with lush brown hair stood before him in an R.E.M. T-shirt.

WALKER
MICHAELS

R ubber gloves on and with evidence bags in his pocket, Michaels stood in the doorway. Though he saw none, he inhaled a whiff of flowers. It tasted like it came from an aerosol can. With Jones behind him complaining like a child about how he couldn't see, Michaels studied the room. He explained his method to the overeager junior detective on his first big case.

First, he would take in the room, undisturbed from the last time Sandy occupied it. He needed to get a feel for her, how she lived, what was most important to her. A teenager's room, as he experienced with his own daughter, held many secrets in plain sight.

He pulled his phone from the inside jacket pocket and snapped photos of the posters on the wall. Standard stuff. Taylor Swift in concert. That scene from Titanic where Kate Winslet stood at the front of the ship, DiCaprio pressed up against her. Trinkets from countries and places Michaels would only see in movies and TV shows crowded the shelves. Next, he took pictures of each of the photos she had on her desk and dresser. Nothing screamed individuality. One word meandered through his thoughts as he panned his eyes over Sandy's bedroom for the third or seventh time: sterile.

"This is the room of a girl who didn't want to be known. Not to her family, anyway."

"Can I come in now? You said, in the car, two are better than one, *right*? I need to learn to case the room. You know... detect."

When Michaels stepped aside, Jones rushed in like a kid into a candy store. Grabbing his arm, the senior detective stopped his partner's momentum toward the dresser. "You wanna learn? Do what I did. Take it in first, before you touch anything."

Obediently, he did as directed, taking more photos on his fancy Samsung folding phone. It made Michaels chuckle, thinking how his old cell used to fold like that. Trying to sound cool, it had a misspelled name: *Razr*. With no fancy screen, no app store, it made good phone calls.

The two detectives examined the room, scrutinizing every detail. When they opened Sandy's dresser drawers, Michaels set the example by being demure as he moved everything and felt over every item. He scribbled more notes and took some additional pictures. His partner followed suit.

After asking Jones to verify that the mother and son were still downstairs, he pulled up the mattress and searched every conceivable hiding spot the room offered.

Nothing.

With a room-filling finger snap, Michaels exclaimed, "Winter clothes."

He had Jones take down the box of packed winter garments from the top of the walk-in closet. When Jones pointed out how they had already checked it, Michaels ignored him. Its existence in the closet was out of place. The young lady lived in a massive home with more space than the Easy-Store-All on Dallas Highway and filled a closet the size of Michaels' kitchen with summer clothes.

"Why'd she have one small box of winter clothes in the closet when her entire cold-weather wardrobe must be packed away somewhere else?"

"Dunno. Maybe she kept a few things handy, in case of a chilly night?"

"Hmm. That doesn't track. This room's like a television studio set or something. A model of what an average girl's room should look like."

"I was thinking Ikea display. Except, with better furniture, *right*?"

"Yeah, that's good too. She lived here, but this wasn't Sandy. This room reeks of Sandra Rawlings, daughter of Deacon Rawlings and his prim and proper wife. The only thing out of place here is this one small box of winter clothes." Removing the items one-by-one, Michaels laid them out on the remade bed. "Why would she keep scarves and gloves here through the long hot summer when she must have another closet full of her winter clothes?"

"They're thicker than all the light summer stuff."

Michaels paused his work to smack his palms for emphasis. "Exactly."

Painstakingly, he massaged every inch of each scarf, heavy glove, and thick sock. The stuffed leg warmer he found pursed his lips. A hat shoved inside that had several socks crammed inside it. In triumph, his hand pulled out a small bag of marijuana.

"*There* you are. We found her, Jones. Our first glimpse of the *real* Sandy."

With a furrowed brow, Jones asked, "How's a bag of weed help us solve the case?"

CONNOR RAWLINGS

What were they doing in there for so long? Connor couldn't help thinking his sister, robbed of her life a day ago, didn't need her privacy and dignity stripped from her on top of that. How did searching her bedroom help these cops catch Sandy's killer?

"Ma, they've been up there long enough."

"Let them do their job. Sometimes you sound a little too much like your father."

"Don't... They should be out there—" He pointed toward the living room. "—looking for the bastard that did this. Not—"

"Connor! Language."

"You're one to talk, Mom."

His mother straightened in her seat as Connor fidgeted in his. "I would never use such vulgar speech. That's never appropriate, not even today."

"What did that guy with the lame tie say about coping? Look at you, wearing her dress… You're already on your second spritz and it's barely four in the afternoon."

"I need to keep my baby close to me." Her eyes dampened.

"Just… forget it. I'm gonna tell those jackoffs what they can go do with themselves. We don't need them here. They need to go find this guy so they can fry him for what he's done."

"'Vengeance is mine, saith the—'"

"Now who sounds like Dad? I didn't think we should still have the death penalty in this country, but now I'm glad Georgia still kills people like that. I just hope that junior dick and his Monk partner catch the guy, and soon."

"Monk partner?"

"From that show… Forget it. They just need to go, to find that Moralist and make him pay for what he did to Sandy. To us."

For the first time since this devastation came crashing down on them, Connor lost all composure and burst into tears. His mom stood and moved behind him, leaned over his shoulder, and wrapped her arms around him. He became a baby in his mother's comforting embrace.

* * *

The room looked disheveled, though Connor could tell they attempted to put everything back the way Sandy had left it. His sister would never have made the bed like that, and the things on her dresser and shelves were all slightly off from their usual meticulous arrangement. It looked more like a normal teenage girl's room now, and Connor had seen a few beyond TV shows and TikToks.

"You guys about done, or do you need more alone time with my sister's bras and underwear?"

The older man flashed a very Dad-like scowl at him while the younger one—Brandon, if Connor recalled correctly—chuckled and raised his hands in surrender.

"We're done. Nothing suspicious in Sandy's underwear, I assure you."

"Just the padding in her bras, then?" Connor made himself chuckle.

"Your sister didn't need any padding. Took after your mom in that department."

The older man jabbed his elbow in his partner's side, and Brandon winked at Connor. While he found her personally repulsive, even Connor knew his sister was attractive. She had been a tough act for a geeky gamer younger brother to follow in school. It was one of many reasons he opted for homeschooling.

"What are you looking for in here, anyway? My sister wasn't killed in her bedroom. You should be out looking for the guy who murdered her."

"We are," Brandon replied. "Well, we have people working on it, and we're following the evidence. It's all part of the process to help us nail this guy."

"How? Sandy slept here, read books on her bed, and scrolled her socials. Nothing in here connects to that psychopath who killed her. She was a pretty normal, boring, teenage girl."

"Do you really think so? With a secret boyfriend?"

Connor found it interesting how the older guy let the rookie do the talking. He might have thought they could make a connection, being closer in age. All Connor wanted was for them to leave.

"Yeah, I think it's pretty normal for a girl to hide the fact that she had a boyfriend. Especially in a house like this. The only thing that would've set my dad off more would be if Josh were a girl."

"Connor," the old guy stepped forward to say, "I suggest everyone take some time to talk with someone... Someone who can help."

"Like therapy's ever helped my mom. Best thing for us is for you to get this guy. I wanna see him fry. To be there to watch when they flip the switch."

"They haven't electrocuted anyone in over twenty years. Jones, take this evidence to the car. They use lethal injection. But justice—"

"What evidence? Who said you could take some of my sister's stuff?"

"Jones, go. Connor, we need a few things to aid in our investigation. You said you wanted us to catch this guy." He nodded. "Then let us do our job. As I was saying, getting justice is important for you and your family, but doesn't make the hurt and pain go away, believe me."

When the guy moved to place a hand on his shoulder, Connor pulled away.

"Do you know if your sister kept a diary?"

"How old are you, dude? I've seen her use the *Journal* app on her iPhone. She had the latest model. Wait, did you find her things with her, um...?"

"We did find her phone, yeah. Do you know her passcode?"

"She used her face. Man, you must be ancient. I guess you can hold it up to her. It's not like being alive is a requirement for Face ID."

"I'm sure our people will be able to access it."

"You really gonna read her journal? Wasn't she the victim? Seems a needless invasion of Sandy's privacy to me. I still don't see how any of this helps you find my sister's killer."

"It does. Look, what do you know about the Moralist? When he was active, I mean, before now. You were quite young."

"I know a little. Why?"

"You know how his twisted motivations are to cleanse young women of the immorality in the world?" Connor nodded. "Think about it. How does he know who needs cleansing—I mean in his view. He must observe potential targets for some time. I believe there are lots of girls out there he watched and chose not to cleanse."

"So Sandy was one of the morally corrupt? He found her more of a slut than other girls. Is that what you're saying? She, she wasn't like that."

The tired looking man sat on the edge of Sandy's bed and exhaled deeply. "Remember, Connor, that man is twisted. *He* makes decisions rational people can't understand. Your sister was none of those things. And no one deserves what that monster does to those girls."

Connor shrugged, slouching his shoulders and wishing for his gaming chair. A silent moment filled the room, and he could almost see Sandy on her bed, pillow under her chest and legs bent, feet swaying above her as she scrolled her social feeds or read a book. Unlike him, she usually left her door open unless she was on a video call or dressing.

"I wanna help."

"You've been a big help already. You've given us a lot of good infor—"

"I wanna do more. I want, let me help you get this guy... for Sandy."

The man sighed and looked up at the ceiling then back at Connor. "There may be a way you can help."

ALLEN RAWLINGS

T o him, this kid looked nineteen or twenty. Allen felt his blood boiling as it surged through his veins. It took all his will to muster up the patience and mildness of his exemplar. *"But ye have not so learned Christ..."* He recalled some key verses he often used to help church members learn to mold their personalities after the perfect example of faith set by Jesus. If not for that, he could have seen himself punching the boy dead in the face.

"Cool, the teachers stand with us."

Allen looked at him with a twisted expression. "Oh, I'm not a teacher. I'm Sandra's father. Are you Joshua?"

His gulp broke through the din of the crowd to reach Allen's ears, and the boy turned white as a sheet. "Josh, yeah—I mean, yes, sir."

"I need to talk to you, *now*." Allen reached for the boy's arm, and he shrugged away. "Look, I just came from identifying my little girl's dead body, and I need to know everything about her life outside of my house. A life I apparently knew nothing about. It seems you were part of that, so I need to talk to you."

This time Allen managed to get a grip on Joshua's arm and yank him forward. The boy protested, shouting for him to let go. Allen only pulled harder to drag him through the sea of partying teenage *mourners*.

He hardly noticed the cellphones pointing at him until one voice pushed distinct words through the blur of chaotic noises. "You're on an Instagram live feed, jerk. The whole world's watching. Let him go."

Shouts of "Let him go" grew into a chant as Allen continued hauling the flailing teenager toward his car. The multitude moved with them, pushing the clearing between the rally and Allen's parked BMW farther away. Something like a hammer dropped on his forearm, almost loosening his vise grip on the kid's arm. He turned to find the biggest teenager he'd ever seen, likely on the varsity football team or a wrestler, raising a fist for a second blow.

When he turned to quicken his pace, Allen bumped into a thick man with a stern face wearing the uniform of a campus police officer.

*   *   *

No matter how much he rubbed them against his soapy palm, the grime buried itself in the valleys of his fingerprints and wouldn't let go. "My girl's dead, and they treat *me* like a common criminal," he muttered into the mirror. The face it showed him was far from Christlike. The uniformed officer babysitting him in the bathroom said nothing. When he had demanded to speak to Walker Michaels, another cop replied with a judgmental look and continued with the booking process.

"Do you know who I am?" Allen didn't look at the cop while he scrubbed under the flow of steaming water in futility.

"Let me guess, you make more in an hour than I make in a year. Friend of the mayor, you can make one phone call, or something like that. Save it. You attacked a kid on public school grounds. Don't matter who you think you are."

"Attacked? I was just trying to talk to him."

"Save it for the judge. And enough with the washing. We don't use ink no more."

After closing the tap, Allen pulled three hand towels from the dispenser. He wiped his hands almost as ferociously as he had scrubbed them.

"Look, I didn't mean… I'm Allen Rawlings… The father of Sandra Rawlings? Dear God, you don't know about the biggest case you've had in years. Does the name Moralist ring any bells?"

"How'd you know about that?" The officer stiffened, and he rested his hand on the butt of his holstered gun.

"Sandra Rawlings… The victim. *Hello*?" Allen slammed the wet towels into the waste basket and tapped his chest with both hands. "I'm Allen *Rawlings*." He stretched his last name emphatically and the officer's face rounded.

"Oh dear. I'm terribly sorry."

"Thank you. Now, may I go? Or could I please speak with Detective Michaels?"

"I meant, sorry about your daughter. You're still under arrest."

*   *   *

The humiliation of being tossed behind bars paled to the fury igniting his eyes as he stared at the dregs of society sharing the common holding cell. Benches for at least four people each had no room to spare as two massively obese men filled one, five Mexicans monopolized another, and a man with wrangled hair and filthy, tattered clothes lay out on the third.

"Rawlings, time for your phone call."

They complied when he had demanded his phone call earlier, but he didn't know the number and they wouldn't let him check his cellphone's contacts. A kind female officer caught his eye, and she agreed to find the number of Charlotte Sellers. Bumping into her son reminded Allen of the favor she owed him and the discretion he knew she could keep.

After her excited babble for their rekindled contact, he shocked her by telling her where he called from and what he needed. She readily agreed to come bail him out.

As he escorted Allen back to the holding cell, the same bathroom officer asked, "Ain't you got a wife?" Allen ignored the question and its implications and quietly entered his cage to rejoin the animals. Standing close to the cell door and gazing through its bars offered a sense of security. Under the scrutiny of dozens of cops and as many cameras, Allen felt reasonably sure none of his cellmates would attack him.

Although it felt like days, it couldn't have been an hour before they called his name again. "Looks like you made bail," that same cop said. He escorted Allen down the hall and opened a security door with a keycard he pulled from a zip string attached to his waist. "Looks like your phone call was a step up from the Mayor's office. Mayor Cambell's a fine woman, don't get me wrong. But this here's a whole 'nother sort of fine."

On the other side of the door stood Charlotte Sellers, the single mom from church. The red dress hugged her curves under the perfectly set golden hair and subtle makeup. She ran into Allen, wrapped her arms around his neck, and pressed those curves into him.

"Thanks for coming. Sorry to bother you out of the blue."

"It's no bother. And I don't need to know what this is about. I know you're a good man, and I can't imagine how you're handling all this. The nerve of these cops, today of all days."

"You know... about Sandra?"

"Doesn't everyone? My Russ told me about the vigil after school. Do they know what happened, how she died?"

The officer quickly jumped in to say, "We can't share any details of an open investigation."

Allen eyed him so sharply his gaze could have sliced through the black polyester uniform.

"Investigation? So, she was...?" Allen nodded and dipped his head. Charlotte hugged him again, stroking the back of his head. "I'm so sorry, Al. You were there for me, and now... I'm here for you."

"Mister Rawlings. We didn't expect to see you here... Ma'am."

WALKER
MICHAELS

The woman in the red dress too glamorous for the police station nodded in reply to Michaels' greeting. He had no idea who she was but grasped the important part—she was *not* Sonya Rawlings. The grieving mother's peculiar conduct back at the house started to find some sense in Michaels' musing.

Rawlings pushed the woman off him. "Detective."

Such a greeting seldom came from respect, and Michaels had no reason to believe this occurrence broke the pattern. Allen Rawlings had been direct in expressing his disapproval at having the man who failed to stop the Moralist heading the investigation into his daughter's murder.

"You plan to make a habit of accosting teenagers on school grounds?"

"*Accosting*? Look, this whole thing got blown way out of proportion. I was just—"

"Investigating my case."

"If you know about Joshua, why didn't you bring him in? Maybe if you'd do your job, I wouldn't have to." Mister Rawlings got right in Michaels' face to yell, "If you *had* done your job, my girl wouldn't be dead."

As if expecting escalation, Jones lifted himself on his toes. With a push on his shoulder, Michaels reattached his hot-headed partner's heels to the linoleum floor. After shooting Jones a stern look, he turned to address the grieving father, showing him his palms. Although Rawlings backed down, the veins in his neck hadn't released their tension.

"You have the full resources of this station working the case, Mister Rawlings. Josh is not a suspect but is a person of interest to the investigation. In fact, we came from your house just now. We're building a picture of Sandy's life so we can trace her activities and whereabouts."

"It's *Sandra*. And shouldn't you be doing that for the suspects and witnesses? Do you even have any suspects?"

"Why don't you come upstairs? We hoped to speak with you earlier, but you left as we arrived at the house."

"Wait, my house... You were just at my house? Who gave you permission to speak to my family without me?"

"We don't need—" When Michaels pushed a stop signal toward him, Jones ended midsentence.

"We weren't aware we needed your permission, Mister Rawlings. We asked to speak, and your wife and son cooperated."

"What did you ask them? You had no... What did they tell you?"

From under a lowered brow, Michaels panned the room. Every eye of a dozen officers focused on observing this spectacle. Like a child watching her parents argue, the woman in red stood frozen. "I think it's better we go upstairs to discuss the investigation. Your friend can go. We can take you to your car when we're done."

"I don't care what you think—wait." Rawlings pointed to the collection of evidence bags in Jones' hand. "Did you take that from my house? How *dare* you. Do you have a warrant?"

"Please, Mister Rawlings. Let's discuss this upstairs."

"I said, did you have a warrant?"

"We don't need a warrant," Jones blurted. Tired of this back and forth, Michaels didn't stop him this time. "We asked permission. And your daughter's the victim, not a suspect. Sonya was happy to allow—"

"*Sonya!*" The man's face burned red.

"Al, maybe we should go."

When the blonde reached for Rawlings' hand, Michaels watched for his reaction. The seething man grimaced at the detectives and jerked his hand away from hers as if from a flame. His lady friend's face contorted to display wide-eyed surprise that morphed into a disappointed frown with an extended bottom lip.

* * *

In the autopsy room, evidence of the medical examiner's progress lay on the table. As if Sandy Rawlings' body hadn't been horrible enough to look at before, what the doctor had done turned it into a bloody prop from a B-grade horror film. Overpowering anything coming off the body, the clinical stench of chemicals assaulted the nostrils. This time Jones needed a pail, which any M.E. worth his salt kept handy.

The other two ignored the lurching junior detective. To look used to this, Michaels stepped closer to the exam table but trained his eyes on the man who'd dehumanized the corpse. Part of him never understood why such extensive work was done when the cause of death was evident. Especially in a case like this, where the body was exactly like the ones before it. Of course, Sandy was *this* M.E.'s first Moralist victim.

"It's exactly like the others, Detective." Young Doctor Young—he could have been Woody's grandson—motioned to the mess of organs and bones unhidden by the girl's peeled-back flesh. He gazed upon it as if looking at a desk full of case reports. Just a pile of evidence.

"I assume you read up on Woody's—I mean Doctor Clayton's—autopsy reports."

"Of course. And long before this new case. Of course, I reviewed them again, to brush myself up." He pulled the fingers on one of the black gloves that ran up the length of his forearms. "I found all the same signs, the Moralist's modus operandi, for sure."

A mumble of agreement escaped Michaels' closed lips. After setting the bucket down, Jones straightened himself and cleared his throat but said nothing, nodding at his partner.

"Anything unusual? Was the girl sexually active or using any drugs?" Michaels removed his notepad and flipped it open. "We have reason to suspect both."

"There was no sexual assault, as per the Moralist's usual M.O." Once Travis wriggled out of one glove, he began working on the other.

"He thinks he's cleansing them," Jones choked out.

"Hmm." Michaels tapped his pen on the open page of the notebook. "I didn't mean from rape. We know his M.O. He never does... *that*. But he nabs them soon after they lose their virginity."

"Or before, if he's quick enough," Jones blurted. "He'd only gotten one girl before she gave it up, *right*?"

Ignoring the reminder of what they all knew, Michaels forced a long exhale through his nostrils. He studied the notebook, turning back one page. "And the chemical agent? Same as the others, I assume."

"Yes. Traces of Flunitrazepam in her blood. As I said, all details match. The leaf told us as much, but I was thorough... to tick all the boxes."

"I'm sure you were." Knowing his eyes were missing something in his chicken-scratch handwriting, Michaels flipped another page. "Delivery method? Of the Flu-ni-traz..."

"Flunitrazepam. It's a benzodiazepine with pharmacologic actions not unlike those of—"

"Doc." Michaels raised a palm. "I've already forgotten what you just said. I'm just wondering if you can tell how it got into her system, is all."

"Right, sorry. Her Seven-Aminoflunitrazepam levels were well over sixty milligrams per liter. I concur with my predecessor's conclusions that a lower dose was likely used to incapacitate the victims and, when he finishes, um, with them... he administers the fatal dose."

"I recall Woody's findings, but he lost me on how he got there. Seems you agree, and that fits the pattern, don't it? But Doc, I'd like to know how he got it into her. Can you tell me that?"

Now Jones had his pad out and the pen in his hand, his thumb clicking the cam repeatedly. Click click click. His face regained most of its color. "You got a hunch, Boss?" When Michaels glared at him, he apologized again for using the unwanted title, his thumb still making that click click click.

Michaels yanked the pen from his grip and squeezed, breaking it in half and ending the infernal clicking with a snap.

Travis tugged off the second glove and set it on Sandy's shoulder. "Give me some more time. I'm sorry, I hadn't gotten to that yet."

"Hmm… Send it to me when you can." Turning to Jones, Michaels said, "Something feels off about this. And how he administered the drug might tell me what."

SONYA
RAWLINGS

t was silly, and she didn't know why she had done it—or wouldn't admit it to herself. Sonya didn't wear the dress for her husband. To accompany him to the morgue, she had put on an Allen-approved dress. When he forbade her to go, telling her how fragile she was and how it would push her to another breakdown, she changed into it. After Allen had stormed out of the house, of course.

Allen didn't care to see her 'showing off her assets,' as he called it. If he had his way, which he most often did, she would have only left the house in frumpy, loose-fitting old-lady dresses. When the detectives arrived and Brandon's eyes shone, clearly informing her how the sundress made her look, she thanked God Allen never saw the thing. Such musing summoned a fresh wave of tears.

The sundress belonged to Sandy.

After he had come home from identifying their daughter's body, seeing Sonya in it set Allen off. Worse than his reaction to her insistence on going with him to identify their child, the dress had started a more heated argument. Looking at her reflection now, she understood why. It went deeper than the dress's immodesty and not knowing she had bought it for Sandy. The two-dimensional woman in her full-length mirror looked like an older, more mature version of his daughter. The woman Sandy would never become.

He'll learn of the boy, Sonya contemplated. How would he react if he found out she knew about Josh? A rush of insurmountable guilt chased the trepidation away and took the strength from her leg muscles. Her knees buckled and she collapsed onto the carpet in her dressing room. The thump and clamorous shattering of the mirror raced down the hall to summon her son.

"Mom? *Mom.*"

When Connor helped his mother to her feet, her legs held her there. Embarrassment reddened her cheeks, and she apologized to her son. Up the entirety of the first night, and hardly sleeping last night, she had a convenient excuse for her loss of balance. As he walked her out of the spacious dressing room, Connor uttered an expletive not permitted in the Rawlings household. She didn't scold him as his limping on a twisted foot stole all other thoughts.

"Are you okay? What happened?"

"I stepped on a piece of glass."

Quarter-sized red splotches on the white carpet trailed them from the dressing room to her four-poster Alaskan king bed. Sonya wondered if the polite young men from Chem-Dry could get those out. It was almost time for their quarterly carpet cleaning.

Like a memory of being mother to younger children, Sonya cleaned her son's foot in the master bath. When she poured peroxide over it, his face shriveled, and he inhaled a wet breath through clenched teeth. She teased him about being a baby, but that was exactly what she wanted him to be at that moment. Although she thought his foot might need stitches, Connor insisted it wasn't bad, and they agreed on a large Band-Aid and gauze wrap, for now.

Thoughtlessly, Sonya pulled her son into a tight embrace. He didn't squirm or complain as he had been doing since becoming a teenager. The unexpected moment brought Sonya to tears. Connor joined her in open sobbing and buried his face in her chest as he hadn't done in years. Gently, she combed her fingers through his hair as his body convulsed, and he wheezed between the bellows. To fill the role of caring mom momentarily diminished her own morbid grief.

* * *

Sonya didn't appreciate not knowing where Allen had gone. When he had stormed out again, he'd said nothing. She had asked him where he needed to go at such a time, begged him to stay. In response, he'd yanked the keys from the wall hook, loosening it from the wooden key rack. Motes of sawdust dripped out of the tiny hole and fell onto the shelf below. Allen had slammed the door to the garage, jarring her as she swept the dust into her open palm with her hand.

The almost silent lifting of the garage door—Allen had insisted on spending the extra money on chainless openers— had sent an ease into her shoulders and her muscles relaxed. When those detectives had come by unannounced, Sonya had felt completely calm. Now the tension her body was reclaiming came not from the quietness of the home or the absence of her husband.

It had often been said no one knew the real you better than those in your household, where all facades were hung on the coatrack by the front door. In church she had heard too many times how the bond between husband and wife was the closest and most important.

He had been gone for several hours now.

Shortly after Brandon and Detective Michaels had departed from their first visit, when they informed them they would never see their baby girl again, Allen had blurted nonsense about needing to do something. He didn't trust the lead investigator and now Sonya understood why. For over three years, Detective Walker Michaels had worked the Moralist case. Never closed, it was shelved only because the killer had stopped killing. Nearly four years had passed since the last poor young lady had been murdered, and now Michaels was again heading the investigation.

The way Sonya saw it, if a trained and decorated detective of Michaels' years could not catch this guy, what chance did an account manager have? True, the detective had only a couple of years over Allen, but he had decades of experience solving crimes. Her earlier web searches found the Moralist serial killer was the only case Michaels had failed to solve. In somber musing, she realized that failure had led to her daughter's murder.

In one hand, Sonya fondled the business card Michaels had given her. He had told her, "any time, day or night." The other hand cradled her cellphone, with Brandon's contact opened, and her thumb hovering over the green call button.

An alert on the little screen snapped her mind out of its pause. Peter and Mary Miller breached the radius of the *Ring* doorbell's motion detector and looked at each other before proceeding up the front steps to press the button that didn't need to be pressed. Mary held two vibrant red roses.

Since they'd started rock-climbing, they both took on a more robust physique. Whenever Mary showed her a video of her and Peter doing what she called 'bouldering,' Sonya marveled at the woman's upper-body strength to hoist herself up those fake rocks. Other than that, she found the videos incredibly uninteresting but always nodded and gave the obligatory responses.

As soon as Sonya swung the door open, she was consumed in Mary's firm embrace. It lasted an uncomfortably long time but could have been a few seconds. When Peter stepped in, Sonya felt like an unsuspecting insect caught in the sudden snap of a Venus Flytrap until he released her and examined the dress. Or, as she saw it more retrospectively, examined *her* in that dress. What she didn't know was if the look from this man cast judgment or meant something else. At times, a discomforting familiarity glittered in his eyes when he laid them upon her.

Before she realized it, or invited them, her visitors removed their shoes and helped themselves to the sofa. After getting a vase for the roses and setting them beside the white ones from yesterday, Sonya asked if they wanted anything to drink. She fetched a bottle of Fiji Water from the refrigerator—she never served guests from the tap—and brought it to Peter with a glass.

An awkward silence sat as a third visitor when Sonya took a seat on her husband's chair. A glance at her watch hinted at the hours Allen had been out, and she wondered where he had gone and when he would be home. She hoped he wouldn't come home to find the Millers on his sofa.

The words that eventually came brought even greater awkwardness than the quiet had created. Once broken,

Sonya longed for its return. She didn't blame the Millers. Not many months ago, she had joined Allen on a similar visit to a church member widowed in her forties by a drunk driver. Sonya had suffered from the same loss for words. Thinking back, she realized her blathering hadn't likely offered any more coherence or comfort than the words bouncing off her now.

"How's Connor handling it?" Peter asked.

It took a great deal of restraint for Sonya not to say the words her mind suggested. These were her friends, doing what they could. Peter served as a deacon at their church and Allen considered him one of his closest friends. Or perhaps, Sonya mused, a protégé. Like all deacons' wives, Mary and Sonya joined the occasional "Wives Night" when their husbands had meetings with the pastor. They had worked on fundraisers and church projects together. Sonya and Mary had known each other since high school, and Allen had insisted on setting up his tag-along buddy with Sonya's friend.

"As good as can be expected. He hasn't said much, mostly stays in his room. But that's his usual. You know how teenage boys are."

Wishing to take that last comment back, Sonya withdrew. Against pastoral counsel, Mary had tubal ligation surgery soon after getting married. She and Peter had said they couldn't think of bringing children into such a corrupt world.

"Your family is in our prayers," Mary said. "I'm sure Connor will be fine. Y'all will get through this. Do you mind if I go upstairs to say *hey*? We left kind of abruptly yesterday."

With a nod of consent, Mary rose and went upstairs. Before the sofa cushion finished reshaping itself into its fluffed state, Peter slid over to take Mary's place closer to Sonya. He laid his hand on her forearm.

"If there's anything you need..."

Forcing a show of gratitude to her eyes, Sonya nodded and pulled her arm from the armrest. The gesture built a wall between them. They sat without words or eye contact for some minutes until a question rattled the cage of Sonya's thoughts, demanding to be let out.

"Do you and Mary really think—"

"Where's Allen?" Peter looked around the room. "Not at work, is he?"

"No. He said he needed some air, to clear his head. He's been in and out all day. It's... I'm sure he won't be long."

Something warm touched her hand and her eyes traced her arm down to where it lay on her lap. With both his hands on hers, Peter leaned forward so close Sonya noticed a gray hair in one of his eyebrows. When Peter saw his wife over his shoulder, he withdrew his hands and sat back.

"Connor didn't say much, and I didn't have the words. We hugged, and I told him he would get through this."

"Thank you. Oh, how's your arm? I'm sure I have some Neosporin if you need."

With a face confused by the question, Mary tilted her head and fiddled with the cuff of her blouse's sleeve. "It's fine. I'm used to it. Happens every time I pick those darn roses." Mary sat beside her husband and grabbed his hand. He cocked his head at her. Trapping a word before it escaped his mouth, she said, "You know we're here for you. Sandy was a lovely girl."

"What a shame what happened to her," Peter said. "Out at night before her first day of school. She was down by the square until late, wasn't—"

"She was coming home for curfew, as always." Sonya's posture stiffened.

Mary took a sip of Peter's water. "As always, when *Allen* is home. We all know he's a bit stricter, isn't he?"

While she didn't reply, the implications of the question swirled through her mind's confusion. Also, Allen could have come home at any minute. In a manner far from her usual etiquette, Sonya said she needed to do 'something' and ushered the Millers from her home.

After changing her clothes and washing her face, Sonya waited.

BRANDON
JONES

The Action Board was fuller now, with photos of the Rawlings family and the name *Josh* with a huge red question mark beside it. Notes scribbled by Michaels resembled Arabic or one of those 'squiggly' languages. One-by-one, Jones asked the grumbling man for the translation and the marker squeaked as he rewrote the information in carefully scribed non-cursive block letters.

Thick red lines connected each point, some with multiple links. After initially criticizing the technique, Jones began to see its value. No computer screen—their station had not been outfitted with wall-to-wall monitors like he had seen on TV shows—could show them such a high-level yet detailed view of the entire case.

Once he finished rewriting his partner's notes on the dry-erase surface, Jones flipped open the coroner's preliminary report. Before adding each new point on the board, he asked if the place he thought of jotting it was good. Each time, Michaels nodded while sipping his coffee and observing through focused eyes—dark bags hanging below them. Once Jones finished, Michaels stood off his lean on the desk and raked his hand through his thick graying hair.

"One more thing."

One of the old case boxes rested on Michaels' desk with the lid removed, and he pulled a stack of photographs from it. Using the round magnets, he placed the photos of the previous victims along the left side of the board, starting from the top. From memory, Michaels spoke each girl's name with a heavy breath as he tacked them up. When he reached the bottom, he continued with a second column. Eleven bright, happy faces—all of them gone, their lives snuffed out by a madman.

A brilliant madman who had evaded capture for seven years.

Jones didn't question his partner's need to see those eleven faces, twelve now with Sandy. They provided added motivation to finally nail this devil. Solving this case, after all these years, would launch Jones' career, likely promoting him much earlier than most junior detectives his age. Staring at the empty space below the last photo, he noticed an imbalance of the two columns of previous victims with six in one, five in the other.

"An even dozen?" The quick deduction slipped out and Jones continued, "Could that be why he's back, after all this time?"

Under a crinkled brow, Michaels replied, "What are you getting at? You think it's a *numbers* game?"

Straightening his shoulders, Jones attempted to firm up his voice. "This guy's methodical, *right*? In what he does and why he does it. He must be some kind of religious nutcase." Michaels nodded a face crinkled in confusion. "Think about it… The number twelve is an important thing in the Bible, *right*? Twelve tribes of Israel. Twelve apostles. Twelve cornerstones of heaven."

The way Michaels' face flattened, Jones couldn't read his reaction.

"I'm not saying this explains the four-year hiatus, but, for whatever reason, he stopped at eleven. Maybe because you did get too close that last time. What if he came back to finish the job? You know, round it up to twelve."

"Hmm. You're saying Sandy Rawlings may be his last victim."

"Dunno. Maybe. Like you said, twisted mind, twisted reasoning."

"We can't assume he's done. The problem with serial killers like this one, with nothing linking the victims besides demographics, is we hit lots of dead ends. We'll go through the motions, putting the usual suspects on the board."

"Why do all that? We *know* it's him."

"Due diligence. When the killings are random, and we don't catch the bastard, we expect him to keep going. God, I wanna be wrong. I'm sorta hoping your twelve-victims theory has legs."

"Michaels." The call came from Officer Bell. On track to make detective, she exuded enthusiasm for the work. Brandon and Melissa had a few drinks a couple of weeks ago, but nothing had yet come of it. Detecting an expectant interest in her for his next move, he hadn't given up.

"What is it, Bell?"

"Sorry to interrupt, sir. Sergeant Carter is asking for you. Both of you, sirs."

As Michaels clutched the working case folder and brushed passed the messenger in a huff, Jones said, "Thanks, Mel." When he smiled, she reciprocated.

With a few hurried paces, Jones caught up to Michaels as he stepped into the sergeant's office. She motioned to the chairs with a straight face. Not a large space, the desk crowded most of it and the two chairs opposite her pressed into the glass wall beside the door when they pulled them out to sit.

"What's this about, Ronni?" The woman, in her early fifties but looking younger with the creamy South Indian skin tone, scowled at Michaels, and he corrected himself. "Sergeant Carter."

"We're creeping toward two days since the body was found. Almost thirty-six hours since time of death. I don't have to tell you how many eyes are on you for this one, Michaels. How many don't want you on this case."

"No, ma'am, you don't. Is that all?" He pushed his hands into the armrests as if he would hoist himself up. Jones thought it was a show and didn't understand the back-and-forth at play over the real wood desk.

"You've got a fresh set of eyes now." She looked at Jones then back to Michaels. "I want to be sure you're using them. Do you have any new leads? Anything besides telling me, and the world, the Moralist is back?"

"Nothing concrete yet. We're just pulling everything together, working the board."

"I saw that. Jones, don't let this dinosaur inhibit you from using every tool and resource at your disposal. You're more up to date on our new computer systems and the AI module chat-bot thing. I want *you* running all evidence and details through it. See if it's worth its ridiculous budget."

"Yes, Sergeant, ma'am." Jones held back a salute, lowering the hand that instinctively started to rise.

Resting her elbows on the desk, Carter steepled her fingers. "Look, Michaels. I stood up for you on this case, back then, and almost lost my career saving yours. I don't have a reserve of goodwill enough to do it again."

"I understand."

"I hope you do."

When Michaels stood, so did Jones.

"Gentlemen. Before you go, let me say this. You need anything; you tell me. You hit any roadblocks; you tell me. I want to know every step you take and every little bit of progress or lack thereof." She leaned forward and came up off her chair. "I want to know when you stop to take a piss. Am I clear?"

"Crystal, Sergeant."

Before Michaels could step over Jones, the junior detective said, "There may be something, ma'am."

Michaels glared at Jones like a bear ready to bite his face off.

"Go on..."

"Dunno. It's Michaels' hunch, I guess. Something about the Chloroform or whatever."

Crossing her arms, Carter grimaced. "And?"

Before Jones could reply, Michaels said, "Chloroform is used in movies. I never remember the name. Flunitrap, or something."

"The point, Michaels?" Carter snapped.

"Nothing yet. I'd not even call it a hunch. A question I asked Woody—I mean that new guy, Travis. Doctor Young. If anything comes of it, you'll be the first to know, promise."

"Promises won't pay your pension. Now get out there and get me something that will close this case. Dismissed."

ALLEN RAWLINGS

The red brick siding wrapped all the way around the modestly furnished Paulding County ranch home. Allen had been here a few times back when Charlotte's husband abandoned her and her son. He helped her and Russel move in. As a deacon in their church, he often rendered spiritual and practical assistance to fellow members.

When his visits increased in frequency, and Sonya started a friendship with his assistant at work, it became harder to "extend" his business trips an extra night. Allen stopped coming around regularly over a year ago. The occasional call for assistance from the single mother brought him back a few times, but it had been months since he last saw her outside of church.

When he called her from jail, Charlotte rushed over without hesitation and still had not questioned him about why he was arrested. Assuming her financial struggles persisted, it surprised him how readily she paid his bail, using a credit card to do it.

Charlotte tossed her bag on the kitchen counter and swung the refrigerator door open. "I still keep your favorite cold ones in the fridge." She lifted her shoulders and smiled. "You never know."

Allen readily accepted the chilled Coors Light and drank it greedily as she watched.

"Russ said he's not coming home for dinner..." she said as she slinked down the hallway.

*   *   *

A good thing about a shower, it washed the guilt away with the evidence and sweat. Clean in body if not in conscience, Allen pulled into his driveway. The garage door lifted automatically once the sensor detected his i3's approach. Sonya had been fuming when he stormed out hours ago, and he had no idea what to expect from her now. Sandra's death had already altered their family dynamic, and none of them acted like themselves. As he exited the car and plugged it in, he couldn't comprehend his wife's thinking in wearing their daughter's dress.

Nothing but silence greeted him when he entered through the door from the garage. The key fob crashed onto the tile floor when its limp hook fell from the key rack. Its clank filled the space then left it to the quiet it held before.

Allen bent to pick up the fob but couldn't find the fallen hook and quickly gave up the search. He dropped the BMW key on the shelf and headed into the kitchen, expecting to find Sonya preparing dinner. Or, at this hour, telling him to sit while she reheated it for him.

When he said, "Hey," to her back, she didn't reply. He didn't think she used the computer for anything besides looking up recipes and the occasional email and couldn't recall the last time he had seen her on it.

"Did you eat out?" she asked.

She still didn't turn to face him. Under her shoulder-length auburn hair, she wore one of her house dresses. A hint of relief filled Allen at not seeing Sonya in Sandra's clothes, a picture of who their daughter would never grow to become.

"No."

"We didn't eat either. Would you call for pizza? I've got nothing in me to start cooking."

"Of course." He stepped behind his wife and laid a gentle kiss on her head.

The positioning allowed him to see what she had on the screen, which she made no attempt to hide. She had over a dozen tabs open to articles and old news reports about the Moralist. The one she was reading in the screen's spectral glow described the last victim and how Detective Walker Michaels had almost caught him at the scene.

Allen rested his hands on the back of her chair. "Unbelievable. If he would've caught the guy, we'd still have our—"

"I know."

"And he's leading the investigation now. After failing for years."

"He got close, almost caught him. A lot of people think that's why the Moralist stopped. I mean, until... now."

"Got close? Did you read the whole article? The suspect he saw was probably nobody. Just some guy at the wrong place, wrong time. Michaels is a worthless buffoon who can barely find the toes at the end of his feet. I don't trust him to find Sandra's killer."

"Is that why you went out again?" Sonya finally twisted her neck and looked Allen in the eye. "You think *you're* going to find this man?"

Allen pulled back, a look of surprise on his face. "I can't do much worse than Michaels." To add a justification, he said, "And not just for Sandra. Who knows who's next... or how many more."

Standing to face him and take his hand, Sonya said, "I know. I want justice for Sandy, too. But nothing will bring her back to us."

"I saw them, you know. Where I went... before. Saw hundreds of them."

When Sonya blinked rapidly, Allen understood the confusion. It was a habit she had when unable to find the words to question him.

"I went to the school. I thought I'd have to wait a while, but they let out early. Somehow, they knew about Sandra. They held a vigil that looked more like a licentious rave. Half-naked girls everywhere. And at school. Those are the ones... Not my..." The lump in his throat swallowed his words.

"Why'd you go there? What did... I mean, *why*? Why did you leave me... your son, again, at a time like this?"

Leading her by the hand, Allen had them sit at the kitchen table. "We know why this guy does what he does." He dry-swallowed hard. "I figured someone at her school has to know who she'd been spending time with. Which boy that... man... might *think* she was fooling around with."

"And you went there to hurt this boy?"

Eyes bulging, he pulled his hand from hers and sat up straight. "*What*? How could... Look. I went to find answers. The cops hadn't even been there. They're doing nothing."

"That's not true. They came here, those same two detectives. They asked me and Connor some questions then checked Sandy's room."

"And you let them take her things. I saw them, at the station, in evidence bags." As if electricity surged through his fingers, he shook both his hands. "Why'd you allow that? How is taking her personal things going to help them catch this guy? They were just hanging around the station, not out looking for him."

Sonya crinkled her face. "You were at the police station?"

"I sort of... got arrested." Dipping his head, Allen stared at his hands as he rested them on the table. "It was just a misunderstanding."

"Allen, what did you do at Sandy's school?"

"Nothing. I just tried to talk to this boy, Joshua. Russel told me he and Sandra had been spending time together recently."

"Who's Russel?"

"Charlotte's son. You know, from church. His father split a few years ago."

"Single, bottle blonde, Barbie figure. Yes, I know who she is. Everyone calls her son Russ."

"And everyone called our daughter *Sandy*, when I named her Sandra."

Allen shot to his feet. The blood that had rushed to his face in rage retreated to the force of gravity and he became lightheaded. To keep from falling, he clutched the back of the chair. Sonya didn't budge.

"They just let you go?"

"What?" He had regained his balance—physically, at least.

"You must have caused a disturbance at the school and frightened those children." Sonya leaned back in her chair and folded her arms over her chest. "They arrested you and then let you go, just like that?"

"I made bail."

"I know."

Allen's mind exploded. "Huh? What... what are you saying?"

Without answering, she stood, sighed, and walked toward the stairs. "I'm going to bed. Don't forget to call Papa John's; Connor must be starved... And it seems you worked up an appetite."

Both their phones alerted them that someone approached the door.

WALKER
MICHAELS

A full Action Board brought both satisfaction and dread. That white plasticky rectangle on the wall had been unmarked for months. Random notes and occasional drawings, some lewd, had decorated it here and there before Michaels wiped them into oblivion. Seeing it filled once again with Moralist case evidence tightened the cramp in his gut.

His stomach's complaint came more from hunger than the sickening feeling from the board. Well past quitting time, Jones stayed and tried to make himself useful. This stage of the investigation meant a lot of staring at the board, flipping through files they had flipped through a hundred times already. And that didn't count the times Michaels had done it years before.

When Officer Bell returned from the lockers in a shiny blue tank top and jeans, Jones told her he needed to stay. Perhaps he thought his role was to stare at that board as long as his partner did. By around 8 PM, Michaels dismissed him. The lovely cop patiently waiting out of uniform to be taken to dinner had been tormented long enough. Since Michaels considered dinner with Jones a worse torture, he wished her luck.

To get Jones to leave, Michaels said he did his best thinking alone. True or not, staring at the board for thirty minutes uncovered no new insights. The buzzing of his phone vibrating again disturbed his process. He mentally cursed whoever decided to label it *Silent mode*. Knowing who it was didn't motivate him to pick it up.

Two people had been trying to reach him, and he only replied to one. How could he explain that to Bonnie? Surely, she had been used to him prioritizing work over his daughter. That's how she always said it. He thought it was an unfair way to put it. To verify Missus Rawlings hadn't been trying to contact him again, he flipped the phone to see Bonnie's incoming call and set it back, face down, on his desk.

Not that he expected Sonya Rawlings to call again, but he had told her, 'any time, day or night.' His ear still rang from the earlier outburst when he told her about his run-in with her husband at the station. Bonnie had phoned six times and sent three text messages, which she knew he hated to receive and rarely answered. He didn't have the thumbs for it. It made no sense to him how talking on the phone was the least thing people did on their phones. In his daughter's defense, she had tried calling first, several times.

"Pick up your phone once in a while, *old* man."

Startled by the intrusion, Michaels turned to find Bonnie at the archway separating the detective squad from the uniforms.

"They said I can't come any farther, father." Her smile lifted the gloomy mood from the room. "I know you're staring at your board, and I'm not allowed to see it. So... are you going to come hug your daughter or do I have to commit a crime to get your attention?"

In a 'dad' attempt to be funny, Michaels trudged over to her. He drew her into a tight hug, lifting her feet from the gray laminate tiles. As he released her, he asked, "Where's Mike?"

"I left him home with the kids."

"How are my grandchildren?"

Sinking her brow, she replied, "You'd know if you came over more often."

"Once a month for dinner not enough for you?"

"Dad, we said we'd do *weekly* dinners." Her grown-up voice mimicked her mother's, especially when scolding him.

"You know how it is, honey."

"I know how *you* are. Come on, old man. Let me take you to dinner. Mike made pulled pork and his grandma's collards."

To counter that would have started a losing argument. He was also starved and beyond exhaustion. It had been years since he woke up so early and had such long days. Four years of starting work at 9 AM. Four years since the Moralist stopped preying on the teenage girls of the city under his protection.

*   *   *

As soon as he stepped into Bonnie's home, the 'grandchildren' ran up to him and stood on their hind legs with front paws on his chest. Michaels always thought a Rottweiler and Labrador Retriever were too big for apartment life. Whenever Bonnie and Mike went out of town, the dogs indulged themselves in *grandpa's* back yard. His son-in-law claimed their morning and evening walks gave them enough exercise. Patting Baxter's belly, Michaels thought he could use a daily run.

Mike's pulled pork and collard greens were as delicious as Bonnie had promised. He would never tell his daughter, but she hadn't inherited her mother's aptitude for cooking. That woman could have outcooked anyone in her sleep. A sudden emptiness entered his bloated, meat-and-greens-filled stomach. It had been years since he'd savored one of Cathrine's meals. During her year-long fight when her breast cancer returned, she'd hardly cooked at all. In the last months, she rarely even ate or got out of bed.

While Mike loaded the dishwasher, Bonnie and her father chatted over the empty table.

"Dad, I know you're on a case, that poor girl is all over the news. The lack of detail in their reporting makes it all too obvious." Taking his hand, she said, "He's back, isn't he?"

Dipping his head gave her the answer.

"You already look exhausted, like you've been working non-stop again. And this is the second day. You can't do this to yourself. Not again."

"I can't, sweetheart... I just can't let him get away. Not again. Not this time."

"But Dad, this case nearly ruined you. No, it *did* ruin you. And look at you. You've only barely pulled yourself back up and now you're at it again. You said Marietta City has more detectives. Let someone else handle this, *please*."

Cocking his head, he said, "You know I can't do that. But this time I don't have you to worry about. You're out of his target demographic now."

"I know you. All you see when you close your eyes is her. Just like the others. What was her name, Sandra something?"

"Sandy. Sandy Rawlings."

"And you won't stop until you catch this guy. Or until it kills you, *one*."

"Baby, I can't—"

"It's his job, Hun." Mike's voice echoed in from the kitchen over the clanking of dishes. "And you always tell me he's the best at it."

She turned her head and yelled back, "He'll obsess, Babe. You weren't there last time. I saw what it did to him." Turning to her father, she continued in a loud voice, "There were times when Mom, on her deathbed, looked better than him. I almost lost both parents at once."

The dogs stirred when Michaels stood. "It looks like you two are perfectly capable of having this discussion yourselves. So, if you'll excuse me, I think I best be going. Been a long day."

"No chance, mister. To the couch. We need to talk."

"Baby girl, we've been talking. I need to get home, shower, and sleep."

"Nope." On her feet as fast as him, Bonnie pulled her father into the living room. "You'll go home, *drink*, and stare at the wall mentally reviewing evidence. I lived at home last time, remember? You'll stay here tonight. You can shower and take the guest room. Billy and Baxter would love to sleep with you."

"You got your boss-of-me ways from your mother."

Chuckling, she slapped his arm. They sat on the couch, Bonnnie nestled against him with the dogs at his shins begging to be pet.

"Mike, please take the kids out. Dad and I need to talk."

CONNOR RAWLINGS

Why couldn't people just leave them alone? First Mary Miller came into his room, his private sanctuary, and crushed him in a hug. Then a stream of people from the neighborhood and church flowed through their home all evening. His parents made him sit in the living room through it all. The pastor spewed nonsense about Sandy being in a better place, and Deacon Matthew said her young life had been delivered from this wicked world.

The youth minister, Brian Downing, insisted on talking to Connor alone. When he resisted, his mother's look made it clear he had no choice. Papa John's boxes filled the kitchen counter, and he found one that hadn't been emptied. These people wouldn't leave, but at least they brought a ton of pizza. Sitting on the back deck, Connor devoured two more slices as the words blew past his ears like a hot August breeze. When Brian asked if he knew where Sandy was Sunday night and who may have seen her, the question pulled Connor into the quicksand of speculation.

He clawed at the memory of his sister's first teenage crush on the handsome young preacher man and how she volunteered to work beside him every Saturday. Latching onto a new realization like an exposed root, Connor tried to hoist himself out of the mire before he drowned in it. Had the youth minister gotten over the theoretical fling as easily as Sandy had?

*   *   *

The pizza crust he tossed onto it toppled the paper plate off the edge of his bed and onto the floor. Gigi would gobble it up, so Connor didn't need to worry about it. Then he remembered that Sandy's Chihuahua ran into the street last month and found a new home under the dirt in the backyard. Like a silly little child, his older sister made them have a funeral for it.

As if his day could not have gotten worse, now he felt guilty for having a negative thought about his dead sister. He didn't know why, but he had heard his parents' bedroom door slam from the other end of the hallway. As Connor changed the bandage on his foot, his dad's muffled voice failed to contain his pleas to know if his mom was all right. How could she have been? How would any of them be all right ever again?

Only when his phone screen dimmed into *Do not disturb* mode did Connor realize how late it had gotten. He had a mission now, something he could do to aid in the investigation and help the cops catch his sister's killer. Though not as addicted to social media as she was, Connor knew his way around the apps. Before now, he never considered it a bad thing he and his sister hadn't followed each other. Their lives had been lived in blissful separation.

Earlier, that ancient detective asked him to help them build a profile of Sandy's social life, her friends, her hobbies, where she liked to go and who with. While he never would have said he knew everything about his sister, her passwords were not difficult to guess. After a few failed attempts to access Instagram, he tried variations of her favorite number— he couldn't understand why anyone would have a favorite number—with the name Josh. Once he got it, he found she used the same password on the other platforms.

With the feeble light of his phone the only thing illuminating his face, he scrolled through her feeds. He found TikTok to be the most annoying and had no idea why she, why anyone, would follow the threads she did. What he saw next dropped his jaw to the floor.

His sister was dead. How did people not get that? So many of her 'friends' tagged her today and added comments to her last posts expressing how much they missed her and were praying for her family. One nutjob sent something obscene in Sandy's DMs about how he'd do her alive or dead. Connor took a screenshot of that one for the detectives. Then he noticed something else he found suspicious.

In one of Josh's IG posts from Sunday, he tagged Sandy and another account called Gigi90210. Sandy's dog and favorite number. It had to be a secret account; one she likely didn't have on her iPhone. Their dad randomly checked their phones, claiming he had the right as long as they were 'under his roof,' and he paid the Verizon bill. Most likely, she logged onto that account in a private browser tab. When it didn't work on his phone, Connor logged onto his computer and pulled up Firefox and opened a private tab.

"What were you up to, sis?"

Day 3

M

S heer curtains did little to hide the young lady's silhouette in the second-floor bedroom window from his binoculars. He licked his lips as she pulled her bed shirt over her head, and he pinched the skin on his forearm to discipline himself. Mitsy Davis always woke early to take her morning run, the first in her family out of the house. Did her parents know about her after-school extracurricular activities?

Not until two days ago had he realized how much he'd missed this. The Lord obviously wanted him to continue his work, had shown him a sign. This young lady had been corrupted by the decadence of the world around her. He knew it wasn't her fault. Peer pressure and the normalcy of what life had become for these kids robbed them of their innocence, their purity before God. Soon, he would correct that.

Another soul to save.

BRANDON
JONES

With eyes pinched shut to block out the bright morning sun slipping through the slit where the two curtain panels met, he pulled the pillow over his head. The Gojira song blaring from his phone woke him, and he clumsily tapped *Snooze*. Three days in a row of waking before six broke his pattern, though not by much. Brandon normally rose by seven to take his morning jog, shower, have a protein-rich breakfast smoothie, and head to the station by nine.

Not today. Today he had to get straight to the action board to work the case of a lifetime.

As he rolled over in bed, alone, the case wasn't the first thing on his mind. This morning was not as he hoped. After a lovely dinner with Mel, they walked and talked a bit. He pulled into her apartment complex just before midnight and received a kiss on the cheek. A simple, "Goodnight. I had a nice time. See you tomorrow," ended the evening.

Up on his feet, Jones pushed one of the panels back to check, but no one usually went to the pool this early. He pulled up his khakis, threw on his blue shirt, and grabbed the same silver tie. In this August Georgia heat, he thought Michaels was insane for wearing a suit jacket,

Ticking too loudly, the wall clock in the kitchen told him to forgo making his shake and grab some coffee and a spinach feta wrap at the Starbucks by the square. He sent a text message asking Michaels what he wanted so he could order ahead with the app and skip the long lines. Before reversing out of his spot, Jones placed the order. With no reply from his partner, he ordered him a grande bold with two sugars and a bacon gouda sandwich.

* * *

As expected, Michaels had arrived ahead of him. He wore the same suit, shirt, and tie as yesterday, only slightly more disheveled. A ripped-open and empty Chik-fil-A sandwich pouch sat atop one of the case boxes on his desk and he stood over it, sipping from a Starbucks venti cup with the lid off. His eyes rolled up to greet Jones through the steam as he approached.

"Looks like one of us got lucky last night."

After flashing a puzzled look, Michaels replied, "I spent the night with a lovely young lady."

"*Young*, huh? I guess we're the opposite then, tiger. I go for the cougars."

A recognizable female voice behind him hissed, "*Really*?"

Turning to Officer Bell, Jones said, "Oh, hey Mel. We're just joking around. You know how men do. Seems our man here got him some last night, *right*?"

"You're a real jerk, you know that?" She grimaced and put her hands on her hips. "And *our man* stayed at his daughter's house last night. I can't believe I thought…"

"But I—"

"Officer Bell, did you need something?"

"Not me. Sarge wants to see you in five." Looking at Jones, she added, "Bring the gigolo." Melissa stomped away.

Jones set the breakfast and one coffee on his desk and sipped his through the little hole in the lid.

"You were gonna let me think you got luck—"

"My personal life ain't nobody's business. Until we solve this case, neither of us got one. I want you in here by seven."

A glance at the phone he placed on his desk showed 7:04. Motioning to the coffees and sandwiches he brought, he said, "Guess you already ate. I got a wrap and sandwich, if you're still hungry."

"Got a Starbucks right next to a Chik-fil-A on my way in. Don't care for Starbucks' food, and Chick-fil-A coffee ain't worth a dime, and they charge a lot more than that for it. Fried chicken biscuit with honey and a bold roast—best of both worlds. But, if that coffee's for me, I'll take it."

"A grande after a venti?" Jones handed Michaels the cup and unwrapped his spinach feta.

"It's one of those days. One of those cases. Check the board."

One glance at the Action Board told Jones Michaels had stayed late or arrived very early. More likely both. There were several new notes and additional pictures. Shots of Marrietta High School and the Rawlings home looked like screenprints from Google Street View. A photo of a young man hung beside the boyfriend's full name, Joshua Sturgill.

"When... How?"

"Detective work, Detective." Michaels tossed his empty cup in the bin beside his desk and started on the one Jones had brought him.

"Wait." Brandon almost dropped his wrap while stepping toward the board and pointing at collages of pictures on several sheets of paper. "These are all screengrabs of social posts. You don't even answer your texts. Did we get into Sandy's phone?"

"The tech guys did, yeah. But most of those aren't on her phone. She had a secondary account." He took another sip and paused, like he expected Jones to react.

"How'd they find it?"

Leaning toward the board, Jones studied the pictures. Sandy had been to parties, splashed around in a skimpy bikini with Josh in a crowded pool, and gone to nightclubs. A more complete picture of what Michaels called 'the real Sandy.'

"*They* didn't. Connor did. I put him on a mission, and he came through. Sent me all that late last night."

Jones breathed out a long whistle. "Looks like our girl led a wild secret life. But what seventeen-year-old doesn't, *right*?"

"Sandy was sixteen. And I'm not sure about all that stuff there."

"What do you mean? She was a party girl. Her father made her go out of the house covered up like an Amish maiden, *right*? And in some of these she's practically naked."

"She's not dressed any worse than anyone else in those photos. And in that one, she's at the pool. I don't know, I just got a feeling we ain't got the whole picture yet."

"Not seeing where this matters." Jones tapped the center of the board, the photo of Sandy's lifeless face replaced by the one her mother said was her favorite. "Just from this, we can surmise the Moralist had reason to think she needed to be cleansed. Shouldn't we focus on him, not the vic?"

"There's no case without the vic." Before Jones could make a snide remark, Michaels continued, "We need to understand his thinking, beyond the obvious. All we know, after all these years, is he takes them once they lose their virginity and thinks he's saving their eternal souls."

"What else can we know? What else do we need to know? We just gotta catch this guy, no matter his twisted thinking."

"He never leaves clues. No prints, no DNA, no witnesses, no nothing." Michaels slammed his cup on his desk and a wave of coffee jumped out and splattered on the case folder's cover. "We need to predict his next move, or we'll never catch him."

"And if I'm wrong about the twelve, he may already be lining up his next vic."

SONYA RAWLINGS

How could it have been past 9 AM? Sonya's internal clock always woke her around seven, even when Allen didn't need to get up to go to work or had been away on business. This also didn't feel like her typical waking up, refreshed and rested. Today she woke with no energy and lacked the will to pull herself from bed.

When Allen had first started taking business trips after his big promotion, she hated sleeping alone. In time, she adjusted, got used to it, and sometimes cherished it. This was one of those times, and he must have taken the hint and slept on the sofa or in the guest room when she didn't respond to his knocks and pleading at the locked bedroom door last night.

Feeling the discomfort of her bra strap digging into her flesh, Sonya flipped the sheet off to see she had fallen asleep without changing. Her wrinkled dress twisted and pulled uncomfortably over her skin, motivating her to get up. Accustomed to lengthy, steamy showers, she stayed under the invigorating flow longer than usual. Trails of tears hid themselves in the streams of water caressing her face, carrying them away from her and down the drain.

After the blower dried her completely, she stood like a statue on the body dryer mat for a while, not knowing what to do with herself. This day, no day ever, would be normal. Would that detective come by again today? Connor had taken to him, too. Sonya shook her head, mentally chastising herself for the thoughts that broke through the unbearable pain, easing it ever so slightly. It was almost enough to make breathing seem like an accomplishable task.

The wide mirror over the double sink had to suffice, since she had broken the full length one in her dressing room. That other detective's eyes crawling over her yesterday awakened something she had thought dead. Allen sometimes still admired the view, but it had been years since he looked upon her as hungrily as that young man had.

Once she had dressed, Sonya leaned an ear to Connor's door and heard the deep breaths of sleep vibrating through the thin wood panel. Out of habit, she glanced into Sandy's room, expecting to see her making the bed and getting ready for school. The room's emptiness wrapped around her heart like a boa constrictor and squeezed. Something else was wrong.

Although they had tried, the detectives' efforts to make Sandy's bed after ransacking her room failed to meet the Rawlings family standards. Sonya had had to make it again when they left. While sure of the memory, she second-guessed herself. The bedspread looked as if it had been slept on. A fleeting hope maliciously teased her before reality set in and she crawled into her daughter's bed. Hugging the pillow, she buried her face in it and groaned.

As Sonya made the bed, she laid the tear-soaked pillow down and smoothed the creases with her hand. She didn't find Allen asleep in the guest bed, and it had been made. Or rather, knowing her husband, it had not been unmade. Expecting to find sheets strewn over the sofa, Sonya found it bare, save for the throw pillows, all neatly arranged in their proper places. That almost silent garage door. Did he leave last night when she didn't let him into her bed? His car was gone, and she had no way to know when he left, until she remembered she might.

Security cameras surrounded the exterior of the house in high-tech surveillance. Those were connected to Allen's computer. Sonya didn't know his password, and he kept his office door locked. Initial complaints about why he felt the need for such privacy, to keep his wife out, were met with excuses about his work and their corporate policy for physical security to any system with remote access. He finally gave in to her 'nagging,' as he called it, and let her in to clean once a week with him watching as she did it.

If she could figure out how to do it, she had a more accessible way to check. The *Ring* doorbell app on her phone had all the premium features enabled and one allowed her to replay older videos. Its *Record activity only* feature meant Sonya only had to search for the most recent records, not scour through eight hours of footage, which she appreciated. The first video showed a dog relieving itself on their front lawn. In the second one, time-stamped 07:21:27, Allen's car reversed slowly down the driveway.

When she closed the app, Sonya noticed the red bubble over the iMessage icon. Fifty-two unread texts from friends, family, and others trying to offer support. Her phone had been in *Do not disturb* mode since Monday afternoon.

Her daughter had been dead for over two days.

Sonya didn't care to read any of those messages. As she scrolled by them, one from Allen at 7:18 AM caught her eye.

Need to go to office for just a bit then can have rest of the week off. Won't be long. Love U.

After a few *good morning* support messages, mostly from people in their church, there was another message from Allen.

Finished at work. Told you not long. Stopping by church for a min. I'll pick us up lunch. Love U.

Although she knew what the phone call would put her through, Sonya opened the phone app to her favorites and dialed Allen's office number. It rang twice.

"Omni Sanitas Pharmaceuticals, Southeastern sales division, this is Emily. How may I direct your call?"

"Allen Rawlings, please."

"*Sonya?*"

"Hey, Emily."

"Sonya... I'm so... I don't know what to say."

"Nobody does, how could they? Listen, Allen isn't answering his cell, and he told me he needed to go in this morning. Can you put me through, please?"

"Oh, but... he isn't here."

Liar! She'd caught him. Sonya had suspected he might have gone off to hassle that boy or try some other foolhardy stunt to catch Sandy's killer. Or... he went to visit someone who wouldn't lock their door.

"He *was* here, got in before me. You just missed him. He said he wouldn't be back until Monday."

"Yeah, Jim gave him the week off."

"Of course. Sonya, if there's anything y'all need..."

"I appreciate that. I gotta go. Thank you."

As she stared at her home screen, Sonya remembered another useful app. When she opened Find My, it defaulted to Devices. She touched the People icon. Like a smack to the face, the app reminded her she only followed Connor. When

Sandy turned sixteen, she removed her parents and, after a lengthy lecture, Allen allowed her that new level of freedom and trust. A trust she abused.

And Sonya had allowed it.

When Connor came downstairs, his mother was sobbing over the kitchen sink, her phone on the tile floor with a crack in the top corner of the screen.

WALKER MICHAELS

Not wearing a smile, as usual, Sergeant Carter absorbed the progress report, not once interrupting Michaels. She reminded her detectives of the pressure to solve the case this time. Michaels needed no reminder and no stronger motivation than the photos on his board. Their boss made it crystal clear they needed some leads, suspects, something more than background on the victim and the name of a boyfriend. Directing them not to neglect the usual suspects and persons of interest, she ordered them not to get sidetracked by those either. Again, nothing Michaels needed to hear.

Perhaps Jones benefited from getting it straight from his sergeant. It took the burden of being his boss off Michaels' shoulders. Since they were paired up, he had been reminding the junior detective of this dynamic in their partnership. While Detective Michaels preferred those times between partners, he had no desire to go it alone on this case. Beyond the need to give Sandy Rawlings justice, the life of the next victim sat on his and Jones' shoulders. Michaels couldn't buckle under the weight of twelve dead girls. The longer they failed, the more ended lives he'd pin on his board.

The call from the M.E. didn't give Michaels the answer to the question he'd left him but did give them their first solid lead. Jones ran it through that chat AI, whatever that was. Throwing on his wrinkled suit jacket, Michaels told Jones to get the car keys. As they passed Carter's office, he told her about the lead.

"Let me know as soon as you have something. Remember, I wanna know when you stop to take a piss." Michaels said the last three words with her.

She had used that line for years. It got old after the first time. Politely, he acknowledged the reminder with a single-finger salute and led Jones to the parking lot to get into their Tesla. He still couldn't believe the city of Marietta footed the bill for a new fleet of cars and upgraded to these. Official department policy had the auto driving features disabled. That suited Michaels just fine.

The instant torque pressed him into his seat. Michaels never drove the thing and, after their first outing together, had forbidden Jones to take off like that. Now they had a lead. The car was electric with the excitement to make some headway on the case. Michaels reviewed a printout of that chat AI's results for the fifth time as Jones sped toward the supply store. The sheet of paper strobed blue and white as the dash light spun, splitting a path through traffic like Moses parting the Red Sea.

Not lifting his gaze from the paper, Michaels said, "Woody says he used a thicker-grade plastic this time."

"Who's Woody?"

"I mean *Travis*, the new young M.E." Michaels lowered the paper and turned to the driver. "Two hands!"

"Travis Young is young. Fresh out of school, pretty much, *right*?"

"I reckon. Been with us about a year and seems to do alright. What kind of a name is *Travis Young* for a medical examiner, anyway? Sounds like a country singer. Travis Young... ain't he someone?"

After scrunching his chin, Jones said, "There's an actor by that name. Was in *The Walking Dead*, I think. So, what's the deal with this plastic?"

"It ain't from a trash bag or thin tarp, like you'd get at the Home Depot. Only store around that carries something like it is where we're going."

"You really think he slipped up, using something traceable like that? You made him sound like a genius or something."

Michaels slapped the dashboard. "Eyes on the road, these don't drive themselves. I may have said 'clever.' Everyone slips up eventually. And he's rusty, if you can call it that. Last one he killed was near four years back. Could be he had a tarp laying around. Didn't think about where he bought it."

"Why not just use trash bags, like before?"

"Jones, if I thought like him... well... I don't wanna imagine what that'd mean. We're almost there, it's just ahead."

They parked outside Kennesaw Building Supply and entered the store. The woman at the checkout called the manager, a stocky man with male pattern baldness, out of his office. Despite the man's cooperative nature, he didn't have promising information to share. In as deep a southern drawl as Michaels had ever heard, he explained the tarpaulin in question was a big seller. Dozens of construction, painting, and remodeling companies bought them regularly. Plenty of residential customers came in for them too. Gardeners liked it for covering areas they wanted nothing to grow through, and homeowners used it under gravel and brick-paver walkways.

"I see you have security cameras. Can we see the footage?" Jones asked.

A fair question under different circumstances. Still, sometimes Michaels wondered if his partner based his investigative methods more on what he saw in cop shows than on his training. After giving Jones a nod, he told the manager, "We got no idea when or if our guy came in here. Could have been months or years ago."

"We only keep a twenty-four-hour video loop. If y'all got a description of the guy or a photo, we might-could be more helpful. Lot of the folks coming in here are regulars."

"I wish we did. Come on, Jones. Let's go interview the boyfriend."

ALLEN RAWLINGS

S itting here in the car was foolish and he knew better. He squinted from the sun in his eyes. If that school cop saw him, he'd be arrested on the spot. Did they know his car? No matter, he didn't have much chance of finding Joshua until school let out, and he'd promised Sonya he'd bring home lunch. One last look before he left. Focusing his view, he panned the classrooms facing the parking lot, but the glare of the late morning sun made seeing through the glimmering glass impossible.

After closing the glove compartment, he shifted the car into Drive, lowered his foot, and made a tight circle to pull out and onto the street. A black Tesla pulled in and he slammed on the brakes, narrowly avoiding a head-on collision. Two familiar faces filled the windshield. One had a look of surprise while the older one wore the worn-out face of disappointment. Detective Michaels lowered his window and waved his arm for Allen to pull alongside them.

As the passenger-side window descended, letting the humid, 98-degree air in, Allen said, "Detectives."

"Morning, Mister Rawlings. Out for a leisurely drive, are you?"

From the other side of the car, Jones yelled, "Do we need to put a restraining order on you, Rawlings?"

"This was my daughter's school. I wish you would stop hassling me and my family and get to catching the man who killed my baby girl." His voice cracked and his eyes filled, but he held the tears behind two invisible dams.

"We're working the case." Michaels leaned out the window. "Do we need to add obstruction of justice and interfering with a police investigation to aggravated assault of a minor?"

"Aggravated... I didn't... Look. I just want answers. Going by your track record, *Walk*, I may need to find them myself, provide my own closure."

"We can give you that right now... behind bars," the driver shouted.

Allen saw a hint of confusion cross Michaels' brow before he said, "We don't wish to take any further action against you, Mister Rawlings, believe you me. But we'll need you to step aside and let us do our jobs. If we find you near this school or trying to contact any of the students or any minors, we *will* act for their protection."

"Like you protected my daughter?"

The man hanging out the window sighed, and it made him look even more tired. "I can't do anything about Sandy, and I'm truly sorry about that. But now you're keeping me from trying to prevent the next one, and the one after that. Go home, Mister Rawlings. Be with your wife and son. I promise, as soon as we have anything, I will personally let you know."

The screen in the dashboard came to life and the car announced, "Call from Charlotte Sellers."

"I gotta go." Allen sped off while the window rose and the call connected.

"Charlotte, this isn't a good time."

"Just a quick sec. When you have time, would you please arrange a visit with Russ? He's never lost a friend like this before. I know you'll say the right thing to help him cope, not to lose his faith."

"*I'm* trying to cope… and help my family. Your son? For Chr—for Pete's sake, Charlotte, my daughter's the one who died."

"I know, I know. I'm sorry." The tires skidded with a deafening screech as Allen stomped the brakes to keep from running a red light. "What was that? Al… Al, are you alright?"

"Fine. Didn't see the light. I'm too distracted to drive and talk. I gotta go. And you can't just call me whenever."

"I remembered. During work hours on weekdays, like before. But I should've known you weren't at work. And I'm sorry I asked about Russ. Whenever you feel up to it. Meantime, I'm here when you need me, Al, always."

"I know. I'll be in touch."

At his subdivision entrance, Allen made a U-turn to go grab the lunch he'd promised to bring home. Sonya liked the new Poke place, but Connor hated it, so after he picked up two bowls, he grabbed his son's favorite, a crunch wrap supreme and two soft tacos, from the Taco Bell drive-through.

The three ate in relative silence, and Connor ran upstairs as soon as he inhaled his lunch. While they had an 'everyone at the table until dismissed' dinner rule, lunch was always flexible. Finished with his Poke bowl first, Allen watched his wife eat and thought about Charlotte's request for him to counsel her boy. How could he help Russel cope with his grief when he had no idea how to talk to his own son?

A job that took him away from home so much, especially in the last few years when his teenage children needed guidance most, took its toll. Looking at his wife, he felt he knew her less now than a decade ago. He'd hardly had a real conversation with either of his children in years. The impact of living in the modern world, he figured. But had he used that as an excuse not to put in the effort? With no way to make that up to Sandra now, perhaps he could rebuild a bond with Connor.

"How can we help our son, Allen?"

It was as if she read his mind, and many things in there were not for her trusting eyes. How many times he had counseled couples from church on the importance of open and honest communication in a marriage. Days long past used to be filled with deep, pleasant conversations, and Sonya had thrived in such a relationship. Now, she put up a good front. A polished shell, the outer layer kept up appearances while the inside shriveled up. Their partnership had long deteriorated into two people living together in shared isolation. Up until now, it had worked.

"I... don't know. Maybe, one of the other deacons could talk to him. An outsider he can feel more at ease talking to. I'm meeting with them later; I can ask."

"He needs his father."

Of course, the boy needed his father. The problem was... Allen's life had become complicated over the last several years, and not only from the change in his job and the move to the bigger house. One half of that life didn't involve his family—couldn't involve them. Yet now, somehow, in a way he still could not understand, it did.

He needed to do something about that.

BRANDON
JONES

It had been five years since he strutted down the halls as a senior in Paulding County High School. On the Varsity football team, he always had a flock of pretty girls, juniors and seniors, around him. Everything about Marietta High seemed designed to impress, and Jones wondered who would be impressed by any of it. Parents rarely, if ever, saw the inside of the school. He knew many considered it a prestigious thing to send their kids here, but he had no idea why.

The Rawlings lived outside this school zone, and Sandy should have attended Lost Mountain. During their private chat with Sonya Rawlings, she had told them Allen used the address of their old house, which they kept as a rental property, on the admission papers. Not something worth reporting, but it raised some questions Brandon's Sunday School education couldn't answer. Surely, Jesus must have said something like, 'Blessed are the honest.' Yet even such church-going folks as the Rawlings found occasion to skirt the rules.

Memories flooded into him as he and Michaels waited outside the principal's office. He'd spent enough time in a chair like this one with a very different anticipation filling the minutes consumed by waiting. Men and women came and went into the adjacent teacher's lounge, and Brandon thought they were more attractive than what he remembered from his high school days. Perhaps another Paulding-Marietta variance, he assumed. One county over, Paulding seemed like another world, more 'country' compared to Cobb.

The principal's assistant provided limited detail about Joshua Sturgill. A Senior, he was a year older than Sandy.

A tall, thin man in a white button-down shirt and a neatly trimmed beard appeared and invited them to follow him. Longer than it was wide, the school counselor's office had two gray chairs facing the desk and a small sofa behind those. Josh was turning the chairs when they entered. The counselor, who introduced himself simply as John, motioned for them to take the chairs, and he and Sandy's boyfriend sat on the sofa.

"Gentlemen, or should I say, detectives?" John began.

"Michaels and Jones will do," Michaels said.

"Alrighty. So, I'm here mostly as an observer to support Josh. I'm happy to help, but for the most part, just pretend I'm not here."

Jones chuckled at 'alrighty' as such a school-counselor thing to say and tried to cover it by forcing a cough. He accepted the water John offered.

"We appreciate you being here," Michaels said to John before addressing Josh. "Thank you for agreeing to speak with us. First, let us say we're sorry for your loss. If at any time you feel uncomfortable, just say so." Josh nodded, and his eyes went glossy.

Jones said, "It's okay, Josh. We just wanna see if you can help catch the guy that did it. You're not in any trouble."

Simultaneously, the boy's reply and Michaels' glare told him he misspoke.

"Why... why would I be in any trouble? You don't think I...?" Josh turned to the counselor with a look of terror splattered over his face.

"Um, no, we just..."

"Just to put you at ease. That's all." John finished Jones' staggered sentence. "Obviously, you wouldn't be in any trouble. You're here voluntarily to help their investigation, and they know that."

"Josh, what my partner meant is, we're just trying to get a full picture of who Sandy was. It helps our investigation to know who her friends were, where she went, and what she did. Were you and Sandy close?"

"We met her sophomore year, didn't go to the same middle school. Got closer over the last few months."

"How long were you dating?" Again, the boy looked at John. Michaels continued, "Don't worry, Josh. You did nothing wrong. We know you dated, and that's fine. We're not her parents. Now, you were an item for... weeks or months?"

"A few months. Well, a few months before summer break."

"Good. Relax, Josh." Michaels showed a softness Jones had never seen. "And were you with her Sunday night?"

"I didn't hurt her. I'd never—" He could no longer hold back the tears. "I loved her."

"Josh," Jones started but John raised a palm to stop him.

"The detective never accused you of anything and *no one* thinks you hurt Sandy. They just need to know the final moments of her life to create a timeline."

Jones sat on the edge of his chair. "Yes, that's exactly it. We know you were together and then something happened *after* you separated. Having the details up to the time you left each other will be super helpful."

After sucking in his sniffles, Josh composed himself. "We were... Together, I mean. We saw a movie, nothing special. They showed the Rocky Horror Picture Show at the Strand and some Seniors acted it out while the movie played."

"I did that once. I was Brad Majors." Brandon got the boy to relax a bit. "What time did it let out and where did you go after?"

"We hit a club. Um, it was... an over-18 kinda place." Shoulders up, Josh looked like a turtle trying to hide his head.

Looking at Michaels, Jones got a nod to continue. "No one's getting in trouble for any of that. We just need the name of the club and time you entered and when you left."

"It's not a club, not really. I mean it is, but it moves. That night they did it in the old warehouse off the square, just behind the Strand. See, it was connected to the movie, had the Rocky Horror theme and all. It was pretty beast. Sandy loved it."

"Okay. Thank you for that." When the boy sucked the dripping mucus up his nose again, Brandon handed him a tissue from a box on the counselor's desk. "And when did you leave and where did you go next?"

"We, we didn't leave together. The last I saw..." He sucked in a breath and looked like he might hyperventilate.

After a pause, Brandon carried on, searching for a gentle way to continue the conversation. It was clearly difficult on the young man. "Do you recall why she left alone, and at what time?"

"It was close to her curfew, and her father was home. She could get away with it when her dad's away—her mom seems pretty cool like that. She insisted I stay. Said she got an Uber."

Detective Brandon Jones jotted that down when he noted Michaels doing the same. Perhaps they found the first break in the case.

"We need to know the time," Michaels stated, losing his softness.

After a shrug, Josh looked at the floor as if to read the answer etched into the laminate. "Her curfew was eleven… So… I guess it was just before that."

Brandon patted Josh's shoulder. "Good Josh, that's a huge help. Did anyone go out with her, you or anyone else? Someone may have exited at the same time, *right*?"

"I don't think so. The place was electric, you know, and was just ramping up. We, I mean, it was the last night before school. I left, I guess, around one-ish."

Michaels looked at Jones, hoisted his eyebrows, and nodded his head toward the boyfriend. The next question needed to be asked, they both knew that. Brandon had hoped the gentle version of his partner would have done the asking.

"Josh, where you and Sandy… sexually active?"

The boy looked at the junior detective like he'd been caught with his hand in the tip jar at Starbucks. With eyes pleading for a reprieve, he looked at John, who said nothing.

"Again, we're not judging. I was seventeen not that long ago. My partner here, well, believe it or not, he was a teenager once, too… a long time ago." The levity seemed to cut the tension in the room, thinning the air between detective and witness. "It will help the investigation and does not leave this room."

"Isn't that a little… personal? To talk about Sandy like that, after…"

"We won't tell a soul." Brandon wasn't sure that was true but saw no reason anyone outside his department, strictly the ones working the case, needed to know. And he certainly wasn't about to tell Mister Rawlings.

The kid squirmed in his seat rubbing his hands. "She wasn't ready… and… and I respected that. I never pushed her to do anything she wasn't comfortable with, I swear."

"Josh, we believe you. When did you think she'd be ready?"

Michaels shook his head. If he tried to communicate something, Jones missed it.

"She wanted to wait until she turned seventeen…" Knees bouncing, he rubbed his hands more briskly. "In a few months."

"Four months is a long time to wait, son. Are you sure you two didn't fool around?" Michaels asked.

"*Fool around*? No. It's like I said, I respected her decision."

Wide-eyed and with raised eyebrows, Jones looked at Michaels. "He was wrong about her, like Sonya said."

Michaels showed him a face filled with a red-hot fury Jones didn't understand.

WALKER
MICHAELS

R eady to explode and lay into his rookie partner, Michaels felt every muscle in his body twinging as he marched to the car. The second the entrance doors closed behind them, he used the parking lot as a stage to exhibit his indignation.

"What were you thinking back there?" he shouted, hands flailing.

"What? I looked at you and you kept nodding me on. What'd I do?"

"You almost divulged key details about the case. And you mentioned our conversation with Sonya Rawlings. What kind of a rookie mistake...? I just don't know... Why do they keep partnering me up with such incompetence?"

Jones showed his palms. "Hold on, Boss. We were—"

"I swear, if you call me boss one more time…" Michaels paused, seething. "If I were your boss, I'd have fired you on day one!"

"What'd I divulge? I didn't say anything. It's not like detectives speaking with the dead girl's parents is any big secret, *right*?"

"Sandy! Her name is *Sandy*. And we gotta be better than this… for her."

Unable to contain it any longer, Walker Michaels bellowed and unleashed the tears he'd kept bottled up for years. This case had broken him; Bonnie was correct about that. Last time, it took three years, eleven dead, and admitting failure to crush his spirit. This was day three and he was falling apart in front of his junior partner. Jones wisely stayed quiet.

As he collected himself, the Tesla pulled up beside him, Jones looking straight ahead to let Michaels finish the moment. He'd been too hard on the guy. Jones hadn't given up any real details. If that kid took Jones' last comment about 'him being wrong about her' to understand the Moralist was back and killed Sandy under the mistaken pretext she had lost her virginity, he could have been head detective of the Marietta police department. He'd probably have caught the guy already.

Once Michaels silently climbed into the car, Jones pulled out, not saying a word. Not even looking at him. It stayed quiet for a while as they made their way back to the station. Ending the silence, Michaels said, "Turn around."

"Where to?" At the next strip mall, Jones pulled over in the parking lot.

"Rawlings' home. No, wait right here. I gotta think for a minute."

After pulling into a spot, Jones rested his wrists on the steering wheel. Unable to keep still, Michaels fidgeted in his seat like a child who needed to pee. Up and down, up and down, his hands could have rubbed through the suit's cheap fabric over his thighs. The words he knew he should say fought to stay hitched in his throat. Michaels forced them out.

"Sorry... by the way... for before. This case got to me, and I unleashed it all on you. I almost erupted last night with my daughter and son-in-law, but she knows how to talk me down."

Not making eye contact, Jones said, "I get it. I'm boiling inside and this is my third day. I can't imagine this case for you, reopening after four years."

"That's just it. It was never closed. Sandy Rawlings is dead because I failed her, like her father said. And I failed the next one and the one after that."

"No one thinks that."

"Sandy's parents do." His head dipped. It became a lead weight, impossible to lift.

"Sonya doesn't... and Allen's a tool."

Michaels laughed. "He's a real jerk, isn't he?"

"Why'd you say you wanted to go to their house?"

"I feel we can get something more from Sonya. Missus Rawlings, I mean. I don't know why, don't know if it's relevant, but there's something more going on in that family."

"He's cheating on her."

Michaels' neck found its strength and he looked Jones in the eye. While he assumed the same, he wanted to quiz the rookie. "Hmm. What makes you say that?"

"Um, hello? Hot blond in the red dress bailed him out of jail, *right*? She's the same one who called him earlier when we saw him leave the school."

"How'd you know that?"

The smirk on Jones' face reminded Michaels of his daughter. It was less becoming on him, but just as smug. "I looked up the report. She had to sign him out and post bail. Charlotte Sellers, a single mom who also attends Allen's church."

"Nice work, Detective." Impressed, Michaels hadn't made that connection. "Now that's the sorta thing we need to discuss with Missus Rawlings."

"You think it's our place to tell her?"

"She knows, believe me. I got a real impression of that woman. I think she's more together and sharper than anyone gives her credit for, most of all her husband."

"Wait. If you just found this out, thanks to my sleuthing abilities," Jones winked over a wry smile, "What did you want to talk to Sonya about?"

"I don't know. Sometimes the gut talks to me. Speaking of which, we get any hits from Missing Persons on the boyfriends of any of the previous victims?"

After digging his phone out from his pocket, Jones bounced his thumbs over the screen. "Looks like they're all accounted for. All alive and well. Another dead end."

"No. It confirms our profile of the guy. He's got an antiquated sense of morality, different for boys and girls. He's not seeing the boys as evil, even though they're the ones he believes are corrupting the girls he kills."

"Sick son of—"

"He is. And he's—" An incoming call stopped Michaels' thought. Bonnie. She told him she would have a check-in call every day while he worked the case.

With a heavy sigh, he took the call and assured her he was fine, having Jones confirm it. They both lied, not mentioning his little episode in the high school parking lot. Talking to his daughter calmed him further, and he thanked her for the loving support. As he hung up, he realized that was what he missed four years ago. Even toward the end of her ordeal, Catherine had been his emotional support, a crutch he leaned on until the day she died.

Once they had aired it out, she never brought up his infidelity again. If only Michaels could have been as forgiving of himself as his wife was of him. She had been in the hospital, the cancer consuming her life bit-by-bit. He spent eighteen-hour days working the case that sucked the life out of him one chuck at a time and slept a few hours each night on the chair at his wife's side. Unlucky circumstances kept him and Ronni at the station alone that one time.

It took months, but Michaels pieced his relationship with Bonnie back together. They never told her, but he knew she knew. When Catherine's suffering ended, he still had the case. His daughter had no one. Eventually, Mike entered the picture and the case went cold. She had said it broke him and that he had pulled himself back together. It didn't look that way to him. When he lost it outside the school, he understood why. He wouldn't be whole again until the Moralist was stopped. His conscience could not bear the weight of one more dead teenage girl.

When his phone rang, he expected Bonnie again.

"Hello...? Oh, hey Travis. What've you got for me?"

SONYA
RAWLINGS

The chirping was driving her mad, purging the house of its glorious silence. Connor sat in his room, on his chair, headphones on as usual. His dad had tried to talk to him but came back down a minute or two later, huffing. Once again, he left them. Sonya opened every drawer in the kitchen. Sometimes it sounded like it came from the left, but as soon as she took a step, the chirp moved to her right.

They had talked more that afternoon than they had in years. It became clear this would change them, change everything. It already had. Allen talked about being a more involved father and tacked on husband as a footnote. To prove himself, he vowed to be home more often, traveling less. Rather than comforting her, the idea summoned other feelings. Her solace raced out the door each time he opened it to enter, much like Gigi used to. Sonya feared with one or two more pulls on that knob, it too would meet the same end as Sandy's Chihuahua. Buried in the backyard with the life she thought she had.

Now it came from behind her. Electronic, she thought. No cricket made such a noise. She opened the laundry room door and sifted through the hampers overflowing with dirty clothes. Never had she let it pile up so high. As she loaded the machine, she heard it again. The door wouldn't close. She pushed again. Again, the washer door bounced back, refusing to latch. With all her might, Sonya thrust the round glass door. When it sprung back, she did it again and again, grunting and pushing harder each time. With a metallic pop, it bounced back and slammed into her hand.

As Sonya collapsed into the fetal position, the spring of her tears became a torrent. On the cool tile floor, her stomach convulsed, and her legs twitched. Lifting her hand, she reached for support. For comfort. For something. Her hand grasped the sleeve of one of Allen's linen shirts. She'd have to iron it right out of the wash. Those took so long and still looked wrinkled when she was done. If only he allowed her to take them to the cleaners. With that sleeve heavy with what came from her nose tucked inside the machine, the washer cycle started.

If she didn't find whatever kept chirping soon, she would surely lose her mind. It sounded closer than ever as the water drizzled over the clothes and the drum of the front-loader spun. The lavender scent of the detergent filled her nostrils.

It lacked the soothing, sun-shiny comfort shown in those commercials.

Allen said he couldn't miss this meeting of the deacons and had gone to the church. Did they even need him there? He missed so many of them when away on business. She knew after a few discussions and votes, the remainder of the time at these 'meetings' turned into card games. Allen never said. Sonya heard it from another deacon's wife. The couple must have applied all that Sunday Service rhetorical nonsense about having open communication in their marriage.

It chirped again, so close she felt a slight vibration. Her hand rested on the square workspace atop the organizer cabinet she had installed in the laundry room when they bought the house. It made a great surface for folding clothes. It also had a small drawer at the top. Sonya removed her sewing kit and scissors, the stain removal pen that never worked, and the dryer sheets, and placed them on top. There, the little culprit that made her want to pull her hair out.

A tiny round smiley face looked up at her from the white disk in the back corner of the drawer. She picked it up and turned it over to reveal a shiny silver back with the Apple logo in the center. With such tiny text, she had to squint to read the writing around the edge. *Assembled in China… Bluetooth LE… Ultra Wideband… AirTag.* She'd heard of those. But why was this the first time she heard one of them?

After a little finagling, she popped the silver disk off the white one and yanked out the battery. The longed-for quietness returned to her day, preserving her sanity. The rumble of the washing machine may as well have not been there. Such common household noises never registered.

Sitting on the sofa, Sonya melted into the setting and picked up a book she had started reading a few days ago. Maybe it would keep her mind off Sandy. The other ladies raved about it last month when the deacons' wives club got together. Though not an official designation, they often spent the evening together as their husbands played cards while pretending to attend to important church matters. She was never one for racially charged stories, but they convinced her to give *To Kill a Mockingbird* a chance. Scout reminded her of Sandy, but she struggled to relate to Atticus Finch.

Now the words swam on the page.

The thought of lingering in her present state of numbness until she went to bed prompted a quick text message to ask Allen to bring home dinner. Before she hit send, she tapped the backspace until every letter was gone. She stared at the blinking line. The last message above from Allen ended with his typical 'Love U' greeting. As she scrolled up through dozens of messages, they all ended the same. He said those words by rote before hanging up a call with her, too. Every time. It had become such a hollow gesture, like saying 'take care' or 'goodbye,' that he once said it to a client at the end of a sales call. While they had a good laugh about it, Sonya didn't find it amusing.

As she texted Connor instead, she thought how sad it was to live in the same house and send texts to each other. He replied much more quickly than if she had yelled up the stairs. For the first time she could recall, Sonya didn't care how Allen would react.

BRANDON
JONES

Memories of his last visit to this room caused a gag reflex. Relief drove the convulsions from his diaphragm when he saw the empty table. The body had been moved to the morgue. His abdominal muscles contracted, but with less intensity when Jones saw the images the M.E. had on the backlit board.

"Michaels, did your follow-up on the plastic tarpaulin yield any results?"

"Unfortunately, no. It was a good lead, Doc. It's just too common an item to get us anywhere."

"They sell thousands of them to hundreds of customers," Jones added.

The M.E. adjusted his glasses by the thick black frames. Brandon hadn't thought he wore glasses, but his memory of this room was a little foggy.

"I'm sorry about that. But I think I have something you need to see. Much bigger than the plastic residue I found on the body."

Travis Young walked toward the LED board and slid his glasses off. Using the temple tip, he pointed to a close-up image of the girl's neck and tapped it twice.

"I don't get it." Jones leaned in for a closer look and squinted. "What's there? What am I looking at?"

"Nothing, Detective. There's nothing there."

Pushing Jones aside, Michaels stepped up, his nose almost touching the picture. "Hmm. You're saying there's no puncture point? No evidence of an injection?"

"Nada."

"Doc… are you *sure*… hundred percent?"

"What am I missing here, guys?"

Michaels turned to Jones and said, "You read the case file. Every victim, each young lady, had a tiny dot, the entry point of a needle, in their neck."

"Doctor Clayton almost missed it." Young crossed his arms. "When the forensics team found it on the second body, he went back and reexamined all data from the first. Hard to find; injection points can close within a few hours. UV imaging shows them a while after, but it was too late for that first victim. So, he performed a histological examination of the tissue to confirm the presence of trauma consistent with a needle puncture."

"The second body was found close to an hour after time of death," Michaels explained. "He concluded the fatal dose of the drug was given to the victims just before they were… displayed."

"That's why the entry point hadn't fully closed." Holding his now folded glasses, Young tapped them on the end of his chin. "Doctor Clayton found evidence of the injection by the spread pattern of the drug through the victim's system and its effect on the tissue at the same location as the needle prick found on the second victim. Factoring for postmortem redistribution, he concluded the same method of injection on both victims. His report stated a light dose of the drug was likely administered during abduction and a second, fatal dose once he finished, um, operating on them."

"He concluded the same for all subsequent young ladies, too," Michaels added. "And we assumed Sandy was no different."

"But she was…. You're saying the method was dissimilar, *right*?" Jones asked.

"Correct. We believe this was the method the Moralist had used in all his prior victims to introduce Flunitrazepam into their systems. This time, we see a change in his M.O."

Jones asked, "What did he do, soak a cloth and hold it over her nose and mouth?"

"Interesting you bring—"

"I swear, Jones," Michaels blurted. "Did you graduate the academy or are you basing your detective work on bad cop shows?"

"What Detective Michaels means is, while *chloroform* on a cloth could incapacitate someone, it would take much longer than they show on television. And that's the interesting thing here."

"Out with it, Doc. If he didn't inject her neck, could it have been somewhere else? Have you checked for it on the rest of her body?"

"Detective Michaels, I'm saying your partner isn't completely off in his assumption."

Trying to hide his self-adulation from his partner, Jones couldn't help but smile.

"Come." Doctor Young motioned them over and turned his computer screen so they could see it. After a couple of clicks, the screen filled with two close-up photos. One showed four fingertips and the other a view looking into the dead girl's nostrils.

Jones didn't see the connection. "Was she a nosepicker?"

"Jones! For God's sake man, we're trying to solve a young woman's murder... Doc, I apologize on behalf of my partner. But you gotta explain what you're showing us here."

"Certainly. When I could not confirm the injection, I followed Doctor Clayton's protocol for tracing the spread pattern, accounting for PMR, of course. That led me here..."

He tapped his glasses on the magnified nose on his screen. "I found trace fibers in the nasal passages and throat."

"Hmm."

"Like from a handkerchief," Jones said.

"Yes. I suspect, like the plastic residue, there will be nothing special or specific about it that would help you. We're running an analysis all the same."

Folding his arms, Michaels stared at the screen and exhaled loudly. Jones could tell he was deep in thought, trying to draw conclusions from this new evidence. Doing the same led Jone's to nothing but more questions.

"What's with the fingers, then?"

"As I said earlier, reaching incapacitation by these means takes longer than they show on TV. A decent dose of chloroform could take up to five minutes."

"You said it was that Flu-trap-azam, or whatever you called it, not chloroform. This one same as the others, *right*?"

"Sandy, dammit," Michaels barked. "For the last time, Jones, her name's Sandy."

"Um, sorry. I know we're trying to catch *Sandy Rawlings'* killer. I'm not used to getting so personally vested on a case, in a vic."

"Look, if you got a problem with how I run my investigation…"

"Detectives, please. May I explain what I found under the fingernails?"

They nodded and Michaels' face slowly lost some of its red heat. This quick turn of emotion, along with the outburst at the school, had Jones wondering how unhinged his partner had become. He thought he should get Bonnie's number and add it to his favorites.

"Nothing," Young said.

After the detectives showed each other blank faces, Michaels asked, "What were you looking for when you found nothing?"

"Skin, hopefully. See, if the Moralist used a cloth soaked in Flunitrazepam, there may have been a struggle. With the injections, the previous young ladies would have passed out without a fight."

"You think Sandy fought for... what did you say... five minutes?"

"Less. While a high dose of Flunitrazepam would work much faster than chloroform, it would be far from instant. And I believe he used a high dose. In fact, I believe that was the cause of death."

Squinting at the photo, Michaels said, "Your time of death doesn't support that."

"Oh, but it does. See, Flunitrazepam, on its own, is often nonfatal. The Moralist used a smaller dose for the abductions, then a lethal dose during his, um, work. In Miss Rawling's case, I don't believe she received a second dose. Combining with the alcohol I found in her system, the drug caused respiratory arrest hours after it was administered."

"Hmm. If the struggle happened during her abduction…" Michaels trailed off.

Jones started piecing things together. "But you didn't find skin, *right*?"

"Because her nails had been scrubbed clean."

Michaels pointed at the computer screen. "He removed the evidence."

"Exactly. I believe this confirms my finding about inhalation of the chemical and a brief struggle."

"But the—Sandy—was an impeccably clean person." Jones looked at Michaels and felt he staved off his wrath by using the girl's name. "We saw her room and the high standards her father set."

"Only minute traces of the dirt at the crime scene were found. No one can go out of their house, no matter how clean their fingernails, for more than a few minutes and not have dust, dander, pollen, residue, and their own dead skin under them."

It startled Jones when Michaels grabbed his arm. He grabbed Doctor Young's arm, too. "Doc, you've made an incredible breakthrough… Jones, we got ourselves a copycat."

ALLEN
RAWLINGS

E ach of his fellow deacons and the pastor took their turn hugging him and saying whatever words they thought appropriate. Some said nothing, just shared glassy-eyed looks and nods with their embraces. Allen preferred those. Not that it mattered, as each spoken condolence fell from his ears immediately after landing there.

The men never dressed for deacon meetings in their 'Sunday Best' but didn't attend in overly casual attire either. Allen wore his 'Casual Fridays' at work clothes. Peter wore a long-sleeved white linen shirt. Before the meeting began, he apologized for his and his wife's comments at Allen's home, and Allen decided to forgive him. Taking the high road, he quoted the words of Jesus about "forgiving up to seventy-seven times." When Allen added, "You're getting close," he feigned a chuckle.

Noticing Allen's linen shirt, just like his but in short sleeves, Peter complimented him on it. Allen's buddy most often hid the now faded greenish tattoos on his forearms under long sleeves. The thin material couldn't adequately hide the panther on one arm nor the sexy woman on the other. "A call back to the sins of youth," as Peter often said. He had convinced Allen and some of the other deacons to try linen to get through the intense Georgia summers. Half of Allen's wardrobe was made of the airy fabric. Several others had also started sporting the magically cooling attire.

The agenda had few but important points they needed to discuss. Some required votes. The first, as usual, concerned the trends and needs of the large flock and how Sunday's sermon would address them. In this non-denominational church, the pastor had some leeway in his services, but the outline the deacons prepared guided what he preached to the congregation. All agreed on a message focusing on coping with grief and supporting the mourners among the flock.

"I'll mention Sandy by name and include her in the group prayer."

With watery eyes, Allen replied to the pastor, "Thank you, Frank. Her name is…" He cleared his throat. "Her name was Sandra. Please call my daughter Sandra. I, I don't care for nicknames."

"Of course. You know we all loved Sandra dearly. She was always such a big help with the youth ministries. She and I worked closely quite a few times. I only had to speak to her about dressing more modestly once, to keep our male members from temptation, and she was quick to adjust. A fine young lady, she was."

"An issue with modesty? My daughter? I always made sure—"

"Yes, Allen, she was a fine example to the other young ladies." Mathew's words kept Allen from yelling at the pastor in front of the deacons. "It's normal when a girl fills out, as Sandra did, to need some time to adjust her habits. I once suggested to your wife she should tell Sandra to wear a bra at church, especially when working with Brian in the youth program on Saturday afternoons. And I reprimanded *him* for flirting with her. She was a very attractive young lady."

"I can't believe you're all saying these things about my Sandra. And now, of all times." His blood boiled, coloring his cheeks. When he shot up to let these men have it, his chair slammed the floor with a loud whap. "She was a good girl. Modest and hard working for the Lord. How could you desecrate her good name like this?" Instead of flying into a rage, he burst into tears.

After the men apologized, praising Allen for his family's reputation, it took some time for Frank to calm him down. He offered to dismiss Allen before moving on to the next agenda point. A sweaty brow and the papers most of the men waved over their faces underscored the item's importance, and Allen feared the majority would be too cheap to get it done.

The air conditioning in the auxiliary offices needed service. Henry said one of their members worked for an AC company and he would ask him to volunteer to repair it over the weekend. With the August heat, all the service companies were booked for weeks. The point passed more easily than Allen had feared. As he rolled up his sleeves, Peter suggested putting a scheduled service visit on the calendar for May of next year, and all agreed.

When it came time for the card game, Allen excused himself. Peter walked him through the door and to his car.

"I don't know what to say… besides how sorry I am. Mary and I came by a second time, just to apologize. You know we didn't mean to imply the Moralist's motive had any justification—with Sandra, I mean. I'm sorry we missed you. We didn't stay long. I figured your family wanted to be alone."

"There's no right or wrong way to know how to act. How many times have I done pastoral visits when a member lost someone? Now… I don't even know how to talk to my own son." When Peter didn't reply, Allen added, "Maybe you could try? Not now, but in a few days."

"Sure thing, of course. You know how much Mary and I love you and your family. I'd do anything for you and Sonya. Anything I can do to help keep Connor on the straight and narrow, I will." After an awkward hug, Peter asked, "Did you discuss the funeral arrangements?"

Allen closed his eyes. "We can't even talk about what to eat for dinner. I... I don't think Sonya is ready to discuss that yet."

"I'll ask Frank to drop his fee for the funeral service, and we can discount the church costs... When you're ready."

A nod of thanks lowered Allen's gaze to the red lines over the panther tattoo. "Is that from rock-climbing?"

"Yeah." He shook his head. "I mean no. It was... when I picked the roses for Sonya—Mary, *Mary* wanted to... She asked me to, rather. Oh! Mary. She made you a casserole. I doubt it's as good as Sonya's, but we figured she wouldn't be up to cooking, and... we thought it'd help."

* * *

With casserole in hand, Allen entered a dark house. Balancing the flat oven dish, he reached for the key hook that wasn't there, and his hand hit the wall. He set the BMW fob on the shelf and flicked on the light. His shouts of his wife's and son's names echoed through the empty home and returned unanswered. A frightful thought rushed in, a conclusion that shot through him like a lightning bolt.

Sonya wasn't strong enough for this.

The glass casserole dish shattered on the tile floor, and its clatter chased Allen down the hall to the living room. Not there. He checked the kitchen, dining room, laundry room, sitting room, and screened-in back porch before racing up the stairs two at a time.

An empty silver frame stood in place of the full-length mirror in Sonya's dressing room. Fractured reflections of him caught glints of light and bounced off the shards in the wastebasket. He looked in horror at the drips of blood on the carpet. Knowing what he was about to find in the master bath, he reached a trembling hand to the doorknob and twisted.

* * *

On the coffee table, a round white paper plate held the crust of a single slice of leftover pizza. He hadn't bothered to heat it up and couldn't finish it. Not in his usual spot, Allen sat on the sofa, leaning upon his arm folded over the armrest. Plagued by soul-crushing thoughts of losing his wife so soon after losing his daughter, he sat in Sonya's seat. She had unofficially claimed the space beside his chair and the children never contested, taking their places on the other two cushions.

Of course, it had been ages since all four had sat together here.

When his phone vibrated, he ignored it at first. Thinking it might be her, and he needed it to be her, he pulled the phone from his front pants pocket and looked at the alert on the lockscreen. Not her, but a message he had been expecting and had hoped to receive.

A new iMessage from Sonya.

Sorry I forgot to text. Connor and I went to dinner. Needed to get out of the house. Want me to bring you something?

He stared at it for a minute, possibly longer. A volley of messages passed mundane information between the married couple of over two decades as between himself and a client. No, with less emotion. When she asked, again, if he needed her to bring him something for dinner, he told her, again, he finished the pizza.

Like an inquisition, she asked him twice what he was doing. He said he was watching the Braves game. To make that true, or less of a lie, Allen grabbed the remote and switched on the TV. The Braves weren't playing, but he had a few games on the DVR. In reply to his question, Sonya said they were waiting for a table, so would be a while.

Ok. Love U.

As soon as his thumb tapped Send, Allen flung the phone across the room.

WALKER
MICHAELS

A copycat. Michaels could hardly believe his own conclusion. The implications ran wild in his head, colliding into ideas, speculations, and... relief. His old nemesis had not struck again. This would have happened even if the Moralist had been caught and sat rotting away in prison or had been executed.

Sandy Rawlings' death wasn't his fault.

"*Walk...?* Did we lose you?"

What had Carter called him? He hated the nickname and never let anyone call him that. To all at the station and in his personal life, he was Michaels. Only Catherine called him Walker. Hearing "Walk" took him back to a four-year-running nightmare. Yet he'd also heard it more recently.

"Sorry, Sarge. Just lost in thought. We got a lot to do now, so if you'll excuse—"

"I said, do you have any leads on solid suspects?"

Sergeant Carter's office became a prison cell, keeping Michaels from the freedom of working his *new* case. He needed to get on with catching this new killer. Would he be a serial killer, following the Moralist's pattern like some deranged loyal apprentice? If so, Michaels had no time for this. Another victim's life was at stake.

"We have our usuals, but now they've been given elevated status. I think we need to treat this like a murder case, for now."

"You sure it's a copycat?" Jones asked. "If so, he'd also be a serial killer, *right*?"

"The gut's talking to me again. I think this was personal. That this guy didn't pick any random young lady to cleanse, like the Moralist always did. I think he meant to kill Sandy Rawlings, specifically."

From her typical lean over her desk, Carter asked, "What's got your gut churning—besides the Moe's burrito your stomach's struggling to digest?"

Michaels grimaced at Jones, who shrugged in reply.

"You were both sucking down drinks from those huge Moe's cups when you came in earlier. I saw you on the cameras... since you *didn't tell me* you were coming back to meet with the M.E." Her scowl could have melted a glacier.

Reprimanded like school children, they said nothing.

"Who are your top suspects?"

Jones said, "I like the father, ma'am. He's a total tool."

"He was with Missus Rawlings all evening and through the night. He is a tool, though, Jones is right about that." The men chuckled but Carter didn't look amused. Michaels added, "Connor was in his room, the parents up all night downstairs. Sonya—*Missus Rawlings*, verified that."

"Wait… You spoke with Sonya Rawlings a couple of times. You guys think she could've been covering for her husband? Do you trust the alibi?"

"I do. Jones and I got a feel for her. And I believe she knows her husband's a cheat. Besides, she wouldn't cover for him if she suspected he had anything to do with killing her daughter. She's a strong woman… ma'am."

"And the boyfriend? We ruled him out, treated him as a witness. Are you looking at him again now?"

"Absolutely, Sarge." Jones sat up straighter in his seat and looked at Michaels. "*Right*? He was super nervous to talk to us. And he got spooked when he thought we were looking at him for it."

Addressing Carter, Michaels said, "Because he's a kid whose girlfriend was just murdered. Look, I'm not ruling him out, but he doesn't look good for it to me."

"I disagree, Bo—um… We know he was the last to see her alive, *right*? He claimed she wanted to leave the club, and he just let her. And no one else saw her. He told us he wanted some, and she refused to put out. I like him for it."

"Alright. You're both working the case, and you have some leeway to pursue it from different angles. But I want you both focused on solid leads. What about close family members, neighbors, friends, school rivals?"

Before his junior partner could blurt out anything else, Michaels replied, "We're getting all that together now. She's got an uncle that looks like a person of interest. We haven't started on members of her church, and I don't think there's anything at the school."

"Don't get sentimental on this one. Just because they're kids doesn't mean one of them couldn't do something like this."

"It ain't that, Sarge. Jones and I got to building a detailed sketch of Sandy's life. Who she was, her friends, her social life, all kinds of stuff. She was popular, but not like the girls in them teenage dramas my daughter used to watch. The ones who have a following while most of the girls hate her. I doubt very much she had anyone hating on her that bad at school."

"What about a jealous girl?" Jones asked. "Josh is a great-looking kid, amazing hair, super popular. He must have girls all over him—Seniors, too. You can't tell me none of them had it in for Sandy, a Junior, taking the hottest boy in school off the market. Hell hath no fury... *right*?"

"The rookie's got a point. Jones, you're on the boyfriend and other schoolmates. Michaels, you look into that uncle and their church, neighbors, any of the usuals. And verify

Missus Rawlings' alibi for her husband, if he's the tool you say he is."

"He is," both men said as they stood.

"Michaels. I know you don't want this to be him… The evidence from the M.E. is circumstantial, and it's been four years. If it's our guy, he's rusty. We can't rule out the Moralist for a slight change in M.O. that could be from nothing more than him working with available supplies or improvising."

After giving her an unconvincing nod, Michaels stepped out. He leaned back into the doorway and said, "Sarge?" She offered him an annoyed scowl. "I'm going to take a piss."

She flipped him off with both hands. Smiling, he marched back to his desk to solve this new murder case.

CONNOR RAWLINGS

A ten-foot-tall mechanical beast of a warrior crested the distant hill. Connor knew he had seconds to act. In full battle armor, he ran at top speed toward the robotic menace that would ravage the town he'd vowed to protect. Tapping A and B together rapidly while pushing up with his left thumb launched his avatar into a spinning jump. In mid-flight, he mashed X then O to draw his plasma sword and—

New Text from Mom appeared on the screen, pausing the game.

In frustration, Connor threw the controller and cursed aloud at himself for forgetting to turn off notifications. He normally gamed on his PC, but this new iPadOS first-person shooter running on the latest Apple chip with its insane number of GPUs beckoned him.

"Read message."

A synthetic voice said, "Hi honey. Want to go out for dinner, me and you? Dad is at his meeting, and I don't want to cook. You can choose the place."

He huffed at Mom for never getting the concept of short texts and abbreviations. At least she started using iMessage more and not shouting up the stairs or banging on his door. Since he turned fifteen, she'd been giving him more 'space,' as she called it. If only his dad could have learned from her example.

While his mom annoyed him, nagged a bit, and made him do things he hated because they were pointless, like making his bed, she wasn't all that bad. Maybe no mom was awesome, but compared to other kids his age, he had to admit his mom was okay. All the other boys who had come over blabbered on about her being smoking hot for a mom. And they all drooled over his sister. Connor didn't see it. He also didn't allow them to spy on Sandy, no matter how much they begged.

"Reply to message… Sure, Mom, you and me for dinner sounds nice."

* * *

Two bright green pieces of broccoli lay like fallen soldiers on a devastated battlefield. Not much else survived the damage Connor unleashed on his plate. He always ordered a medium-rare Flo's Filet at LongHorn Steakhouse. Mom took a bite of her salmon and smiled as she chewed. He knew she had something to say but would never speak with her mouth full.

"What is it, Mom?" he teased with a smirk.

After working her jaw more deliberately, she swallowed. "You remember what you used to call those?" She pointed at his broccoli with her fork.

Connor pursed his lips. "You mean when I was, like, *three*?"

"You said it a lot longer than your teenage pride will admit."

He chuckled. She was right. "Baby trees."

They shared a laugh, and his mother reached across the table and caressed his cheek. Dropping his eyes into his drink, he pulled back, but not immediately. The clatter of forks and knives on ceramic plates competed with the din of dozens of conversations swirling in the air around them. With a final gurgle, Connor sucked the last of his sweet tea through a straw. The scent of the soggy lemon wedge buried in the ice at the bottom of the glass filled his nostrils.

"I miss those days. We're not as close as we were when you were young."

He looked up at her. "Mom, please."

"How was your steak?" It seemed she picked up on his mood. More reason to think she was an okay mom. Why couldn't he tell her that? She took the last piece of salmon from her fork.

"Delicious, as usual. Thanks for bringing us here."

"I needed to get out of the house. I think we both did."

The server, an overly friendly guy who looked no more than eighteen and had acne problems, took his mother's plate and nodded at Connor's. He looked at his mother.

"He's done," she told the guy while smiling at her son.

For a moment, he'd thought she would make him finish his vegetables, as he always had to at home. Smiling at him, like she used to, his mother looked almost... happy. She looked more like herself than she had in days, and that made Connor smile back at her. They sat like that, quietly staring at each other, until the server came back and ruined it.

His mother encouraged him to get dessert, anything he wanted, but Connor was full. She ordered a decaffeinated coffee and said she didn't really want it but wasn't ready to leave the table, to let the moment end. As the waiter walked away, Connor asked if they needed to bring anything home for his dad. She shook her head and said he finished the leftover pizza. Connor's response surprised him as much as her.

"I love you, Mom."

Teary-eyed, she grabbed his hand and said softly, "I love you too."

"Mom... are you, okay? I mean... What a stupid question. None of us are okay."

"I know what you mean, honey. Yes, I think so. I had... well, the hardest day of my life. I lost it a little these couple of days, I know. No, I'm not… *okay*. You're right, none of us are. But we will be. We have to believe that."

Connor nodded. The waiter set the coffee down and asked his mother if she needed sugar or milk. Shaking her head, she kept her focus on her son.

"I'm so proud of you. Not only for how you're handling… this… but for the man you're becoming."

With no idea what to say, Connor stared into her glossy eyes. For a second, his eyes blinked rapidly. His mom placed another hand over the one she had intertwined with his.

"You and me, Connor. *We'll* get through this, and we'll be okay. Do you understand me?"

Connor believed he did. A mental image of the ensuing eruption snapped into focus and flattened his lips. He squeezed his mother's hand and smiled.

BRANDON
JONES

B efore heading out, Jones perused the Journal entries on Sandy Rawlings' phone. Skipping ramblings about her diet, exercise, and church volunteer work, he read the ones featuring Josh. The good-looking Junior had caught her eye on the first day of her sophomore year, and he noticed her. Several entries followed, showing her clear infatuation with the boy who regarded her as a friend. A few scriptural references came after each of those, reminding herself to have chaste thoughts.

Two stood out from the notes about the first buds of their relationship sprouting into romance. After detailed entries about their first and subsequent dates and their first kiss, Jones read of Josh's wandering hands and how Sandy pushed them away. He jotted that in his notebook. Requiring more than a jot, he snapped photos of ones Sandy entered last week, the day before she was killed, and one from that last fateful afternoon. What he found fueled his suspicions of Josh.

Today I get to be with him again. How I miss seeing his beautiful face every day. So glad the summer break is almost over. The last time we were together, he pulled me behind the pool shed and tried to untie my bikini top. I felt so bad for slapping him. I tempted him too much, wearing that. Dad only let me keep it because I promised I'd only wear it to sunbathe alone in our yard. 'For this is the will of God..., that ye should abstain from fornication.' —1 Thessalonians 4:3. (At least until I'm 17 :)

Update: We met later, after the pool party. He got handsy again at the park and said I was so beautiful that he couldn't help himself. I think I blushed. It felt weird, but in a good way. When I reminded him about our agreement, he said I was close enough to 17 and he knew good girls from his church who started way earlier than me. That didn't make me feel any better about it. He apologized and told me he loved me. HE ACTUALLY SAID IT!!! He's so awesome and I think... I love him too.

The last sentence of her final entry brought a tear to Brandon's eye.

He's taking me to see The Rocky Horror Picture Show tonight and then to a secret club. ON OUR LAST NIGHT BEFORE SCHOOL!! So exciting!!!! I really think he'll wait for me. (For our LOVE) December isn't too far off now... Can't wait for 17!

* * *

More ostentatious than the Rawlings house, this white-with-black-trim colonial spoke of money—old money. Off

Whitlock Avenue, these homes went back generations. The Sturgill family was well off, there could be no doubt. Brandon wondered why they didn't send their son to a fancy private school. Marietta High had a great reputation and a fair bit of prestige for a public school but was still a public school.

The Sturgills didn't look at all pleased to find Detective Jones and Officer Bell at their door. Sergeant Carter had assigned her to accompany Jones as part of her track to making detective and because she said having a young, soft-spoken female cop might help loosen the interview's tension. The ride over went about as poorly as Jones expected, and he didn't think he could dig himself out of the hole his juvenile comments buried him in with her.

Sturgill's wife wore a smart business suit and had her dark hair in a bun. Put a pair of glasses on her, and Jones thought she'd fit the role of sexy librarian. Learning Josh's stepmother—who kept her family name, Whitehall—was an attorney heightened Jones' senses to tread carefully. The father never said what he did for a living. Above his designer jeans, the white golf shirt hugged his muscles.

Asking to speak with the boy alone met with near hostile rejection, and Josh's father looked ready to plant a fist in Jones' face. Not too thick a man, he looked fit enough to make his point. It took some convincing after that, but they called Josh to the living room and had him sit between his parents. It may have been a Victorian-style sofa; Brandon only knew the crimson with gold accents looked like they raised it from the Titanic. He'd seen something like it in an exhibit last month.

The boy's eyes kept searching the room, and Jones thought he might have preferred the school counselor over his parents for this. It didn't take a detective to know he was nervous, possibly frightened out of his wits and shaking in his new pair of Vans sneakers. Mel introduced herself simply as Melissa and thanked him for agreeing to talk with them. Jones knew they would soon have no choice and would likely lawyer up. His stepmother worked as a real estate attorney.

"Listen, detectives, I am not at all pleased you spoke with my son at school without my consent."

Jones replied, "We do apologize, Mister Sturgill. Understand it was voluntary, and the school counselor was present. My partner and I spoke to Josh as a witness to aid in our investigation."

"And now they have a few follow-up questions. Dear, let them proceed. Maybe Joshua can help them find his friend's killer."

"Thanks Missus, I mean, Miz Whitehall. Josh, we just want to clarify Sandy's last moments, if we may." He looked at his father with eyes full of panic. "You told us she left... *your friend's* house, a little before 11 PM. Can you be sure of that?"

"It's like I told you and the older guy; it was close to her curfew."

"Right, as you told us. But are *you sure* you didn't walk her out? It was late, dark, and not the safest part of town, *right*?"

"I object," Whitehall exclaimed. "It sounds like you're trying to cast blame on Joshua. If that's what this is, we'll ask you to leave right now."

"No, ma'am," Mel said. "I wasn't at the school earlier and Detective, I mean, Brandon, is confirming for my benefit. Josh, are you sure no one exited with her when she went to meet the Uber?"

"Yes." The boy stared at his interlocked hands.

Jones followed up by asking, "Did you *see* her use the Uber app?" The stepmother cleared her throat deliberately. Mister Sturgill scooted to the edge of his seat and leaned forward like a lion waiting to charge. "I mean, do you know how long they said before the car arrived?"

When he shook his head, Mel said, "We have record of her placing the order from her phone at 10:39 PM. The driver arrived at 10:48 and reports seeing no one outside the cl— um, house."

"Josh." The father turned to his son, still holding the ready-to-pounce pose. "I thought you said you went to the movies then hung out at the Taco Bell after."

"Yeah, like I told them." His eyes begged for Jones' corroboration.

"Right, sorry. You told us Sandy left you and your friends there. I don't know why I said house."

"You both said it," Whitehall corrected. "His father will deal with that later. Our dinner will arrive soon, so please carry on and be quick about it."

Jones nodded acceptance of the terms. "So, Josh. She ordered the Uber. It was going to take about ten minutes, and you walked her out to wait with her…"

"What? No. I told you. *No one* went outside."

"Did you follow her after, then, try to convince her to stay with you, or to go somewhere with—"

"Enough!" Mister Sturgill's deep voice shook Jones like a summer storm's thunderclap. "You said my son was a witness, and now you're trying to accuse him of something. Get out, now."

As Sturgill ushered him toward the front door, Jones turned back and shouted, "You went after her, didn't you? Couldn't keep it in your pants a few months… Did you kill her? Did you kill Sandy?"

When Jones staggered backward, covering his eye, Mel almost tripped over him. She apologized to the Sturgills while Jones pushed her out the front door.

"That was a huge mistake," Jones yelled, walking quickly. "Assaulting an officer and impeding an investigation."

The seething man picked up a baseball bat from its lean by the door and stepped onto the porch. A DoorDash guy stood in the driveway, a spectator to the scene. The force of Sturgill's swing smashed the wooden banister. Mel and Jones jumped into the car and slammed the doors shut.

"I'll have your job for this, Detective!"

WALKER
MICHAELS

This church far surpassed Walker's memories of his Sunday school and weekly services. His grandfather's Southern Baptist church held maybe a hundred people. This place rivaled a small arena. An eeriness filled the silence in such an empty space with its vaulted cedar plank ceiling stretching more than a hundred feet from floor to peak.

Compared to the wooden pews his little bottom had fidgeted on for two hours, these cushioned chairs would have made those childhood Sunday services endurable. When he behaved, his granddad took him for an ice cream afterward. His father never cared much for church, and his mom was Pentecostal. Her efforts to refute her father-in-law's insistence little Walker be brought up Baptist had all failed.

A man who introduced himself as Pastor Frank met him halfway down the center aisle. He said a few of the deacons were still there but Mister Rawlings had gone home. At

Michaels request, Frank stepped away to invite the deacons to stay to answer a few questions. Assurances from the bearded pastor came with his return through the door on the side of the altar—or stage, as Michaels considered it.

The man, who looked odd in 'normal clothes' even though Michaels had never seen him in his pastoral garb, opened up with little prompting. He spoke well of the Rawlings family and praised the work Allen did as a deacon, emphasizing how it was voluntary, not a paid position. Sonya Rawlings had a stellar reputation as well and always supported church bake sales and other projects. While Connor attended Sunday service, he never seemed into it, sometimes falling asleep. In support of the youth ministry, Sandy volunteered on Saturdays and came early with her father on Sundays.

"Sometimes he'd let her drive his electric car to church," Frank said with a smile. "A lovely girl. Such a shame, what happened to her."

"Did you work closely with Sandy?"

"Sometimes, yes. A lovely girl. All the deacons will tell you the same. We had some problems when she… *matured*. You know, the transition from girl to womanhood, when men start noticing."

"Hmm… Did she have any boyfriends at church? Was she close to any boys? Or any of the men here look her way?"

"Men look, Detective. We try to purge ourselves of inappropriate desires, by the grace of God, of course. It's all around us, though. Blatant immorality permeates this debauched world." He waved a circle over his head. "A young lady like Sandy can't be blamed. She was a fine young woman and responded readily to suggestions to present herself in a more... *modest* appearance. We had no trouble with her after that."

As the pastor rattled on, Michaels took extensive notes. Similar sentiments came from the three deacons who remained to speak with him. How great the Rawlings family was, especially Allen and all he did for the church. More praise for Sonya Rawlings, with too much adoration in the eyes of a man named Peter as he mentioned her. That glint dulled when he said, "She wasn't as strict as a parent needed to be to raise a teenage girl in today's world."

It was uncomfortably warm in the office where he spoke with the deacons. Only Peter had long sleeves. When Michaels asked if he wasn't hot, he gave a dissertation on how he had convinced his fellow deacons of the benefits of quality linen to the point where Allen wore nothing but the airy, light fabric in the summer. "In fact, most of us wear linen now. All summer long."

A deacon named Matthew also spoke of Sandy's 'blossoming into womanhood' and her need to be more modest, especially around certain men she worked with in her volunteer service. From specifics Peter added, Michaels gathered the youth minister had paid more than a wholesome amount of attention to her. He jotted down his full name, phone number, and home address. When Michaels asked where Brian Downing worked, Matthew didn't know.

Before running out, Peter said, "He's a house painter, a good one. Since he did ours last month, Mary can't stop telling people how much she loves how it turned out. Of course, once he completes his training and gets ordained, he'll be our fulltime youth minister and won't have to paint anymore houses."

"House painter. *Hmm*."

Michaels wrote that down with the word *Tarp* and double underlined it.

M

How foolish, he thought, to be out mere days after a young woman had been killed. And on a school night. A logical assumption, he blamed the parents and the world around them. A world of moral decay they let into their home through television, movies, books, music, and electronic devices. Poor Mitsy Davis, her eternal soul in turmoil, needed redemption.

From his car across the street, he watched. She looked twenty, and his eye stumbled over the temptation in its sight. He kept from fully turning his face, looking upon the form of Mitsy Davis through his left eye. Jesus once said, "If thy *right* eye offend thee, pluck it out, and cast it from thee."

On the street corner, surrounded by boys with raging hormones, she pranced around in clothes as revealing as a Victoria's Secret model's. "Might as well hang an open for business sign over your genitalia." Barely seventeen and that store had already celebrated its grand opening. The price?

Her dignity. Her morality. Her righteous standing before God.

The Lord, in his grace, called him to redeem such lost souls.

These children tested their fake ID's and entered a nightclub on the Paulding County border. He could have waited for her to exit, do the Lord's work in haste. Sucking a drop of blood from his thumb, he reminded himself this was not the time.

"Tomorrow evening, Mitsy Davis, I will lead you to redemption."

SONYA
RAWLINGS

An obnoxiously loud alert blared through the interior of her Toyota Prius. Sonya only thought of lowering its volume when her phone rang while she was driving, forgetting by the time she'd park. It startled her every time someone called.

"Call from Mary Miller…"

Sonya pressed her thumb into the green phone button on the steering wheel. "Hello?"

"Hey, sweetie. How y'all doing?"

"As well as we can. I'm in the car with Connor."

"Oh. Hey, Connor… Look, I just wanted to check in. I still feel awful about what I said. I never meant to give you the impression—"

"Don't worry about it. I never know what to say or how to say it. Just ask Allen."

After a polite chuckle, Mary said, "As we hear in Sunday sermons all the time, and know better than most from our husbands' work with the church, too many girls are corrupted by this world. But Allen raised Sandy right—I mean, you both did."

Shaking his head, Connor held a finger over the *End Call* button on the touch screen.

"Mary, I can't talk while I'm driving. Really, don't worry about it."

"Okay. I won't keep you. I just want to assure you that I know you and Allen did the best you could with Sandy. But 'the whole world lieth in wickedness,' as you know."

Sonya replied dryly, "First John chapter five."

"I wish my parents had found Christ. If I could have had a dad like Allen… I know my uncle wouldn't have… I…"

"Mary, Connor's with me. I think it's best if we talk later."

Before she could answer, Connor pushed the button.

After an awkward silence, Connor asked, "Was Sandy… Did Uncle Richie ever—"

"No!" Her word had more power than she expected, making Connor wince. "Don't you even think that."

"Then why doesn't he come around anymore?"

"Your dad… He reads into things."

An announcement blared again. Sonya welcomed the opportunity to end that conversation. Although she missed her brother, she never talked about him.

"Call from Detective Michaels…"

"You have his number saved?" Connor shook his head judgmentally.

"He *is* leading the investigation."

"Ah-ha."

Pressing the green phone button on the steering wheel, she said, "Hello?"

"Hey, Sonya—um, Missus Rawlings. Sorry to disturb you unannounced. Is this a bad time?"

"No, Detective. I'm in the car. We're headed home from dinner."

"Oh… Am I on speaker?"

"Yes, Connor is with me."

"Where's Mister Rawlings?"

"He went home after his church meeting. Said he was watching the game."

"I was hoping to talk to just you. There's been some developments in the case."

Connor leaned toward the dashboard display. "Anything you can say to my mother, you can say to me."

"Hey, Connor. How you doing?"

With a red face and open mouth, Connor looked ready to rip into the detective.

"He's fine. We both are… doing as well as can be expected. What's the development?"

"I'd prefer to speak with you privately, ma'am, as soon as possible. At your convenience, of course."

"You're talking about my sister, so just tell us already."

"Fair enough... If you're okay with that, Missus Rawlings?"

"Please, Detective, tell us what you found out about my daughter's murder."

"I need you to find a safe place to pull over first."

* * *

Something crunched beneath her foot as she stepped through the door from the garage. A male voice, not her husband's, traversed the hallway from the living room to greet her. The announcer for the Atlanta Braves, a voice she knew well. From April to September, Allen often had the game on the hundred-inch television when he was home.

Not willing to miss a second, he always kept the volume blaring so he could hear it as he walked around, grabbed a beer, or used the bathroom. No distractions were tolerated when the Braves were playing. Once, in a memory Sonya wished she could forget, he ignored her plea to turn off the game on the bedroom TV as they made love.

It made her question the expression *making love.*

Sonya cringed whenever she heard that announcer's voice.

Shards of broken glass littered her natural stone tile entry. Mushy lumps of... *casserole?*... tried to flee the sharp pieces but lost the battle and lay there dead. The disgusting mess aggravated and puzzled Sonya equally. Remembering her mirror and the cut on Connor's foot, she told him to step carefully around it.

With feet a safe distance from danger and shoes removed, they entered the empty living room. Sonya asked Connor to turn off the TV and expected to hear the typical, "Hey, I'm watching the game," response from the hall bathroom. It didn't come.

"I'll clean it."

An unexpected offer from the boy who hated to make his bed or put his socks and underwear in the hamper right beside the pile of dirty clothes in his room was welcomed with a smile. As he busied himself getting a dustpan and mop, Sonya called Allen's name. When he didn't reply, she left her bag on the kitchen counter and went upstairs.

In the master bath doorway, she watched Allen shower through the steam-laden clear glass. He hadn't noticed her yet. As he climbed to his upper forties, he hadn't lost his looks or toned physique. Despite the sight before them, her eyes had lost their luster for him. She didn't know exactly when that happened but knew his had lost their hunger for her first.

"Oh, hey." He tossed her a boyish smile and faced her as he rubbed his fingers in his full head of dark brown hair. "You... used to join me, sometimes," he said expectantly. "There's plenty of room."

With her arms folded under a blank face, Sonya did not remove herself from the doorframe. "What's that mess downstairs?"

"Oh, sorry. Mary sent a casserole. Peter gave it to me at the church, and I dropped it on the way in." He shut the water and stepped onto the body dryer. "I meant to clean it up."

"Connor's doing it."

"Really? So… we have a little alone time."

When he brought his naked and not fully dried body closer, Sonya turned and ambled away. From behind her back she said, "I'm sleeping in Sandy's bed tonight. I need to smell my baby girl."

WALKER MICHAELS

The phone screen faded to black like a soundless death scene in a movie. A strange and familiar loss crept in. On his computer monitor, an email detailed a complaint from the Sturgill family against Detective Brandon Jones and Officer Melissa Bell. He'd have to deal with that in the morning.

Bonnie called again for her apparently twice daily check-in. Ronni would be furious if she knew he'd told his daughter about the working copycat theory. To Michaels, it was no theory. He knew this was not the work of the Moralist and would not allow the terminology his sergeant insisted on using dampen the high it brought to his spirit. Of course, higher than its previous state might not have been much of an accomplishment, as he was keenly aware.

Funny, he thought, in the ironic sense of the word, how the station changed its mood so quickly. Last night, several detectives and officers worked well past 9 PM. Even Ronni—Sergeant Carter when people were around—stayed beyond her firmly-held-to quitting time. One privilege of her office, she could be responsible for the work done by those under her without needing to be there while they did it. Despite the overwhelming toll it took on every aspect of his life and being, Michaels preferred his job. He never wanted to be anyone's boss.

Electricity buzzed around him, surging into his veins, and he felt more energized than he had in years. He had a new killer to catch and an innocent young woman whose blood cried out in the streets for justice. He thought that term might have been in the Bible but didn't know scripture all that well. No, it was from that U2 song, *One Tree Hill*. While he didn't care for the singer's political views, Michaels couldn't deny the brilliance of *The Joshua Tree*.

For the first time in ages, Michaels was humming.

Advancing from person of interest to suspect on the Action Board, Sonya's brother, Richie Phillips, had left town unexpectedly the night of Sandy's murder. Though he'd allegedly driven to Macon for a rental property emergency around 10 PM, no one could verify the time or give him an alibi. When questioned about him, Sonya said little beyond him not having had come around in a while. Allen had grimaced at the mention of the man's name but said nothing.

The more talkative of the church deacons, Peter, had told Michaels how Allen forbade Sonya's brother from coming to their house when the children were younger. Beyond that, he said little more than how much Allen hated the guy and that he had made his wife cut her brother off completely. Reading between the lines, Michaels assumed some inappropriate behavior with his niece… or nephew. Macon police had dispatched officers to take him in for questioning.

Bonnie arrived as promised with Chinese take-away from House of Lu. She mentioned how much better her father looked. As she described it, he still looked tired, but a healthier kind of tired. Michaels thought he understood her meaning. With everyone having gone besides the uniforms downstairs working the night shift, he and Bonnie sat at his desk eating out of black plastic containers.

"They always do this in cop shows. Jones would love it."

Looking up at her dad, Bonnie smiled like she did as a child. "TV cops always eat out of those white paper boxes. I asked for them, but they only had these."

Michaels chuckled. "This'll do. Thanks, baby girl."

As he scooped up a forkful of Singapore Noodles, he marveled at his daughter's skill with chopsticks. The Szechuan chicken she balanced between them smelled way too spicy for his innards to handle. As Bonnie ate, she studied his board.

"You're sure this isn't him?"

"You shouldn't be looking at that. The sarge'll have my keester if she finds out you were even in here."

"Did she know you had another board at home last time?"

"In my *locked* office." His tone feigned aggravation.

"So... Detective Michaels..." Bonnie stood and marched toward the board, folding her arms. "Who done it?"

"Would you believe... you're the first person to ask?" The smirk came to his daughter's lips as expected. "That's exactly what this board will help me answer. Can't hit the fast-forward button and skip to the reveal."

"Maybe... do a Scooby-Doo ending. Pull the mask off to reveal the real killer. Gasps from the group as they see his face. 'And I'd have gotten away with it too, if it wasn't for you meddling detectives.'" Her grumbly voice made him laugh.

"Since your *kids* can't talk, I'll have to do this the old-fashioned way. I liked the uncle for a spell. He's there to the left of Sonya—um, Missus Rawlings."

"He must not have been around when God handed out good looks."

"Looking at his sister, you'd never have guessed the relation."

"*Dad*...? 'Sonya—um, Missus Rawlings,' is a grieving mother. And she's married."

"Hang on now, baby girl."

"I'm just teasing. Besides, I know how obsessive..." When her father scowled, she corrected, "*focused* you get on a case.

You said you *liked* the uncle. Got someone else as suspecto numero uno?"

"The youth minister at their church. See, I think Sandy had a little crush on the guy. Even volunteered to work Saturday afternoons and Sunday mornings with him."

"This him?" She tapped on the photo of Brian Downing. "Sandy had good taste. He's a hunk. Why didn't we have a youth minister like that at Mom's church? I'd have volunteered to work there too."

"*Nice*. Sandy wasn't journaling back then. Her first entries started with high school and Josh Sturgill." When she looked closely at Josh's photo, he said, "Don't say it."

Leaning closer, she studied Brian's picture. "If I were her, I'd have stuck with the hot youth minister here."

"Her infatuation with Brian made it into an early journal entry. Without mentioning a crush, Sandy wrote how he was too old and how much more... *light* is the word she used, I think... Josh was than Brian."

"The word's lit, *old* man. Let me guess, *he* didn't lose interest in Sandy. Kept his 'How *you* doin'?' eyes on her. Maybe there's a reason he became a youth minister."

After a shrug, he said, "There were complaints at the church, but not about Brian. About Sandy needing to dress modestly and wear a bra, especially around him. None of those complaints *came from* Brian. Get this... He's a house painter and one of our early clues, that looked like a dead end, was that the killer used a black tarp like a painter might use."

"Open and shut case." She held an open hand toward him. "Let's go nail the bastard, partner. Gimme the keys, I'm driving."

"Yeah, you are. Home to your husband."

"Seriously, Dad. He looks good for it. Why not bring him in?"

"We need hard evidence. We're working on it and hope to have something concrete tomorrow. Plus… I'm not off the father yet."

"You said he was home, and the wife and son were there."

"There's something about that family. I think they got big marital problems. I know the look. Seen it in your mom's eyes." An awkward silence floated between them for a moment. "Allen Rawlings is a pompous tool. Jones' word. What I don't know yet is if he's a two-faced tool."

Day 4

SONYA
RAWLINGS

When she woke, her arms were crushing the pillow into her face and chest. Sonya pressed her nose into it and extracted her daughter's scent. The fragrance of lilacs transformed the room into an enchanted garden. Sandy loved that shampoo. Sunlight split the curtains down the center to fracture the room. The radiating pale-yellow satin-finish paint on the walls couldn't wrest Sonya from the bed. Gravity's pull on the shattered mother's bones and muscles had increased exponentially while she slept.

The phone she pried off the nightstand displayed the time: 8:09 AM. It complained about not being plugged in overnight by showing her a yellow 11% in the top right corner. What did it matter? Her parents' flight from Paris wouldn't get into Hartsfield Jackson until the afternoon. They'd taken the trip of a lifetime only to have it cut short and come home a week early. Allen's parents phoned and said they would come for the funeral. They lived a six-hour car ride away in Raleigh, North Carolina.

After soaking the pillow once more, Sonya mustered the courage to lift herself off the bed and make it, pulling the bedspread taut. A note fell from the door when she cracked it ajar. From Allen, it told her he'd gone to the gym and then had some errands to run. Reading it lessened the morning's crushing weight.

After a shower, Sonya descended the stairs and went into the kitchen because she didn't know what else to do. She needed to do something. She made scrambled eggs and avocado toast. The avocado had ripened and wouldn't last another day. Most of what she made landed on a plate she set on the counter for when Connor woke up. Playing with her eggs more than eating them, Sonya counted the tiny brown dots peppering an overripe slice of avocado. Nine. To confirm what didn't matter, she counted again, going in the opposite direction.

Staccato rumblings of Connor stirring upstairs animated her. She traced the pounding of his heavy morning feet as he lumbered to the bathroom. A minute later, the toilet flushed. It had been years since she needed to remind him to wash his hands. Lighter steps made their way back to his room and he closed the door.

Despite the gap stretched between them by his teenage angst and digital isolation, he always kissed his mother good morning when he came down for breakfast. This morning's greeting had a deeper impact. Sonya sensed affection where obligation used to reside. Although the eggs had cooled, Connor devoured them and the toast—after setting the avocado slices aside. She fully expected him to run back up the stairs after his "Thanks, Mom." Instead, after rinsing his plate in the sink, he sat beside her at the counter.

"Dad?"

"At the gym, then running some errands."

"And you?"

"I need to get the house ready for your grandparents."

"I'll help."

"No, sweetheart. Thank you. I think… if you're up to it, you should do some schoolwork. I know, just hear me out. The routine and occupying our minds will be good for us."

Connor agreed less reluctantly than she expected.

"I need to go out, just for a little bit. And get a few groceries at Publix. I can bring something home for lunch. What would you like?"

"Anything but Taco Bell. I've told Dad like, a million times, I wouldn't even feed it to Gigi. Only reason I ate it the other day's 'cause I was starved and there wasn't anything else."

"He thinks it's your favorite."

"Yeah, when I was like, *five*, and you wouldn't let me have Micky D's. As much as he tells me I *need* to listen…"

Putting a hand on his, Sonya said, "What then? You name it."

"You could get me an Italian sub from Publix. With everything but vinegar."

*   *   *

After asking for a porcelain coffee cup, Sonya fidgeted it in her hands. Carrying it from the counter to the table, she had nearly dropped it. The coffee didn't taste as good as the espresso she made at home, and she didn't want to drink anything. To sit at a table without ordering something didn't seem right. The setting of this meeting made her as nervous as the person who asked to meet her here. He said the Starbucks was close to her house and he didn't want to drag her down to the station.

A pink-haired young lady behind the counter called out something that sounded like 'cricket.' A tall, professional-looking woman walked up to take her drink and said, "Bridgett. Thanks." Sonya used to wear suits like that when she worked at McDuffey Development until she quit in her third trimester with Sandy.

Each ding of the door opening lifted her eyes from the trembling black liquid's surface. The businesswoman leaving. A couple of young men in white shirts and ties entering. The nametags she couldn't read identified them as Mormon missionaries. Sonya wondered if they were the same two who regretted ringing the Rawlings' doorbell last month when Allen happened to be home. He seemed to enjoy goading them into a scriptural argument.

Lost in thought, she missed the ding that announced Detective Michaels' arrival. Four minutes late. As he took his place third in line, he waved at her like they were old friends. Looking around at the crowded tables for the first time, Sonya wondered if anyone would recognize her.

"Hey, sorry I'm late. Traffic on Whitlock was horrendous, as usual."

The man sat across from her and removed the lid from his large cup of coffee. They didn't call it 'large' here, for some reason, and Sonya didn't care to remember what they said instead. He ripped open a brown paper sugar packet, dumped it in, and repeated the process. He swirled a wooden stick around, making a whirlpool in his cup. The bitter aroma lacked the silky-smooth notes she had come to love since her trip to Italy.

"Thanks for meeting me. I wanted this to be a more… *casual* conversation. And thanks for coming alone."

"I'm not sure why you couldn't say what you needed to yesterday, on the phone. I don't want to leave Connor too long, so please tell or ask me whatever you need to."

"He's the reason. I mean, I didn't want to talk in front of your son. And I didn't think you'd want what we're gonna discuss said in front of him, neither."

"Allen wouldn't like this. If he finds out…"

"We'll jump off that bridge when we come to it. I need to ask you about Allen, actually." Her eyes widened, and she knew he could read her anxiety. Leaning over his coffee, he whispered, "You and him having marital problems?"

Any fear she had turned to shock, and Sonya blushed. She looked around at all the faces buried in their phones and paying this conversation no attention.

"Sorry, ma'am. I know it's personal, but *it is* relevant to the case."

"What makes you certain it wasn't him?" In a softer tone, she added, "The Moralist, I mean."

"I shouldn't be telling… We don't release every detail of a case. The drug he used was in the papers, but not the method of introduction. The Moralist used a hypodermic needle. In your daughter's case, the man likely came up from behind with a cloth doused in it."

"Like in the movies?"

"Yes. Only, it takes longer than they show. We believe she may have struggled and likely scratched him during the abduction. See, he scrubbed under Sandy's fingernails."

The idea of her little girl struggling worsened the images that haunted Sonya behind her eyelids since learning her daughter had been killed. Her vision clouded and she raised a knuckle to the corner of her eye.

"We believe your daughter's death may have been personal."

With an already straight posture, Sonya pulled her shoulders back. "He said that. After you first told us, Allen said... well, I thought he was speculating wildly... He wondered if someone meant to hurt our Sandy and did those... *things* to throw you off."

"Hmm. He said that? Interesting."

"Interesting how?"

"Well, Missus Rawlings—"

"Please, Sonya."

"You told us he was home in the evening and all night with you. That's one of the things I need to verify."

After a few rapid blinks, Sonya said, "First you come in here and ask me if we have marital problems. Now you think I lied for him?"

"No, ma—Sonya. I think you were devastated and confused by the horrific news my partner and I came to deliver that morning. Now I'm asking you to think about that night."

Sonya dropped her eyes back into the undrunk and cold espresso she still clutched between her hands.

"When did your husband come home?"

"At eleven."

"Eleven, exactly? You're sure about the time?"

"When he's not away, he doesn't usually stay out past Sandy's curfew... To make sure she's home on time. He came home right at eleven."

"And he was home with you all night? Did you go to bed or fall asleep?"

"My daughter didn't come home, Detective. We didn't go to bed, and I assure you, I didn't fall asleep. He wanted to go look for her, but we had no idea where Sandy had gone. Allen was in the house all night."

"Hmm. Okay. Thank you for confirming that. Now, I gotta ask… Why'd your mind go straight to me implying that you lied about his alibi? Did you assume your husband was a suspect?"

"Don't you always start with the family? Or is that just something they do in those crime shows Allen watches? And it wasn't my brother either. I heard you had him arrested."

"Macon police cleared him. The tenant at his rental down there confirmed the time of his arrival. Even leaving when he said he did, he had to have been flying down I-75."

"He never touched Sandy, if that's what you cops are thinking. Allen forbids contact with our children because Richie's an atheist. My husband won't stand for any free thinking under his—Sorry. I mean, that's all it was. Richie would never do anything to hurt a child."

"We gotta follow every lead. But, like I said, he was cleared."

"You went to the church. Do you have suspects there?"

The detective turned his full cup of coffee on the table and examined the logo on it. "I'm not at liberty to discuss the details of the investigation."

"So, we're meeting in secret for you to get information from me, *unofficially*, and you're telling me you can't answer my questions *about my daughter's murder.*"

The raised volume attracted unwanted eyes and Sonya stood to go. Michaels grabbed her hand and they both froze, looking into each other's eyes for an elongated moment.

"Sonya. Let me walk you to your car, please."

"You haven't even sipped your coffee. Good day, Detective."

"It's a to-go cup. And I'm Walker."

ALLEN
RAWLINGS

Invigorated from his morning workout, Allen stood in the shower and let the water flow over him, soothing the pain that bled from his heart and made his skin ache. Physical activities helped, distracting the mind and body from the cold realities of his life—a life his daughter was ripped from in an instant.

As he dressed, Charlotte called his name from the kitchen. The pangs of hunger set in, so he accepted her offer of pancakes. She said she had a mix, so it was no bother. What Allen saw in her eyes when he entered the kitchen and kissed her went beyond 'no bother.' Years ago, Sonya used to look at him that way. That thought made him wonder when his wife last saw the face he was wearing now for this woman.

As they ate, Charlotte asked about his day and where his wife thought he went that morning. Allen dismissed the mention of Sonya, preferring to keep himself in one life without it bleeding over into the other. When he told her about his investigative efforts to supplement the police department's ineptitude, she bounced on the balls of her feet, giddy as a child.

"Can I help? I can go with you."

"That's not such a good idea." He pulled a piece of instant pancake from his fork and chewed. "People can't see us together. And I don't know how you could help."

"We don't have to go together. Give me an assignment. Oh, I know. I can spy on someone. I'd be good at that. Come on, Al, I wanna help," she whined.

Allen's eye twitched. "I know. You've been an amazing help already, believe me."

"What? A bail out and sharing my bed. Is that all I am to you?"

"Come on, Charlie, that's not fair."

She blushed. "You haven't called me that in a while."

"Look, I wish you *could* help…" Studying her as she bent over the table to remove the plates, a new idea narrowed his eyes. "Maybe you can."

*   *   *

While Charlotte kept Frank occupied in the auditorium, Allen snuck into his office to search for… well, he didn't know what. The pastor's comments last night about Sandra put him on Allen's suspect list, and he thought he might find something. Drawer after drawer, file folder after file folder, he found nothing connecting this man to his daughter's death. Nothing saying the church preacher was anything but virtuous and focused on his duties to the congregation.

When his phone rang, Allen answered and wished he hadn't. Not only because it was Sonya. He was trying to be quiet, sneaking around in the pastor's office. When she confirmed his theory about a copycat, he exclaimed, "I told you," and reflexively covered his mouth with one hand.

When he climbed into his i3, he found Charlotte crouching down in the passenger seat. He had told her they needed to take separate cars, but she said her old clunker wouldn't start.

Laying a hand on his thigh, she asked, "Anything?"

"No. I think Pastor Frank's a good man."

"Me too. When I told him about my concerns for Russ dealing with Sandy's death, he was so kind and compassionate. He read me some verses and offered to speak to Russ."

"He'll do a better job than me. I can't think straight, let alone provide guidance to anyone else."

"Who's next?"

"Do you think your seductive charms will work on a younger man?"

*　*　*

All he could do was watch from the car down the road and hope Brian didn't know where Charlotte lived. She looked like she fit in, the trophy wife of one of the rich twats in any of these enormous houses. Fortunately, the friendly lady at Brian's answering service gladly provided the name of the subdivision where he was doing an exterior painting job. Allen had pretended to be a potential customer with a huge job and asked for the location to see Brian's work.

The timing needed to be right, to look as if she happened to notice him as she walked by. If only they had Sandra's Chihuahua to sell the charade. After stalling in front of the house before the one outlined in black tarpaulins, Charlotte made her move. When Brian came around the side into the driveway she strolled by.

To get a better view of the scene, Allen fumbled through the glove box and found a pair of birdwatchers. He wished he could read lips. Brian's reaction to Charlotte's flirtatious nature and how she looked in that sundress left no question she had his attention. "Take it slow, Charlie," he said to his windshield. "Let it flow naturally before you start with the questions."

A sweet, though naïve, woman who would do anything for him, Allen doubted she had the acting ability or brains to pull this off. With the threat from the police for him not to investigate, he couldn't approach Brian. The youth minister also knew him and his family, so any questions Allen asked would give up his motive of accusing the young man. This woman was his only shot at this.

The conversation lasted longer than he expected, and Brian never looked upset or uneasy. Allen assumed the small talk hadn't slid into the subtle questioning they had rehearsed in the car. It ended with her giving Brian a kiss on the cheek and him walking back behind the house. With a skip in her steps, she pranced toward the BMW, opened the passenger side door, and slipped in beside him.

"I got it," she said, smiling widely.

"Got what? What did he say?"

"I got what you asked, like we practiced. It's obvious he was into your daughter, even from, like, fifteen. I mean her, when she was fifteen. He's older." Allen rolled his eyes but didn't interrupt her. "He said he realized she was too young, but it sounded like *she* pulled away from him. It was all inuendo and inference, mind you." Through a bright smile, she added, "I'm good at being coy."

"God, woman. Sunday night—where was he?"

Allen's words came out hard enough to crush bone, and she pouted like a child.

"Look, Charlie, I'm sorry." He took her hand, and her cheek muscles relaxed. "I'm too anxious about all this. I need to know who killed my daughter."

"I understand. So, yeah, he said he was home on Sunday."

"Aha! So, he was home alone, without an alibi. I knew it."

"No, Al, sorry. You didn't let me finish. He hosted a Zoom with the kids from church. A sort of 'reminders for going back to school' thing."

"With the kids? It must have ended early. He had time." Allen reached for the door handle. "I'm going to kill—"

"*Wait.* Some of the parents stayed on. Even Pastor Frank was online. Brian said some kept him on 'til late. After eleven. I mean, I could ask some of them, see if it checks out. I think I'm good at this."

Allen sighed deeply. "It must not have been him, then. The cops say Sandra disappeared just before eleven. But we have another suspect to check."

WALKER
MICHAELS

To catch up to the brisk walk of Sonya Rawlings, Michaels raced out the door. Some coffee leaped from the filled-to-the-brim cup to stain the cuff of his sleeve. It had cooled considerably under the icy conversation that passed over it on the table. Sonya didn't say anything or acknowledge his presence beside her as she marched to her car. The stern mask the woman wore turned to aggravated surprise when Michaels leaned his hand on the top of the doorframe, keeping her from opening it.

Words weren't necessary for Michaels to discern her thoughts. Her heated scowl screamed volumes. Looking into her eyes as if he could make her understand, he let the situation settle before speaking. Three days ago, when this ordeal was the continuation of the worst period of this detective's life, he felt what little remained of his soul draining from him. The moment he saw Sandy's body, he had blamed himself. This woman and her husband blamed him for not protecting their daughter.

Now the case had evolved into a new murder investigation and became even more personal. The bond he had forged with the dead teenage girl over guilt hadn't dissolved with his liability. Something his mind couldn't articulate about the Rawlings family drew him like a magnet. Raw hatred for Allen Rawlings had become a raging fire in his gut, ravaging his intestines like a cancer. He wanted Sonya to have been wrong. He wanted to find the opportunity in the darkest minutes of that night for that man to have left the house and killed his daughter.

"We have a lead, Sonya. Telling you now will only have negative consequences. Trust me, I know. Hatred will grow inside you like a weed, choking you from the inside out."

"How *should* I feel toward the man who killed my little girl?" Tears welling in the glassy orbs around her hazel irises became powerful magnets.

Walker gently placed his hand on her upper arm, and she fell into him, sobbing. His first instinct sent his eyes roaming through the parking lot. Before he could push her away, she straightened, ran her knuckle under her eyes, and lifted her key fob. He hadn't seen a woman so broken, so vulnerable, since Catherine. It wasn't the cancer that did it to his wife, and he knew what he saw now wasn't forged exclusively from this woman losing her daughter.

Michaels took a half step back, his now cold coffee a dead weight in his hand. "I'll let you go."

"Brian. The youth minister. He had eyes for Sandy, and she had a crush… for a while. One of the deacons told me to have her dress more modestly around him. She was a child, not even sixteen at the time."

"I'm aware of the situation. I assure you; I'm looking into all angles. Every lead is being taken seriously."

"I should hope so."

Silence stood between them like a chaperone at a middle school dance. It drove Michaels to the edge of sanity, and he needed to say something. He could have kicked himself for saying, "What kind of car is this? It looks futuristic."

"Toyota Prius… Prime. Allen bought it for me four months ago."

He squinted at the splotches of sunlight glinting between broken patches of shade. The breeze fondling the nearby tree cast waves of light and shadow over the shiny metallic paint. It looked like a living creature with shimmering skin. "It's not exactly white. It almost has a hint of blue. Must be the sun playing tricks on the eyes."

"Wind Chill Pearl. The color cost extra. But I loved it, and Allen let me order it."

"Hmm. I like this one better than that little boxy thing your husband drives."

Looking blankly back at him, Sonya said nothing. Since Michaels ran out of things to say before he mentioned the car, he kept his lips together and waited for her to break the silence that reassembled itself into a chasm between them.

"Thank you, Walker..." She placed her hand on his forearm. "For sharing what you couldn't tell me."

Having already blundered by leaving his mouth in gear and his brain in neutral, Michaels nodded but didn't speak. Besides, he still needed to make his way to the subdivision where he knew he would find a certain youth minister/house painter.

*   *   *

As Michaels neared the house his GPS said was less than fifty feet away, he was sure he recognized the woman walking up its driveway. A second, closer look verified his assumption. That attractive blonde woman wasn't a random neighbor striking up a conversation with the shirtless house painter. Her name escaped him, but Michaels had a clear mental recollection of where he had seen her. Jones had investigated her when she bailed Rawlings out. His findings painted a picture of someone who wouldn't be in this neighborhood unless she was cleaning one of the three-quarter-million-dollar houses.

With a foot on the brake to maintain his distance, Michaels puzzled over her presence here—beyond the obvious connection of attending the same church. The woman had a son, and the painter was his youth minister. Dolling herself up and tracking him down to discuss her son's pastoral care while the minister was painting a house, roasting under the intense August sun, didn't make sense.

It didn't *feel* right to Michaels.

Chasing away his next question of whether the blistering heat would help or hinder the thick tint's absorption into the fiber cement board siding, Michaels parked one house back and pondered the scene. That slinky dress wasn't the uniform of any housecleaning service. Why was this woman here, talking to his next suspect? It didn't add up... until it did.

Allen Rawlings.

In his outrage and desperation, he could have been stupid enough to bring her here. As the thought meandered through the detective's synapses, the woman kissed the youth minister's cheek and strode away in the opposite direction from Michaels' position. Brian watched her for a minute then disappeared around the side of the half-painted house. Michaels noted the black tarpaulin protecting the landscaping that wrapped around what, to him, was a small mansion.

While trying to shut off the car with no engine or key, Michaels spotted the silver BMW i3 approaching from behind a Dawn Redwood tree. Its dense lower branches hung just over the grass below, hiding Mister Rawlings' car from his earlier view. The blonde sat beside the driver, who held a steel gaze under a focused brow. Michaels put on the sternest judgmental glare his face could muster but the i3 whizzed passed with neither occupant noticing him.

The door swung open, and Michaels pulled himself out of the government-issued Tesla. He still couldn't believe these were the new fleet of unmarked cars. He missed his Chevy Caprice. Tires screaming behind him pulled his gaze. False alarm. Someone in a grayish white import made a U-turn a couple of driveways back. All these houses looked the same and each street in the subdivision had the same name with Road, Street, Court, or Way appended in smaller text on the street signs.

The questions he had mentally rehearsed slid behind the one hammering in his skull, trying to break through his forehead. What did Brian Downing discuss with Allen Rawlings' mistress?

BRANDON
JONES

This morning may have been worse than the one that started with a pre-dawn call that took him to his first murder victim's body. At least that had the excitement of plunging him into his first big case. The way Sergeant Carter's voice shrilled when she screamed his name would likely crawl between his skin and bone for days. His ears rang for twenty minutes after the chewing out he sat through in her office. Her tongue lashed him like a whip, and he could almost hear the open wounds crying for soothing consolation.

Instead, he received another fiery blast of Carter's indignation when she received a call from the Commissioner. The Sturgills—Amanda Whitehall, specifically—had phoned the mayor. The mayor informed Carter of a meeting in the commissioner's office at 12:45 and left no room for interpretation. She and Jones were to clear their schedules to attend. Whitehall and Sturgill would be present to file their formal complaint.

Unsuccessfully hiding evidence of the altercation under his aviator glasses, Jones trudged back to his desk. Since the suspension he expected hadn't come... *yet*... he had work to do. It seemed pointless; he knew Josh killed her. The kid had produced no alibi for himself in the club, and no one saw Sandy leave or could verify he didn't follow her. A child of privilege. Jones figured the boy thought he could get away with anything. Rich mommy and daddy would protect him. Although, he had the distinct impression it was the well-to-do stepmom who had the power in that family dynamic.

"You really think the boyfriend did it?"

He hadn't noticed Mel walk up to his desk and read his mind.

"It's dead obvious, isn't it? He had motive and opportunity. He wanted some, pushed her for it, and she wouldn't put out. He followed her out of the club, probably pulled her into an alley, and tried to take what she wasn't giving."

"But there was no sign of struggle, no bruising, and no sexual assault."

"So, you're a detective now?"

"Why do you have to be such a jerk sometimes?" She crossed her arms. "I know going with you last night doesn't make me a detective, but I've seen the case file and the evidence. Your theory doesn't fly. If that boy forced himself on her, her body would show it. It doesn't. *Detective*."

Imitating that red-headed TV detective he thought was cool, Jones pulled off the aviators and stood to look her in the eye. "Sorry, Mel. You're right. I was a jerk. And not just now, even… I snapped, and I'm sorry. You make a good point, actually."

Relaxing her arms to let them hang at her sides, Mel replied, "Thank you."

"Doesn't mean he didn't do it. I guess he didn't try to rape her. Or…" The pop of his finger snap startled the uniformed officer. "That drug, the Flunitraz whatever… It can be used as a date rape drug, *right*? What if he planned to do it but gave her too much, and she OD'd? To cover it up, and to get vengeance for her shutting him out, he did the FGM and exhibited her in the park."

Mel put her hands on her hips. "That tracks better than your first idea, I'll give you that. But I'm not seeing it go down like that, not with what was done to that poor girl."

"What do you mean? It's like I said. He was angry. A spoiled rich kid didn't get what he wanted, so he tried to drug her and take it from her."

"Yeah, that would all work if he didn't try to frame it as a Moralist killing. He'd be suspect number one. But what was done to Sandy Rawlings? That took an insane amount of forethought and planning."

Jones exhaled loudly and sunk back into his seat. "You're right. Maybe you should be the detective, and I should get back in a uniform."

"No, it's just... You're only looking at it one way, like you do lots of things. There's more to things, to people, than carnal desire. You take a girl out, and your mind goes straight to whose bedroom it will be after you paid your dues suffering through dinner and conversation."

"*Suffer?* Nah, Mel. I had a nice time the other evening. I'm not like that."

"You are. You haven't stopped talking about Sonya Rawlings and Charlotte Sellers since you saw them. And that's all you see in Sandy's murder, even though she was never the object of a sexual crime. You gotta look at this from another motive."

He scratched his head. "The cleansing? Josh wasn't the type of kid who thought she needed to be cleansed. No, he wanted to do the dirty deed with her."

"But it wasn't the Moralist's goal. *His* motive was the cleansing. This new guy just used that to cover his tracks."

Shooting out of his chair, Jones leapt toward the Action Board. "No. No, that's not it. Something Michaels said, when this case first started. He said these serial killer types have fans."

"Fans?" Mel joined him at the board.

"People that idolize them and the work they do. This one was sick. I mean really deranged stuff with the female mutilation under the guise of saving these girls from the immoral world."

When he tapped a photo on the bottom of the board, off to the side, Mel asked who he was. George Odom had been added as due diligence, but no one thought of him as a proper suspect. Calling him a person of interest seemed a stretch when Michaels put him up there.

"Next-door neighbor. As religious as the Rawlings, but from another church. Only reason he's even on the board is Mister Rawlings told us they had it out once when he caught the man perving on Sandy sunbathing in the yard."

"So, a pervert with a morality motive? Twisted."

"Yeah. And we were looking at a Moralist killing, so we ruled out a fifty-something-year-old man ogling the neighbor's girl in a bikini. And now, like you said, it's not a desire *for* her, for Sandy. It's a desire to *protect* her, to save her… in a warped sorta way."

"I'm lost. Then he's still not good for it. If he got his jollies peeping on a teenage girl, he didn't want to save her."

"Allen Rawlings blew up and left it at that. But Connor told me later there was more to the story. This George fella, they didn't catch him ogling. He approached the Rawlings— well, Sonya. Allen wasn't there. Said he was concerned about Sandy. Then Sonya told us the guy saw Connor's friends pressed into an upstairs window, gawking at her daughter. He also said he had seen Sandy sneaking in after curfew and that her parents needed to protect her. That it was a dangerous world out there."

"Now you're on to something. What's our next move?"

Jones checked his watch: 12:34 PM.

SONYA
RAWLINGS

When she spotted a black Tesla in the Odom's driveway, Sonya slowed to a stop. George and Ellen were at work, so why would a car be in their driveway? She had seen a car like that earlier, but Teslas had become rather commonplace in Cobb County in recent years. Not for good old Southern boy Republican George Odom. He drove a Chevy Tahoe, and his wife had a newer model Cadillac Escalade.

Confirming Sonya's initial instinct, Walker Michaels stepped off the Odoms' front porch. He walked past his car and down the driveway toward her. For some reason, her nerves turned to Jello. Watching the nonchalance in his stride, she realized she hadn't been caught anywhere she wasn't supposed to be. One house away from home, she had stopped when she saw a suspicious car parked at her neighbor's empty house. So, where did the guilt come from?

"Afternoon."

She lowered the passenger-side window. "Something wrong, Detective?"

"Walker will do just fine, as I said." He leaned and rested his forearms on the door. "I got no need for formalities."

"And may I ask what you're doing at my neighbors' home?"

"I told you we were following every lead."

"Oh, you can't mean that little incident from last month. It was just a misunderstanding. George and Ellen are good, church-going folks."

"Yeah, a good Christian man who got off watching your teenage daughter lying out practically naked."

"Detective! She always wore her swimsuit and was in our fenced-in backyard. And we already told you; George was simply concerned about my daughter's well-being."

"You did tell us…"

To escape another unwanted conversation, Sonya raised her foot. The car inched slowly forward, and Michaels straightened.

"Good day, Detective."

"Sonya, wait." She stopped and he caught up. To her surprise he opened the door, plopped into the passenger seat, and pulled the door closed. "We need to talk."

"Didn't we do that already?"

"I know it seems unfair, you being the mother and all, to keep things from you. It's to preserve the integrity of the investigation. And it protects you."

"You already checked into Brian—um, I mean, have you? You arrested my brother. My husband accosted a teenage boy. You accused him of killing his own daughter. Now you're looking at poor George. It doesn't look like your investigation has very much integrity to preserve."

"We follow every lead. We now know it wasn't the Moralist. It could be a copycat who will select more girls and continue his mentor's work. I know. It's how these sickos see it. But I believe, with all my heart, your daughter's killing was more personal than that. So, we gotta pursue every angle."

"And where's that getting you? Are you any closer to finding her killer? *No.* Does any of this even matter? Nothing you do, nothing anyone does, will bring my baby girl home."

The buildup reached volatility, and the dam holding her tears in check burst. Sonya didn't know which happened first, her leaning onto his shoulder or him pulling his arm around her. Her body went limp, and her foot slipped off the brake.

Neither of them reacted to the subtle movement, but both straightened and jerked their heads when the sound of scraping metal rippled through the open window of the Prius. As if she could push it through the floorboard and stop the car by driving her heel into the pavement, Sonya slammed her foot on the brake pedal. A mild expletive slipped from Sonya's mouth, and her hand covered it in haste. With his head out the window, Walker said the front wheel "got scratched up pretty good on the curb."

He rested his hand on hers as she squeezed the shifter and guided it to put the car in *Park*. A moment passed like a decade and the man beside her sat no longer a stranger. She didn't know what they shared, but being thrust together over such an unbearable tragedy forged a macabre connection she didn't understand but also didn't reject.

"You said you needed to talk to me."

"*Huh?* Oh, yeah. I wanted to see you—I mean, I needed to talk to you—because we *have* made some progress. We've ruled out several suspects."

Thinking she needed to say something, Sonya opened her mouth but lacked the cognition to push anything out of it.

"I know." Walker raised his free palm. "It doesn't sound like much. But the process of elimination is progress. It narrows the list. Narrows our focus."

Sonya sighed and felt her energy for this police business rush out of her with her breath. "I don't think this is good for me."

"What do you mean?"

Looking down to see it was still there, Sonya pulled her hand from under his. "My son and I need to mourn and support each other. I think I need to leave the investigation to you and not be involved."

"Involved?" His softened face reclaimed the gruffness it sometimes carried. "Why'd you ask me if I had checked into Brian?"

The Jello nerves returned, and Sonya turned up the fan on the air conditioning.

"That was you. The U-turn in the driveway."

Putting on her most convincing look of shock and innocence, she said, "I really have no idea what you're talking about."

"How'd you know where to find Brian Downing? Did you follow me when I left the Starbucks? Oh, oh. You followed Allen." Sonya settled. "That's what I wanted to talk to you about, actually."

With a puzzled expression, she looked at him for clarity.

"I know you and Allen have been having problems... *marital* problems."

"How dare you, Detective. My daughter is dead and instead of looking for her killer you're putting your nose into my marriage... *Where it doesn't belong.*"

"Sonya." His soft face returned. She preferred it. "I know you're much more than the persona you show the world. I also know you know things maybe you never admitted, not even to yourself. And I don't suppose you've ever confronted Allen about it, either."

Sonya's neck muscles weakened, and her head dipped.

"You know... don't you?"

An eternity squeezed into the span of a few seconds. She nodded.

WALKER
MICHAELS

Did he lie to the mother of the murdered young lady? Elimination of suspects in *this* case didn't feel like progress to him. It was good detective work, following leads and corroborating stories and verifying alibis. Like a bee on a windshield, he felt as if he'd hit an obstacle at a hundred miles an hour. This case had become a mess of splattered guts, and he needed to sift through them.

The youth minister's story sounded credible. Michaels pulled the lever to spray the windshield with cleaner. Specific people had been in an online meeting with him until a time that would have made it impossible for him to have reached the center of Marietta to abduct Sandy.

"Virtual backgrounds," he exclaimed as he turned into the station.

Upstairs, he found an empty desk where he hoped he'd find his partner hard at work. After the fiasco with the Sturgills, Michaels assumed Jones would have faced a suspension. If nothing else, it would appease the mayor and make the Sturgill family think they were getting justice.

What about justice for Sandy?

It eluded him like a dog's tail, yet around and around he chased after it. Alone at his desk, he practically inhaled his Chick-fil-A chicken salad sandwich. Having chosen the healthier option, he rewarded himself with a side of waffle fries. They fared no better against his voracious appetite.

Could Brian Downing have been somewhere other than his house, as he claimed, when he led that Zoom meeting? If he had been near the Square when the call ended, he might have had just enough time to nab Sandy before her Uber arrived. That was a stretch and would have required amazing luck to time. Or brilliant planning. Michaels dragged himself from his chair and wrote *Virtual background?* next to Brian's photo on the board. With a steady hand, he drew a red line from him to the club to Sandy.

Dropping people from the suspect list narrowed it down, as he told Sonya. If Brian's whereabouts checked out, the number was a big fat goose egg. Every time he looked at that board, studied the photos, perused the casefile, read the post-mortem report, or closed his eyes, one name floated to the top like oil in water.

Allen Rawlings.

A solid alibi: his wife vouched for him. From that evening through the night of Sandy's death, she never fell asleep, and he never left home. Michaels wondered if her shame was powerful enough that she'd lie to keep her husband's nocturnal activities with Charlotte Sellers a secret. Somehow, Sonya found that house where Brian was working. Perhaps she had a habit of following her husband.

What about the Rawlings family confounded him so?

Would Allen have killed his own daughter? Why would he kill her? He could have learned of the secret boyfriend. There was the embarrassment at church of the pastor and a deacon speaking to Sandy and her mother about modesty. She had repeatedly broken curfew, and the neighbor and Connor's friends got their jollies watching her sunbathe. All of that must have been a bit too much for the 'holier than thou' father.

"Would he kill his own daughter?" Michaels asked the board.

"He would. But he didn't have the opportunity."

When Michaels turned his head to the voice, he found Officer Melissa Bell behind him. Jones had blown his chance with her. He also called her Mel, which Michaels didn't like. Not only because last names were the station standard, but also because 'Mel Bell' sounded like a cartoon character.

"Bell. You like Allen Rawlings for it?"

"I would, yes, if his wife didn't alibi him."

"Hmm." He tapped his chin. "Any news on Jones?"

She looked at her watch. "Should be just about done. Their meeting was set to the strict time constraints of one Amanda Whitehall. If I wasn't a lady, and thought less of dogs, I'd have just the word to describe that woman."

"In the commissioner's office?"

"Yeah."

Michaels grabbed a sheet of paper from his desk and marched out.

ALLEN RAWLINGS

The rusty trailer at the end of the line of dilapidated, unkempt corrugated metal homes didn't look fit for occupancy. Allen never liked going into Paulding County, especially not Hiram. The 'Haven on Earth' mobile home park was across town from Charlotte's place. At least her walls were made of brick, and a stiff breeze wouldn't rip the roof off it.

"What are we doing here? I don't like this place, Al."

"I found you in a place just like this." He unclicked his seatbelt.

"That's not fair. You know Billy left us with nothing. I was thirty-one with a thirteen-year-old boy whose father just abandoned him—abandoned us."

"And now you're thirty-four with a sixteen-year-old son and living in a real house in a decent neighborhood. Thanks to me. And you don't need that good-for-nothing Billy. You've got me."

"Got you? *Seriously*? Al, you helped us out. I'm not saying I don't appreciate that. We'd never have gotten that house on our own. And you never asked back a dime. I'm grateful. I truly am. And you… well, when you and me… It was wonderful. I felt like I had value again, as, as a person."

"I don't have time for this, Charlie."

"I just wanted to say, I missed you. You not coming around and all. I was ecstatic when you called. And now… well, getting back to seeing each other like we are… I don't want it to end, not again. I don't think I can handle that."

The air became suffocatingly thick, and Allen felt the interior of his i3 shrink around him. He didn't want to stop seeing her either, but the hardest thing about being with the woman was walking that fine line between a fun and wild relationship and her obsessive neediness. He opened the door and inhaled a refreshing breath of humid ninety-seven-degree air.

"We'll talk about this later."

"It's always *later* with you. Last time you said that I didn't see you for months… until you needed me to bail you out of jail."

As if acting independent of his conscious mind, Allen's hand flew and Charlotte pulled back, banging her head into the side window. To mask the rage she had driven him to, he dropped his hand to her chest and pulled the fabric of her dress to one side, then the other.

"Show more of these. This guy's a little unhinged, and I imagine quite a loner. He won't be able to resist such... titillating temptation."

"Unhinged? Will I be safe?"

"You said you wanted to help. Said you'd do anything for me."

"Of course, Al. You know I would."

Reaching over her, Allen pulled the handle of her door then pushed it open. "He won't answer the door for me or anyone. Make sure he sees you, gets a look at what you have to offer. And when he opens the door, I'll be right there."

"Promise?" He nodded. "Who is this guy, anyway? If I'm going to risk my life, you could at least tell me why."

"My daughter was... well she was killed by someone who made her death look like the Moralist did it."

Charlotte gasped and covered her mouth with both hands. "He's back?"

"You never listen. The guy pretended to be the Moralist. It wasn't him. I knew that from the start, and it took those dim-witted detectives two days to figure that out."

"Where does this guy come in?"

"He was a fan... of the Moralist. Obsessed with him. He wrote blogs and posted on forums and praised the work the Moralist had done saving young women's souls."

"Wouldn't the police come after him, then?"

"Maybe. Even *they* figure some things out, eventually. The guy operated only on the dark web. He's a nutcase, but he's not an idiot."

"And you're sure he'll fall for this ploy? A busty blonde randomly knocking on his door—seems a little obvious to me."

He walked his eyes up and down her body. "Most men have the same fatal flaw."

Satisfied or not, Charlotte crept up to the dingy trailer. She looked back at Allen as he sneaked to the side and hunched over. She knocked.

Nothing happened. He motioned for her to knock again. Nothing. When moving his mouth to mimic speaking only made her squint in his direction, he cupped his hands around his mouth and nodded to the filthy mobile home.

"Hello…? I'm sorry to bother you. I tried a few other homes. I have car trouble, and my cell is dead. I just need to borrow a phone… *Hello*?"

A gray curtain that looked like it used to be white separated slightly from the bottom of the window with the torn screen. Beady eyes studied the damsel in distress. She played her part by fidgeting and twisting to be sure he'd want to open the door to get a better look. A guy like him, Allen thought, would imagine he'd get more than a look in exchange for helping her.

The door squeaked open on rusty hinges thirsty for oil. Allen saw the scraggly beard on his chin first, then the rest of his unwashed face leaned out, granting his eyes a close-up view.

"Broke down, you say? In that fancy car there?"

Like a trained soldier, he looked left and right. Allen feared he had been spotted ducking behind a rain barrel, but the man didn't panic.

"It doesn't plug itself in." She shrugged blushingly.

"Need to use the phone, eh?"

"Ya… yes sir. I'm terribly sorry to disturb you. It's rather an emergency."

Again, he looked around. "Not many's home during the day. Working folk, most. I expect I'm the only one around. I'd guess you'd be mighty grateful for coming in to use my phone."

Do it, woman, Allen thought, as if he could telepathically control her. He had told her she needed to get him to step back, not to see Allen charging. Even if she needed to step inside, he had promised to be right behind her.

Charlotte reached for the door handle and lifted her foot to the first metal step. "I'd be in your debt, of course."

When she stepped inside, Allen came thundering in behind her, knocking her to the floor. His hands clasped the man's throat as he pushed his back into a miniature kitchen counter piled high with dirty plates and pots and pans with the moldy remains of whatever slop was cooked in them. The clatter of cheap aluminum crashing to the floor and plates shattering into jagged shards of porcelain rattled the trailer as much as Allen's manhandling of the suspect.

"Did you kill her?" His voice bellowed in the poorly lit, crowded space. "Tell me, you sick psycho. Did you kill a girl copying the Moralist? Did you?"

Allen shook the man and applied greater pressure around his windpipe. Trying to pull Allen's arms down, he gasped but took in no air.

"Al, he can't talk. Al... Al... If you kill him, we don't get anything out of him." Charlotte yanked his leg to no avail.

The man's face lost its color, and his eyes bulged.

"*Al*," she shrilled.

Relaxing his grip, he let his hands fall to the man's chest and grabbed his grimy shirt. With a twist and thrust, he threw the man to the floor atop the mess of pots and broken dishes. On his knees straddling the man, Allen slammed a fist into his face and gave his cheek another blow as he screamed, "Did you kill my daughter?"

Charlotte tugged Allen's arm to stop the onslaught of near-death blows.

"I didn't kill nobody," the man shouted in reply. Anger filled his voice more than desperation or fear. "Get out before I kill *you*."

The man swung his hand toward Allen. That hand clutched a shard of a broken plate, its jagged edges converging into a sharp point. It caught only loose linen fabric over

Allen's chest. The momentum of the man's arm fell toward Charlotte. A gash in her forearm spouted blood like a fountain. As she shrieked, her wound seized Allen's attention.

With wild eyes and an intense severity on his face, he moved behind the crouching man. Wrapping his arm around his neck, Allen squeezed. The man dropped the makeshift weapon. Pulling and clawing at Allen's forearm didn't loosen its hold from his neck. Allen yelled obscenities at the man as he continued to crush his windpipe and watch the life drain out of him.

BRANDON JONES

T he woman's tirade reached the twenty-minute mark, and Brandon sat quietly through the torture. So did Mister Sturgill. He looked just as downtrodden as Jones felt. All Amanda Whitehall's 'sexy librarian' vibes melted away from the heat of her anger, and she looked like a goblin now. Nodding every so often, the Commissioner said little. Sergeant Carter said nothing.

Whenever the seething real estate attorney cast her gaze at Jones, her vampiric eyes hungering for his blood, he shrunk into his seat a little more. A suspension was sure to come. At this point, he would welcome it if it allowed him to leave the room.

"…and we demand compensation along with Detective Jones and Officer Bell's immediate suspension."

"Honey, the officer didn't say anything. It was just Mister Jones."

The look Whitehall gave her husband almost made Jones feel sorry for the guy. He wondered what that poor man was in for when they got home. Then he thought he'd gladly endure whatever it took to be married to a wealthy, powerful, attractive woman like that.

"I spoke with the mayor, as you know. She assured me you would be fair and do the right thing, Commissioner. And yes…" She glared at her husband again, before turning back to Commissioner Smalls. "I hold both accountable. Officer Melissa Bell is culpable. I have already consulted my attorney; she's drafting the lawsuit as we speak."

Just as the commissioner began his reply, opening with an apology, Michaels barged in. The flung-open door rebounded off the wall and slammed into his shoulder.

Carter's eyes widened with shock. "Michaels, this isn't the time."

"I disagree, Sarge. Commissioner, sir, I have the charges against Mister Sturgill right here and was about to go downstairs to file them."

"*Charges*?" Whitehall stood and rested her hands on her hips. "What charges could you possibly file against my husband?"

Looking at the Commissioner, Michaels replied, "He attacked Detective Jones during a completely legitimate interview. Charges include assaulting a police officer, impeding an investigation, and threatening an officer."

"This is outrageous," Whitehall shouted.

"Sir, Detective Jones asked probing questions during an interview granted by the parents of Joshua Sturgill in their presence. Roger Sturgill physically ushered him out of the house and punched him in the face. As Jones and Officer Bell fled to their car, Sturgill pursued, swinging a baseball bat with enough force to destroy the handrail on his front steps."

A stop gesture by the commissioner stifled Whitehall and intensified the redness in her face. Commissioner Smalls stood and faced Roger Sturgill. "Do you have anything to say regarding these charges, sir?"

"Well... I... That's a one-sided version of what happened."

"There's a witness," Michaels replied.

"Irrelevant," Whitehall blurted. She held a flat palm toward her husband. "He's not the one who incited the incident. Detective Jones insulted our family, wrongfully accused Roger's son of horrible crimes, and rudely yelled at Joshua. We sanctioned an interview under the pretense Joshua was a witness to aid the investigation, not a suspect."

"And none of that excuses the charges against him." Turning to Smalls, Michaels said, "Sir, Miz Whitehall is not a legal guardian of Joshua Sturgill and wasn't involved in the altercation beyond being a witness. Any complaints or charges against Detective Jones or Officer Bell are only valid if Mister Sturgill wishes to file them."

"*What?* Now look here you… you—"

"Settle down, ma'am."

When Michaels cut her off, Whitehall's face blanked, her jaw hanging. Jones assumed that sort of thing didn't happen to her often, if ever.

Addressing Mister Sturgill, Michaels said, "Sir, we all deeply regret how the situation in your home escalated. I'm sure you understand how urgent it is for us to pursue all leads in our efforts to catch a killer who preys on innocent young women." Sturgill nodded. "We also understand your position as a father. I propose we drop both sides of the complaints and charges. I'm sure Detective Jones regrets his words and is eager to apologize. If you accept that, I'll tear up these charges against you right now."

Michaels held the folded paper with both hands in a ready-to-rip grip. Sturgill nodded and Jones rose to his feet and removed the aviator glasses.

"Mister Sturgill." He extended his hand and Sturgill took it. "I'm truly sorry for disturbing your family and for the way I spoke to Josh."

Sturgill nodded, and Michaels ripped the paper in two, put one half over the other, turned them sideways, and ripped them again. The tearing sound ended an ordeal Jones was sure would have cost him his job.

* * *

A wide smile glowed from Jones' face as he and Michaels returned to their desks and sat. Seeing this, Mel's shoulders slackened at the situation being settled. When Brandon said he'd be glad if he never saw that woman again, Mel sat on the edge of his desk and leaned toward him.

"I'm surprised. I'd have expected you to say you enjoyed being dominated by such a powerful woman. I saw how you looked at her at her house, in front of her husband."

"No, she scares me. Plus..." Brandon smirked at Mel. "I've matured."

"In a day?"

"I didn't say I was done."

They shared a smile until Michaels cleared his throat.

"Can we get back to the case, now that you're still allowed to work it?"

Jones had one question he needed to ask first. "Sure. But I gotta know, did you think your charges against Roger Sturgill would have stuck? I mean, they filed a legitimate complaint, *right*? And then we bring him up on flimsy charges for his reaction... in his own house."

Michaels smiled dryly.

"No way," Mel said. "Is that why you grabbed the expense report you printed out?" She bellowed a deep laugh.

With a palm slap on his desk, Jones said, "Who knew your habit of wasting paper would come in handy one day?"

"So... can we all please get back to the case?" As Mel stood to leave, Michaels said, "No, Bell, stay. You're part of the investigation now, and we need all the help we can get. I cleared it with the Sarge."

When Mel smiled, Brandon looked at her with renewed admiration for a competent officer and more than decent company.

"When you told me of your hunch on the neighbor, I went by his place. He was at work, but I bumped into Sonya Rawlings." Michaels paused contemplatively. "She downplayed the whole thing with him. Said he showed concern for her daughter and was a good man. I trust her instincts."

Jones got up and walked to the board. Tapping George Odom's photo, he said, "All we got is this guy and the kid."

"Hmm. You still like Josh for it?" Jones nodded. "It's going to be difficult to pursue that now. The family will never allow us to talk with him again after... Unless we arrest him. You got *anything* we can use to justify that?"

"All circumstantial. Like you say... the gut's talking to me. But it's also shouting, 'Check the neighbor.' I think he's got motive for the copycat stuff. You know, the cleansing."

Michaels said, "I'm not so sure, but let's see if we can make a detective out of that gut of yours. Take Bell and go pay a surprise visit to Mister Odom at work. Be discreet. Bell, change first. Ask him to come speak with you without making a show of cops harassing him at work. Don't ruin someone's reputation over asking a few questions."

On his feet, Michaels yawned and joined Jones at the board. A stack of names without photos rose from the lower right side of the contacts/suspects area. He pointed at them and looked like he fell into deep thought. "It's worth checking into the youth minister's Zoom call, but I think it'll be a wash. Let's regroup here after you see Odom. We need to put our heads together on these church deacons."

M

After school on Thursdays, Mitsy Davis went to the library. Her parents likely thought she went there to study or read, the wholesome activities associated with such a place. Once again, he laid eyes on those corrupting her. He only began observing her a few days ago but had easily caught up on her activities via her public social media profiles. A life put on display for the world to see. A morally bankrupt world.

A righteous warrior, King David couldn't build God's temple. Doing the will of God had drenched his hands in blood. Jesus later said this implement of the Lord's sacred work had not ascended to his reward in Heaven. It didn't matter. Join those he cleansed in Heaven or suffer everlasting damnation in Hell; like David, he would loyally carry out all the Lord had consecrated him to do.

Parents needed to be more attentive, he thought, as he watched Mitsy Davis and a group of boys and girls smoking marijuana behind the library. The joint made its way around the group, loosening these girls' inhibitions. Leading Mitsy Davis down the path of sin.

"Was there someone else?"

Looking past the guilt that pulled his eyes down more than once, he studied Mitsy Davis. What happened next looked like a practice session for more licentious conduct to follow. The girl's need of redemption reflected in his eyes like a divine omen. Sometimes he wished the burden of this calling to be lifted from him.

"No," he said to the distraction clouding his thoughts.

The time had come to save Mitsy Davis from this debouched world. For her to be in the arms of her Savior for all eternity. Her cleansing would come tonight.

CONNOR
RAWLINGS

After sending those screenshots to that detective, he wanted to do more. Violating his sister's socials— which would have been cringe under any other circumstances—had given Connor a role to play in catching her killer. Now all he could do was sit and wait. Mom thought he was busy with his schoolwork, but he couldn't concentrate. He didn't want to, either.

Struck by a realization he had missed earlier, a sudden trace of panic crawled up his back, removing it and the rest of him from his gaming chair. In Sandy's closet, he paused and wondered if his mother had come home. She had told him she wouldn't be long, and his stomach rumbled, anticipating the Italian sub. As quickly as the anxiety had overtaken him a moment ago, a new and irrational concern flooded him.

Swiping up, he unlocked his phone with his face and opened the Find My app. He didn't think it was fair when

Sandy got to remove herself and he didn't. His parents could always track his location unless he left his phone behind, which he never did. The one time he tried, his parents didn't buy his excuse of forgetting it. He had gone to Rachael Weller's house when he'd told his parents he was going to GameStop. Somehow, his mother found out. His dad came home two days later and gave him the worst scolding he ever received, along with a one-month grounding.

Never had he bothered to open this app. He didn't care where his parents went, only that he had the house to himself—which meant sitting in his room so didn't change anything. The only name and contact-photo face under the People section was Mom's. It was his favorite picture of her. In a memory, she held a younger version of Connor on her lap and had the biggest, brightest smile. A close-up of her once joyous face filled the little round icon.

On the map in the Find My app, her face overlapped the blue dot over their house. With his headphones on, he would not have heard her come home. He had muted alerts from the *Ring* doorbell app. Connor spread his thumb and index finger apart on the screen three times to zoom in. His mother's face separated from his location dot.

With a twist of the plastic rod, he cracked open the vertical blinds in his sister's room. The light breaking through the slats painted stripes on the wall like prison bars. Peeking through the narrow opening, he saw his mother's car on the street. She had almost run it up the curb onto the lawn.

*　　*　　*

Connor devoured the sandwich while his mother slowly ate her salad, laying her fork on her napkin between bites. A sound from a memory crossed the kitchen table, and Connor's recollection of those days on his mother's lap brought a nostalgic warmth to the room.

Connor smiled at his mom. "You're humming."

"Am I? Sorry."

"No. It's... it's nice... to hear, I mean. You look better."

"So do you. How was the sandwich?"

Nodding enthusiastically, he said, "Thanks for bringing it. I was starved."

"Would you be a dear and clean this up? I have something I need to do upstairs."

His mom headed to the stairs and Connor crumbled his sandwich wrapper into a ball. Curly strips of shredded lettuce fell from it, and he picked them up—which proved a more tedious task than he imagined. Those olive oil-drenched strands clung to the glass tabletop, avoiding the pinch of his fingertips. He dumped everything into his mother's cardboard salad bowl and tossed it into the trash.

One step into his run to the stairs, Connor stopped. Mom had asked him to clean up, not just to throw out the wrapper and container. With the glass cleaner and a rag in hand, he wiped the table clean, bent and leaned to check it from different angles, and removed the smudges the best he could. He raced up the stairs to resume the game he'd left on pause.

A thud from his mother's bedroom roiled down the hall from the opposite side of the house. When it hit him, Connor raced out of his room toward hers. Anxiety tightened his chest. He stopped his run at her doorway, twisted the doorknob and entered.

"*Mom*...? You okay?"

On all fours, she turned to face him and smiled. "Give me a hand with this, please."

A large blue suitcase lay on the floor beside the bed. It had tipped onto its side and his father's clothes had spilled out. He didn't ask, didn't need to. Kneeling beside his mom, he helped her lift the luggage onto the bed and lay the clothes back in it. She neatly folded each item and placed them in a tightly packed and methodical way to keep them from wrinkling.

They did the same with a second bag, getting about half of his father's summer wardrobe packed and ready to go.

WALKER
MICHAELS

C omputer work never suited him. He kicked himself for sending Jones and Bell to talk to Mister Odom while he sat at his desk, doing research. In the screen's blue glow, Michaels questioned how his faith in Sonya Rawlings had grown this quickly. She dismissed her neighbor and, for some reason he didn't care to identify yet, that was good enough for him. Since it had no answers for him, he took the last of the coffee from his cup. It tasted like burnt tar, but a walk down the hall didn't take as long as a drive to Starbucks.

The question plaguing him as he ran background checks on the pastor, deacons, and youth minister heightened the urgency of the case—again. He could only guess if this copycat was a one-off crime to kill Sandy Rawlings or if there would be a next victim. Second to that, his mind went back to the dark place that held his memories of the three-year pursuit of the real Moralist.

The question of why that butcher had stopped tormented him. He couldn't imagine how having a copycat honoring his legacy would impact someone like that. If he didn't sit back and let someone carry the torch, there could be two deranged killers on the loose.

Another terrifying possibility manifested like a sucker punch to the kidney. It had been almost four years. Despite fighting the point, such a subtle change in technique, when everything else matched, was hardly conclusive proof of a copycat. If he was wrong, Michaels might just have sent this case on a wild goose chase that would result in more dead teenage girls.

No, he knew it in his gut, felt it when he first examined Sandy Rawlings' body in the park. This killing was personal. Now his only leads were in the family's church. When he had stood there admiring the grandness of the structure, imagining the throngs worshipping there, he tried to reconcile such faith with the brutality he had seen. It was unimaginable someone from this group of the faithful, let alone the pastor or one of the deacons, could be capable of murdering a young woman.

Jones had liked Josh for it, but thinking of him left Michaels' intestines at ease. Even though he may have pressured her despite her resolve, he didn't seem the type. A crime of passion, maybe. But a calculated and planned murder clever enough to throw off the investigation? No, this kid didn't—*couldn't*—do that. No amount of convincing by Jones would make Michaels think otherwise. Perhaps if Josh *had* been the son of Amanda Whitehall... .

His phone vibrated. A vocal message from Connor Rawlings.

"I know you found it. It was mine. Dad sometimes searched my room. Sandy saw it and only agreed to keep it for me so I'd have to ask for it, and then she would try to stop me from smoking it. She didn't think I knew where she hid it."

Michaels typed his reply. *Thanks.*

In another vocal message, Connor said, "I know I could get in trouble. Don't care. I don't want anyone thinking it was my sister's weed."

After struggling with the tiny keyboard, Michaels sent a vocal reply. "You won't get in any trouble. I appreciate how you want to protect Sandy's reputation."

The deeper he got into Sandy's life, the more personal this case became. She was a good girl and Michaels now agreed with Sonya's comment from days ago. Though he had originally dismissed her words as naïveté, she had emphatically stated she had raised her daughter right.

An email alert brought his eyes back to the computer screen. Brian had done as promised and sent him the link to the recorded Zoom meeting from the night of Sandy's murder. While he had no idea what the inside of the youth minister's home looked like, Brian hadn't used a virtual background and hadn't even blurred it. At one point toward the end, a gray cat crawled over Brian's keyboard.

"Narrows it down," he said to the computer. "Which leaves all those other good Christian men as persons of interest."

When the background checks finished, the report flashed on the screen. As expected, these men were squeaky clean. A parking ticket or two, a misdemeanor from when Matthew was eighteen… "Wait, who's this?" An allegation had been filed against a deacon Michaels hadn't yet interviewed. Nineteen years ago, a nurse reported suspected domestic abuse by Gerald Porter. His wife said she tripped in the shower and didn't press charges, adamantly stating her husband would never do that.

That deserved some digging. Within a few minutes, Michaels had his answer. As much as he hated to admit it, the new AI chat thing made that easy. The seventy-seven-year-old man suffered from Cervical Spondylosis and had limited mobility as a result. On his best day, he couldn't move even a small child's body.

Michaels had met and spoken with deacons named Matthew, Peter, and Harold. No red flags raised an alert on them or the others whom Michaels still had to contact and interview. This couldn't wait until Saturday. Michaels asked the detective squad's administrative assistant to arrange to have the pastor and all the deacons come by the station for interviews on Friday afternoon.

Another vibration in his front pocket signaled an incoming call. It was about time for Bonnie's check-in. Caller ID listed the number as *Nerd Herd*. Michaels had given the tech forensics team that name. It came from a show he and Bonnie used to watch years ago where the characters couldn't work for the 'Geek Squad' unless the producers wanted to be sued. They gave him some unexpected information about a connection to the Moralist they found on the dark web. Michaels had no idea what that meant other than it being something he would never have found himself.

* * *

Even if there hadn't been a dead body in it, the trailer looked and smelled like a back-alley garbage dumpster. Now a crime scene, it didn't add up. Why the Moralist or his copycat would have done this, Michaels couldn't guess. Rowland Jenkins had been a fan of the most notorious serial killer of the last decade—*ever*, in Marietta. He praised the man for his work in saving all those young ladies and purifying their souls.

In one of the more troubling of all his disturbing posts, he called for others to join the crusade. Michaels considered the possibility he had taken up the mantle. The only one lured in by his own twisted recruitment efforts. Could he have been the copycat? If so, why was he lying dead in his home? Someone had strangled this man to death. With no other wounds and no lacerations on the body, whose blood was that on the floor? Those answers eluded Detective Michaels.

The forensics team examined Jenkins's body and confirmed no cuts or bleeding. Michaels ordered a rush on a blood analysis. "Find me a match, *now,*" were the exact words he barked at the agent assisting in the crime scene investigation. He knew it would take too long to find a match, and he needed to know who had done this sooner than possible.

"Sir, we might have something," a voice called from the back of the trailer. "He had a surveillance camera."

The camera and computer must have cost more than the mobile home. An officer working with the surveillance software on the computer did what he called 'scrubbing' to roll over the footage from the current time backwards. Lying from the ground, its view spanned the patchy brown grass. The screen fluttered as the camera flew up and mounted itself on the side of the trailer beside the door. An ample chest in a revealing dress filled the screen and the officer paused the playback.

Pointing at the cleavage, Michaels said, "I know who those belong to."

After he said it, the footage reversed in slow motion and zoomed out to show Charlotte Sellers knocking on the door.

"There was a blur just before… er… *after* she knocked." The officer rewound frame by frame. "After he zoomed in on her rack. Sir. This is all we've got."

With the camera zoomed in as it was, all it captured was the arm and part of the back of someone in a white shirt entering the trailer. Michaels asked them to play it again without speeding it up, and the officer told him it was normal speed. Slowing it down didn't show them any more detail, but Michaels knew exactly who had been there—who had killed this man.

BRANDON
JONES

The conversation filling this car ride was a vast improvement over the last one. Brandon and Mel mostly discussed the case and found room for bits of personal dialogue. As Michaels had predicted, nothing came of the talk with George Odom. He seemed deeply disturbed by Sandy's death and had a solid alibi. Not only was his wife at home with him, but their grown son had also been passing through town on his way to Jacksonville and had spent the weekend with them.

On the ride back to the station, the call came in. Centrifugal force pressed Mel into the passenger-side door as Jones took a hard left turn and floored the accelerator.

The siren screamed and the blue light on the dash spun as they raced down Weeping Willow Way and pulled into the trailer park. Michaels stepped out of the last rusty mobile home and pulled off his blue rubber gloves. He ducked under the line of police tape into the afternoon sunshine. Squinting, he stepped up to the car as Jones and Mel hopped out.

"Another girl?" Jones asked, his voice trembling.

Michaels shook his head. "Something else."

After the update from his partner, Jones looked over the scene. When she had stepped to follow, Michaels told Bell to wait outside. That gruff voice calling his name from outside cut Jones' examination short. Just as well, it smelled worse than the county dump in there. When he stepped through the banged-up doorframe of the trailer, Michaels tossed him a key fob.

"Have Bell take yours with one of the cruisers and go pick up Charlotte Sellers. You're with me—*now.*"

They hopped into the vehicle and Jones reversed down the narrow alley between mobile homes.

"You think he'd go home?" Jones asked as he screeched onto the road.

"I don't know what brought him here, or what made him strangle Jenkins. But I bet he wants an alibi, and he knows his wife is a more reliable one than his mistress."

"Did we confirm he's sleeping with her?"

Michaels gave him a knowing look. "If he's unhinged, Sonya may be in danger. I know this thing can move, so move it. I need to get there *now.*"

*   *   *

A faint blue light raced across the late afternoon shadows on the house and came again as Michaels ran up the front steps. Michaels gestured to the officers to stay in the cruiser that pulled up behind them. Jones could see him pushing the bell repeatedly and banging on the door. After a few seconds, Connor opened it, and Michaels ran in before Jones made it to the porch. Jones had learned more about his partner in a few days than he had since they were paired up. A witness to his emotional breakdown outside the high school, he questioned the balance Michaels had between professional and personal investment in the case.

Never had he seen this level of panicked frenzy in the man.

Stepping from the kitchen at the back of the house into the living room, Michaels' eyes trembled. They raced over the space, even searching the ceiling. "Where is she?"

After removing his loafers, Jones joined them on the living room carpet. Connor's attempts to get Michaels to comply with the no-shoes-in-the-house rule were ignored. An older couple sat on the sofa. A puzzled look deepened the wrinkles carved into the man's face. The woman's wide eyes raced around the room and her knees bounced. With palpable worry for her daughter, she looked like an older version of Sonya when they told her Sandy had been killed.

Shaking the boy by the arms, Michaels asked again, "Where's your mother? Is she home? Is everything alright?"

"Chill, dude. She's in her room." Michaels turned toward the stairs, and Connor grabbed his arm to stop him. "Taking a shower."

When Michaels froze, Jones asked, "Is your father home?"

"No, not anymore."

"What is this about?" the older man asked.

"He was here, *recently*?" Michaels asked Connor hurriedly.

"He was gone when I got up this morning and been out most of the day."

"Did he come back?"

The harsh tone of Michaels' question caused Connor to take a step back. A look of terror fell over the boy's face. With two detectives racing over with lights flashing, pounding on the door, and screaming questions at him, Jones feared the kid might lose his cool and erupt in an outburst.

"Listen here," the man complained, rising from the sofa. "You have some nerve speaking to my grandson in this manner."

"Connor, it's okay." Jones spoke in a calm, soft voice. "We're looking for your dad to ask him some questions and just wanted to check in with you and your mom… to make sure you were alright."

That seemed to work. Jones could see the tension leave his neck. Concurring with Jones, Michaels apologized for scaring Connor. He turned to Sonya Rawlings' parents and apologized to them as well.

"I wasn't scared, just… confused. Why'd you think we were in danger? My dad?"

Finding a disapproving grimace on his partner's face, Jones turned to Connor. "Why would you say that?"

"Well… you come charging in here like… like someone was being murdered. And after what happened to Sandy. Then you keep asking about my dad."

Michaels cocked his head and stared at the kid. "Why'd you immediately connect us thinking you might be in danger with your father? Does he lose his temper? Has he ever been violent?"

"No. He's pretty strict, sure, but not like that. I've never seen him like that before today."

"That man does have a temper." The lady on the sofa shook her head.

After stealing a glance at the woman, Michaels turned back to Connor. "Before *today,* as in just now? Was he here in the last hour or so?"

"Yeah. But he's been gone near an hour now."

"Did your father say when he'd be back?" Jones asked.

"He's not coming back. Mom and I packed his bags, and he took them with him."

Looking out the open front door, Michaels asked, "She kicked him out?"

"Yeah."

A blank look washed over Michaels' face. "And he left, just like that?"

"After they had a pretty huge fight about it. Massive. I've heard them argue before, but never as bad as that."

"My son-in-law isn't used to not getting his way," the older man interjected.

"Even Mom lost it, yelling at him at one point. She calmed down right away, but he kept screaming. I even heard some things smashing before he ran down the stairs and out the door."

Michaels' expression of disbelief turned to wide-eyed concern. "How was she, your mom, after? Did he hurt her?"

"I didn't see her. Like I said, she went up to take a shower. My father came home, they argued, he left. I went to check on her and heard the water running."

"For an hour?" Michaels darted up the stairs.

WALKER
MICHAELS

The pounding in his chest didn't come from his run up the stairs. Fear of what he was about to find tore through him like a chainsaw. Allen Rawlings may not have murdered his daughter, but he killed a man and came home to find his marriage shattered in pieces. What had he done?

Walker flung open the door to Sandy's room and stood in a haze of confusion. Behind the next door, the unmade bed, gaming chair, and rock band posters clearly identified Connor's room. The hall bathroom was the size of Michaels' bedroom. This house was a maze. Another room had a neatly made queen bed but looked too small to be the master bedroom in a house like this.

Every door that didn't open to Sonya piled more trepidation onto his already overwhelming dread. He *knew* Allen had killed her. Michaels would never believe that man would take being kicked out of his house with his tail between his legs. Connor said there had been a fight, sounds of things being thrown. A physical altercation between a man pumped on a rage-fueled adrenaline high and a helpless woman had one likely outcome.

When his phone vibrated, he mindlessly pulled it from his pocket. Not Sonya. He'd missed Bonnie's earlier check-in call. His thumb touched the message icon, and he selected "Sorry, I can't talk right now." Jones had shown him how to do that last week.

The process of elimination took too long. A freight train of chaos barreled through his mind. All Michaels had to stop it was raw logic. It failed. He pulled the handle of the next door and took a long step forward. It was the largest linen closet he had ever seen. Shelves of towels rose up the custom wood shelving. Colum after column. Someone could have run a small hotel from here. The broom closet came next and left him with one more door to try.

A clearer head would have tried it first. On the opposite end of the other bedrooms and buffered by the two closets, the door at the end of the hall must have been the master bedroom. A narrow table lay on the floor before his destination, the Chinese-looking porcelain vase it was there to display in pieces on the floor. With a shaky hand, Michaels clutched the brass doorknob and twisted. Hesitantly, he pushed the door open.

The master suite spanned the space of the entire first floor of his modest home. Even though it was the largest one

Michaels had ever seen, the room dwarfed the four-poster bed in the center. Photo frames and jewelry boxes had fallen from the dresser. The space glowed in the rays of light spilling through the lace curtains of the massive window to the right. Like spotlights, they fell upon the blood splotches on the plush white carpet.

Michaels followed them from the bed to another room beyond an open archway. An ornate powder blue dresser or desk or makeup station of some sort filled the far wall. A dressing room, he presumed. The metal frame had once held a full-length mirror. Broken shards filled the trash basket beside it. Clear signs of the altercation. And something Rawlings could have used as a weapon to kill his wife.

Only then did Michaels notice the noise. It sounded like no shower he had ever heard. Given the drastic difference between this and any normal home he had been in, he figured it might have been an elaborate shower box installation with marble tile and the best hardware fixtures money could buy. Or the bathroom could have had a powerful exhaust fan.

This was it. He had come up to find Sonya, to see what Allen had done to her. A mental picture formed of her lying in the tub, covered in blood. He touched the doorknob and pulled his hand away as if it had shocked him. He tried again. Not wanting to see what he knew awaited behind this last door, he turned the knob and pushed.

SONYA RAWLINGS

Water streamed over her like a sun shower's soft drizzle. She had chosen the setting to feel the soothing caress of the hot liquid as it coated her and trickled down her skin. Something new and invigorating under the power of the shower's magical spell felt like liberation. As she ended the glorious flow, Sonya couldn't remember if she had used shampoo or body wash. It didn't matter. This shower had masterfully fulfilled its purpose to wash away the stress, the worry, the pressure she had lived under longer than she had realized until this day.

Once the rush of warm air dried her, she stepped off the mat. As she reached for the door handle, she heard Connor in her bedroom, so she wrapped herself in a silk bathrobe. It enveloped her in comforting security. She was just getting the knot tied and tucked in when the door flung open, startling her.

Sonya gasped and stepped back. Her foot slid out from under her on the wet tile and she fell back, landing on her backside between the shower's glass wall and the towel dryer. The bulging eyes examining her looked like they might pop out of their sockets. Sonya checked her robe; thankful her tumble hadn't exposed her.

"*Walker*?"

"*Sonya…* Oh, thank God."

He leaned over and hoisted her up. Before she could say anything else, he pulled her into a tight hug. Arms at her sides, she didn't reciprocate but closed her eyes and leaned into him as he squeezed her. With ideas surfacing as to what was running through his mind and why he seemed so… *relieved* to see her, she welcomed the concern and tender care.

Talking into his shoulder she asked, "Did you think Allen would do something?"

Walker released her from his embrace. "Yes."

"I asked him to leave. Connor and I packed his bags earlier, and I told him when he came home. He left not long ago, just when I was getting into the shower."

"I know. Listen, there's been some developments… In the case, and with Allen."

Looking down at her robe-covered body, Sonya said, "Maybe you could let me get dressed before we continue this conversation."

Michaels excused himself so Sonya could put on a dress. When she called him into the bedroom, he entered with his shoes hanging from his fingers. She motioned to a reading chair. Sitting on the bed beside it, she took his shoes and laid them on a towel. As he explained his 'developments,' she couldn't believe Allen would have killed anyone. She did, however, believe the part about Charlotte Sellers being with him.

"Why would Allen have gone to see this man, this Jenkins, and, and… do *that*?"

"As you know, your husband's been doing his own investigating. I believe he thought Mister Jenkins was the copycat who killed Sandy."

"Was he?"

"No. He was just some sicko who idolized the Moralist back in the day and wrote about it on the dark web. Not a copycat, just a fan."

"*A fan*… of a serial killer." She shook her head. "And now?"

"I'll protect you… I mean, we'll keep an officer outside, day and night. In case he comes back."

"Walker, he was here, and in a rage like I've never seen. If he didn't hurt me then, I don't think that's necessary."

"I'd feel a whole lot better with someone outside."

"And the real killer? Are you any closer to finding him?"

Without words, his dipped head supplied the answer.

Sonya took his hand.

ALLEN
RAWLINGS

ome. A word he'd thought he understood now mocked him, devoid of all meaning. For years he kept the delicate balance of his two lives like the ends of a tightrope walker's pole. These last few days threw years of practiced equilibrium off kilter. Never had he been so careless, acted with such reckless abandon.

Walker Michaels. That must have been who told Sonya about Charlie. Allen had no other explanation. The detective had seen her at the station when she bailed him out. Of all people, Allen pondered why he thought to call that woman. A poor attempt to save face. Shame kept him from phoning his wife. None of the deacons could know of his arrest. How would he ever regain such lost respect? What took years to build required less than a minute to destroy.

Was trust any different? Sonya would never trust him again.

No. He was being fatalistic, and he knew he needed to stop that. If he looked at this as a setback, a rift that could be stitched back together in time, the pain would go away. His balance would be restored, eventually.

"Al, you sure it don't need stitches? He cut into me pretty deep."

She had bled on the seat of his BMW, and now it needed to be cleaned. When he had dropped her off at home, he'd resolved never to see the indigent woman again. Charlotte had been a great distraction from the spiral of turmoil his life had become over the course of four days. Before he'd bumped into her son at Sandra's school, he'd almost forgotten how Charlie had been an oasis in the desert of this other life.

Almost.

After a few arid months apart, they rekindled their relationship as if it hadn't skipped a beat. And she never asked him to leave his family. Perfect balance. Now his two lives swerved into a head-on collision, and he had forgotten to wear his seatbelt. Could he face the deacons in church once they knew he and Sonya were no longer together? The death of a child had been known to wreck the strongest of marriages. Yes, he felt secure in his position at the church. Maybe, one day, the same would prove true with his family.

If not, Charlie was all he had left. Examining her slip her glistening body into a slinky robe, he thought this woman could be enough. The passion between them hadn't waned. If anything, it had intensified this time around. After thinking she wouldn't let him in when he came back to her house, suitcases in hand, she welcomed him eagerly and opened more than her door.

"I'm sure you'll be okay. The bleeding stopped, and it will heal. Just keep applying the Neosporin."

Allen paced the tiny 'master' bedroom while Charlotte went into the bathroom to reapply the bandages her vigorous exertion had loosened. Shrewdly, she had texted Russ to go to a friend's house, order a pizza, and not come home for a while. Allen couldn't imagine the boy's reaction to him being there. Perhaps a new pair of the best noise-cancelling headphones on the market would soften him to the idea.

"Hey, babe? Come in here, please. I wanna check your arm."

Stepping up behind her, he pressed himself against her as she leaned over the sink, looking in the mirror. Holding her by the waist, he smelled her hair. When he kissed the top of her head, she smiled warmly. The bathroom had everything in one tiny open space. A single sink, toilet, and shower. He had paid to have it redone when she moved in, and she kept it sparkling.

It amazed him how the episode in the trailer park hadn't phased her. Or it did. If anything, it acted as a stimulant, invigorating her. He never anticipated this merger and now envisioned her becoming more deeply entrenched in the half of his life that had slipped closer to whole. If this gave him such fulfillment, perhaps he didn't need what Sonya called 'love.'

"Let me see." When she turned to face him, he lifted his forearm. Her fingertips gently caressed the lines etched in his flesh. "He really dug into you."

"Yeah."

Charlie massaged a generous dollop of ointment on the scratches.

"About a year ago, Russ and his friends were roughhousing… like boys do. One of 'em pushed Russ into that hawthorn bush out back. His arm looked a lot like this, and the Neosporin fixed it right up. You can't even see the—"

Allen pushed her away, and she dropped the small tube of medicated liniment. His face shown with a revelation that launched the logical part of his mind into a ferocious battle with his quickly building rage.

"Peter, from church. He had scratches like this on his arm. He said Mary asked him to trim the rose bush and the thorns got him."

"Like my Russ. I'm sure Mary's got Neosporin or something like it."

As Charlotte reached for his arm, he pulled back, swatting her hand away. She pouted. Allen stumbled into the bedroom, his hands in fists, knocking on his forehead. Following his every step, she tried to calm him with words that bounced off without impact.

"He did it. He killed my baby girl… No, it can't be. Peter loves my family. He looked after them whenever I was away… That's it… He had eyes for Sonya, and maybe… Yes. I caught him looking at Sandra, too. Saying how she matured. Do anything for my family? That son of… He killed her!"

"Al, what's going on? You're scaring me."

"Peter Miller. He called my girl a *whore*. My daughter! Said she deserved what she got. I'm gonna kill him!"

"Don't you think you're jumping to conclusions?"

When she grabbed his arm, he stopped pacing and stared at her as if she had materialized from nowhere. Not the epiphany he needed now.

"Al, please slow down. Now tell me, do you really think Deacon Pete had anything to do with this? Like you said, he's a good man, and he loves you and your family. Why would he do anything to hurt you… I mean… to kill Sandy? He wouldn't."

Plopping on the edge of the bed, Allen buried his face in his hands. "I don't know what to think anymore. *I have* to do the cops' job for them. *I found* Jenkins. They probably have no idea who the guy was or that he had any connection to me."

"And you killed him."

He raised his head and drilled through her with his eyes. Those words added realism to the blur the last few hours had been.

"In self-defense. He… he hurt you."

Allen put his hands on her hips, and she straddled his thigh.

"I know, babe. I know. He would have killed me. You defended me, saved me from that lunatic. You were so brave and strong." Pressing his face into her chest, she stroked his head.

He jumped to his feet. "I gotta go. I need to know. If it was Peter… I'll…"

"You'll call the police. Or… I'll talk to him, like I did Brian. I can find out where he was on Sunday night. I'm good at it, you said so."

When she reached to caress his cheek, he slapped her hand away.

"No. He does dinner at his in-laws on Thursdays. I'll confront him when he gets home."

"Then why are you going now? Stay with me," she whined.

"I've got something I need to do first."

*   *   *

It must have been meant to be seen, there as a deterrent. Two uniforms sat outside his house in a marked police car like stalkers. He imagined them with their binoculars. Sonya liked to keep all the curtains open until she went to bed. He stopped a few houses away. Dusk's darkness lay over the road, disguising his car enough not to distract them. Allen doubted their eagle-eyed caution did anything more than ogle his wife.

He couldn't walk up to his own home. Sitting there, he considered what *this* part of his life had become. Perhaps it was time to accept the dominance of the other one. It was always the stronger of the two.

WALKER
MICHAELS

Tomorrow Michaels would interview the pastor and all the deacons from the Rawlings family's church. He wasn't sure any of those men looked good for the murder. What motive did any of them have to harm Sandy? If one of them had done it, they made it look like a Moralist killing. Perhaps they thought they were saving Sandy. Or they may have done it to throw the police a red herring.

And why was he still in Sonya's bedroom? A warm, soft hand lay on his. Michaels hadn't moved since he sat there, clasping the armrests as if the chair were ticking up the track of a towering roller-coaster, nearing the precipice of a steep drop.

Tick tick tick...

"Walker? You haven't said anything in a while. You look beyond exhausted." Leaning in, she peered into his bleak, unfocused eyes. "The police car is here. Why don't you go home and get some rest? There's nothing more to do tonight. Maybe your interviews tomorrow will turn up a lead."

A deep sigh escaped as he stood and grabbed his shoes. Bonnie called again. He left the phone in his pocket; he didn't need to look. An earlier text from Bell told him Allen's BMW wasn't at Charlotte's home. Since they were in an unmarked car, he had them stake it out in case Allen showed. If Sellers moved, they were to follow her before taking her in for questioning. Michaels' feet felt heavy, but not due to his physical exhaustion. Robotically they moved one in front of the other, inching him toward the door. He had no idea what to do next.

"Will I see you tomorrow?" Sonya asked.

"I expect so. I hope to have an update after those interviews." Looking back at her, deep into her eyes, he saw something that looked like… promise. "I mean, I would like that."

"Okay. Tomorrow then."

"Wait." He paused. "I'm still trying to work something out about Allen. He strangled that man to death with that woman, Sellers, there with him. And he comes here. Was she here, in his car?"

"No, I don't think so. Connor watched him toss his suitcases into the car. He would've said."

"Hmm."

"You don't have to dance around it. My husband killed someone. And I know where he's gone. This thing with Charlotte Sellers isn't new."

A look of surprise on Michaels' face was met with pursed lips on Sonya's.

"No, I'm not surprised you knew. Look, Sonya, I figured you for a smart lady. I guess, one day, I hope you'll tell me why you stayed with him."

"You're a father, Walker. You know the answer to that."

"Well, we've got a car at Charlotte Sellers' home. Allen may not know we found Rowland Jenkins. If not, he's got no reason to think we're looking for him."

"No, he wouldn't think you knew about that. He... he said you were incompetent. That's why *he* had to solve our daughter's murder. He seems to have a particular distain for you."

"I felt that from the get-go. Understandable when he thought I failed to catch the guy that killed his daughter." After another step toward the door, he paused again. "Is there anything else you can tell me about him, his behavior, anything, when he came by earlier?"

A contemplative look created a slight crease between her sculpted eyebrows. "He changed his shirt. I'm not sure if that helps at all."

"Did he leave it here? Was it white?"

"No and yes. He took the shirt. It was one of his nice white linen short-sleeve button-downs, but the front was torn. He put on a blue one... with long sleeves. I guess because of the scratches."

"Scratches?"

"His forearm. The right, I think, was all scratched."

Michaels took Sonya by the arm. "I need you to think… Did they look like *fingernail* scratches?"

"That's exactly what they were. Once when he got…" She blushed and studied the carpet. "He got a little, um, *rough*… in… and I scratched him. It looked just like that. I figured Charlotte must have done the same."

"Sonya, you may have just solved this case. I… I gotta go."

* * *

"I know, baby, I know." He had to shout. "Come on, Jones, move it. Look, Bonnie, I'm fine. More than fine. I was in the middle of something when you called, is all. Watch out!" The car swerved and Michaels steadied himself. "Nothing. Some idiot doesn't know what police lights and blaring sirens mean…. Look, I gotta go. I think we're about to nail this guy. I love you, baby girl."

As Jones slammed the brakes, the sudden stop pushed Michaels forward. The blue light carved into the dark edges of cars, trees, and the Millers' home. It encircled the detectives' car, round and round like one of those kiddie rollercoasters at a county fair. The pulse of the dash light was the only disturbance rustling behind the windows of the natural stone-fronted house.

As if it were about to explode, they bolted from the car, leaving the doors open. A hand wave sent Jones around back, gun drawn. Michaels unholstered his weapon and crouched as he toed along the walkway to the front entrance. The throbbing of his heart pulsated in his ears. He left the exhaustion he had dragged along for days on the reading chair beside Sonya's bed.

Too early for them to be asleep, he reasoned. If they weren't at home or were waiting in ambush, Michaels couldn't know. With his back to the wall at the bottom of five wide steps, he ascended sideways, one foot over the other. Five or six thumps on the door yielded no response. After another series of pounding, he mashed the doorbell repeatedly.

Michaels raised his foot and kicked with all his might. He nearly fell down the steps from the push back. The door and frame were more solid than he expected. Slightly dazed, the door opening was a jolt of caffeine to his senses. Instinctively, he jerked his gun into an unsteady aim. Jones held up his hands, his own pistol clutched in one.

"Anything?"

"House looks empty. I'll search upstairs." Jones disappeared inside the home. The beam of his flashlight sliced through the darkness and bounced away until it retreated down the upstairs hall.

After letting his nerves settle, Michaels pulled his cell phone from his pocket. He holstered his weapon so he could retrieve his notepad from his jacket. Crinkling pages flipped rapidly until he stopped, turned back a page, then another, and found what he needed. Hands shaking, he unlocked the phone and dialed the number.

"Hello?"

"Pastor Frank. This is Detective Michaels. I need some information."

"Good evening, Detec—"

"Look, it's imperative I find Peter Miller... *now*. Is he at the church?"

"No. I'd be happy to give you his home address."

"We're at his house; he's not here. Do you know where I might find him?"

"Oh, it's Thursday. He and Mary usually have dinner with her parents. I'm sorry, I don't have the address."

"I have Peter's number. Can you give me his wife's?"

M

The *Ring* doorbell app on his phone alerted him again. His eyes spun, and he felt the rage mounting inside at seeing those two detectives outside his home. Without telling her where he was going, he left the house in a frenzied hurry. Too much happened at once. This was not going according to plan. Justice would be served, all in God's due time. He couldn't tell his wife where he was going. How could she understand? He left her with her parents to fulfill his assignment.

The Lord wanted Mitsy Davis to be saved.

Her tank top hugged her breasts but didn't cover enough of them. He pinched his arm. When she turned around, the bottom of her buttocks crested below the too-short denim shorts. It wasn't her fault. He reminded himself of this as he pinched again. The world had done this to her, made her a victim. Now it was time for her soul to be redeemed.

Mitsy Davis and her boyfriend, both too young to be courting, went inside the pizzeria. Calculating the time to get there and back against the couple being seated, ordering, and eating, he pulled away. "Don't worry, my child. Tonight, you will be in the bosom of our Lord."

SONYA
RAWLINGS

W hen Sonya went downstairs, her father asked her what that man wanted. Her mother asked why he'd kept her upstairs so long and why a police car was still parked outside. Called back when their granddaughter died, her parents had come from the airport a couple of hours ago. They had shared hugs and cried with her and Connor, witnessed the biggest fight she ever had with Allen, and seen him getting thrown out of his house.

As if that welcome weren't enough, they watched two detectives storm into the house, frightening Connor, to then keep their daughter from them for almost an hour. Now Sonya had to leave them.

As her thumbs ran over her phone screen, she looked up at her son. "Connor, stay with Memaw and Papaw. I need to run an errand."

Hands trembling, Sonya double-checked her message. Someone needed to know, in case…

I need to do this.

She pressed *Send*.

"An errand, at this hour?" her father questioned.

"It's what, just after nine? I won't be long."

"Ma, where're you going? I don't think you should go out."

Taking her hand, her mother nodded. "Connor's right, dear. We came here to be together. Whatever it is, it can wait until tomorrow."

"No, I need to go."

"Then I'm coming," her father insisted.

"No, Dad. You two stay with Connor, please. It's why you're here."

Before any further complaints could be voiced, Sonya grabbed her key fob and rushed out the door to the garage. While she was still trying to set the navigation in the Maps app, Connor knocked on the car window and she lowered it.

"You're not going to find *him*, are you?"

"Your dad?" She sighed. "Look Connor, things are complicated now and happening fast. I need to do something, and I need you to trust me. I love you."

With her eyes locked on her son, she reversed before he could say another word. The crash and sounds of splintering wood startled her. When she pressed the button on the garage remote, the buckled door lifted a few inches and the silent opener's motor moaned. Pressing the second button opened the door on Allen's side.

Connor darted out of the way as she used the ample space of the massive garage to shimmy the car over—forward reverse, forward reverse. As she swung the Prius through the open door, she heard a crunch and bang. In the haste of her hectic escape, she had ripped her sideview mirror off.

The tires screeched in protest as she pressed the brake with both feet—narrowly in time not to smash into the police cruiser. Throwing the car into *Drive,* she stomped the accelerator. With the phone's Maps now displayed on the dashboard screen, she rushed off to connect her blue dot to her destination.

WALKER
MICHAELS

T hree black and white Marietta police cars added their strobing lights to the scene that pulled neighbors from their homes. No evidence surfaced from the Miller house, but a roll of black tarpaulin lay in wait in the shed out back. On a shelf above it, Jones found a half empty bottle of Flunitrazepam.

Someone at the station ran a DMV check. Peter drove a Dodge Durango. Not a van, as suspected, but a vehicle that could easily transport a body. All the pieces snapped into place.

They had him—only, they didn't. Phoning Peter would be a risk. To play coy and pretend he had a question before tomorrow's interview might throw off any suspicion. Or tip him off. That's why Michaels had asked for the wife's number. But if she answered, he'd need to instruct her immediately not to let Peter know who was on the phone and to go somewhere to talk in private. And he hadn't met the woman. If she were anything like him, she wouldn't answer a call from an unknown number this late in the evening. It went to voicemail.

"How'd you connect Peter Miller to Sandy's murder?" Jones asked.

"The scratches on his arm. And we suspected Brian, the youth minister-slash-house painter, because he seemed to have motive, has a van, and used black tarps." Jones squinted and pursed his lips but didn't interrupt. "The Millers hired him to paint their house last month. So, I figured he had access to the tarp material used to transport Sandy's body."

"And the scratches on his arm… What the M.E. said about her struggling with the killer. Him scrubbing her nails. You think Sandy scratched him while he held the drugged cloth, *right*?"

Nodding, Michaels said, "I didn't think anything of it until Sonya said Allen had scratches on his arm. He had that Jenkins guy in a chokehold and his arm got scratched, same as Peter Miller's. And Travis identified those fibers in Sandy's nose were linen, just like the long-sleeved shirts Peter always wears."

"Do you think he only meant to kill Sandy and throw us off with that Moralist stuff? Or is he a sick fan who'll keep going, continue the legacy, if we don't nail him?"

"I still think Sandy's murder was personal."

After slapping a gloved hand on the thick black roll, Jones said, "But he's got more tarp and more of that drug. What's our next move?"

They exited the shed and headed down the driveway.

"Get these cop cars outta here… And get those people out there back in their homes. We wait here for the Millers to come home. Then we arrest the sick bastard."

"They'll know we're here." When his partner's words blanked his face, Jones explained, "The *Ring* doorbell. Peter Miller knows we're here."

A vibration on his thigh rattled him. He froze. Jones asked what was wrong. Probably Bonnie again. He didn't have time for her now. Imagining the consequences of ignoring her after she chewed him out for doing it earlier, he pulled the phone from his pocket. His eyes threatened to pop out when he saw the name on his screen.

"Connor, what's wrong?"

"My mom, she's gone out."

"Where? Where'd she go? Why?"

"Wouldn't say. She was acting crazy. I've never seen her like that before."

"Think, son. Did she say anything? Any clue where she might be going?"

Michaels paced the length of the driveway, his head shaking anxiously.

"No... But I think... I think she went to find my dad." The boy's sporadic breathing came through the connection in huffs breaking through the static.

"Relax, Connor. Try to calm down. We have a car at Char—I mean, where we think your father may be going."

"Yeah, I know who Charlotte Sellers is. If my mom goes there, confronts him in the state he's in..."

"I won't let that happen."

As the words escaped, Michaels heard his own chastisement of his junior partner replay in his mind. "Never promise." He looked at Jones knowingly and kept pacing.

"Find her, Detective. *Please*. You gotta find her." The kid's voice squealed desperation. He had lost his sister, his parents' marriage was falling apart, and his father had left home. Now he had a justifiable fear that his mother was in danger.

"Have you tried calling her?"

"Yeah, like, a hundred times. Straight to voicemail. Tried iMessage, too. I get the 'She's driving now...' message and can see she hasn't read any of my texts."

"Let me try. I'll call you back."

As quickly as he could move his thumb, Michaels hung up, tapped Favorites in the Phone app, and pressed on Sonya's name. Straight to voicemail. "Sonya, I just heard from Connor. He's worried. You need to go back home. Call me back."

He dialed Connor.

"Anything?"

"Straight to voicemail. Look, Connor. I need to know where she's going. Think, son."

"Wait! I can find her."

M

Yes, he had timed it well. The young couple sat; he with an empty plate and she with two pieces of crust growing cold on hers. At the counter, he asked about a pickup for a DoorDash order and the bogus number he gave them drew a look of confusion on the young cashier's face.

Looking at the cracked screen on his phone he said, "Oh, sorry. The order is for Marietta Pizza Company. Thanks anyway."

He stepped out of Johnny's New York Pizza and leaned against a Ford F-150 parked near the entrance. After his first kill in years, he felt ready for this. He hungered for it. This was his calling, the Lord's work. In the Gospel, Jesus told his followers doing it would be refreshing despite any hardships it brought.

Such chivalry. The boy paid the bill, and they made their way around the crowded tables to the door. Toward him.

With his phone in hand to feign distraction—he was intensely focused—he pulled the door open and bumped into

Mitsy Davis as she stepped out. A flowery smell saturated his nostrils as his eyes fell over her young body. She must have dabbed the cheap perfume behind her ear. For that momentary fall into temptation, he pinched his arm. It hurt more this time.

"Hey, watch where you're going." The boyfriend played the strong protector.

Hiding under an Atlanta Braves baseball cap, he said, "Sorry," and pushed by them.

No, the boy was no protector. A part of the immoral world corrupting the soul of Mitsy Davis, the kid was her destroyer.

She rubbed her neck under her ear and said, "Dang mosquitoes."

Letting the door close on the next guy coming out, he watched as the happy couple walked hand-in-hand to the boy's car. Stepping off the curb, Mitsy Davis stumbled. Her valiant escort tried to help her catch her balance. The curb hadn't tripped her up. Gallantly, the young man helped his now woozy girlfriend to the car. Loss of muscle control set in, and she turned to gelatin in his arms.

The boy fell back, landing on his backside with Mitsy Davis slumped over him.

Sneaking up from behind, he whacked the boy on the back of the head and hoisted the girl to her feet. She could not support her own weight, so he wrapped one arm over his shoulder. With her pressed into his side, he walked around the back of the small shopping plaza to where he had parked. Barely conscious, Mitsy Davis dragged her feet along as he pulled. If anyone noticed them, hopefully all they saw was a couple who'd had too much to drink and couldn't keep their hands off each other.

A spark of bright light startled him.

CONNOR RAWLINGS

After Connor tapped *Speaker* on the phone app, he swiped it off the screen. Pulling down with his thumb brought up the search field. He typed *F* and tapped the Find My app from the list of suggestions. In the *People* tab, he saw his mother's face, joy emanating from it in a memory.

"She's not far from the Square."

"How do you know that?"

"The Find My app." Connor didn't have time to explain how smartphones worked to this old guy. "I can see her current location, in near real-time."

"Can you send it to me?"

"It won't let me add you to track her, but I can send you her current location."

"Yes, do that. And Connor, I need to know if she moves. Stay on with me while I go to her."

The chaos of hurried commotion spilled through the speakers of Connor's iPhone. His grandparents looked at him expectantly. He tapped *Mute*.

"That detective is going to find Mom."

"Oh, thank goodness," his grandmother said. She hadn't moved off the couch and looked haggard from traveling all day.

"Good, Connor, that's good. You do whatever it takes to help those men find your mother."

"Of course, Grandpa."

"Connor, where's your sis—" His grandmother burst into tears.

Sitting beside her, his grandfather rubbed her shoulder then put his arm around her. "I know, dear, I know," he whispered. His own eyes clung to the remnants of spent tears.

Connor saw a picture he would never see of his parents at that age. They had been like that once. There used to be a sense of security here, hung like a tent over them in this house—well, the one before this one, mostly. Things hadn't been great between his mom and dad before they moved. The four years in this house had done nothing to improve that. He and his sister often thought it was the stress of dealing with teenagers—with *them*.

"Connor," his phone yelled, snapping him back to the moment. "We're close. Has she moved?"

When he looked at the map on his phone, his mother's face had left it. He zoomed out to find her then zoomed in on her icon.

"Looks like she's on Dallas Highway now. Going away from Marietta, back this way."

After he tapped to *Unmute* the phone, he repeated himself.

"That's good. She's coming home," his grandfather said. "You see, dear. She's fine."

"Move it, Jones. Maybe she's going back home. We're still following, in case she's not."

"Please, Detective. Keep following her." As Connor pleaded, his eyes glazed over. A forced cough did little to mask his worry.

"We're almost at Barrett Parkway. How far is she?"

"Not far. She's near The Avenue."

"Jones, Avenue at West Cobb. Step on it. We're almost there, son. We'll find her."

SONYA
RAWLINGS

nsure of what he could have been up to, Sonya observed her husband as he slipped into the derelict garage. As she had correctly assumed, he hadn't gone back to Charlotte Sellers' home. If only he had, this would have been over. Perhaps he had another 'other woman.' A sardonic chuckle escaped her lips as she saw the poetic justice in her husband cheating on his mistress. Sonya wondered if any of that mattered now.

Her husband had killed a man.

If she could get Walker to arrest him, this part of her life would be laid to rest. When the detective had raced out of her house, a fire for catching her daughter's killer had burned in his eyes. Sonya contemplated each of the nightmares her life had become. Both could find a measure of closure on the same night. Her breaths evened out, and memories chased away active thoughts.

What she had buried inside herself for years had now surfaced, and her mind raced to stack events in chronological order. Their marriage had endured some rough patches, as most couples hit. They also had many happy memories. Those faded in time, and for the last several years they were parents to their children, sharing a bed. So much of Allen's life had been a secret, kept from her as if she wasn't his life partner, the trusted companion and confidant all those church sermons said she should have been to him.

Her Find My app lost its usefulness when he abandoned the car with the AirTag she had placed in the trunk. It had led her to the garage behind the old church, which was the last place she thought she'd find him. Watching Allen change vehicles, Sonya assumed he knew the police were onto him for killing that man in the trailer park. The thud of the door rattled her. In the darkness beside the old church, she regretted lying to her father about wanting to do this alone. When the van pulled away, the Prius followed at a distance. Not to lose him as he raced through the light evening traffic, she needed to stay closer.

Chilling panic overtook her for a second, thinking she had lost him. Sitting at the red light at Barrett Parkway, the old church van idled two cars ahead of her. Training her eyes on it, Sonya said aloud, "Our new huge bus with the vibrant green 'Holiday Inn' church logo would be easier to spot." A fleeting chuckle sliced off a small piece of the tension inside the cramped hybrid.

Pulling in behind him, Sonya kept a cautious distance and pulled into a parking space across the aisle with a few large cars buffering hers and the church van. She didn't want to be noticed before she figured out who he might meet and where he would spend the night. When Allen walked around the building, she knew she should have called Walker. Or 911. Let the police end this now.

She waited.

Curiosity tugged at her, and she fondled the door handle, ready to follow him. "Better to wait in the car." She nodded. The only things here were nail and hair shops and a couple of restaurants. The Hibachi place wasn't bad. Allen liked it. The size of the to-go bag would tell her if he'd picked up dinner for one or two. She took the opportunity to get a better view by turning the car around and backing into the space.

Her suspicion was confirmed when he came around the building. That little brunette half-naked hottie was not Charlotte Sellers. No, this was something else entirely. As she pressed the send arrow on a text to Walker Michaels, the car filled with a blue light, darkened, and filled again.

WALKER
MICHAELS

With the most recent location from Connor, who said his mother hadn't moved in more than ten minutes, Michaels directed Jones to turn right at the light. Connor announced the map showed his mom behind the small shopping plaza or at the orthodontist place behind it. At the entrance to the shared parking lot for the plaza and dental office, they turned in, and Michaels yelled for Jones to stop.

He'd found her.

Relief swelled his heart, and his mind raced with questions. What was she doing here? Had she hoped to catch Allen in the act of what she needed no proof to accept? Why had she come alone?

Connor's muffled voice cried from the floorboard through the phone's speaker. A new text alert lit the screen. Thoughtlessly flinging the door open, Michaels stepped into the night's darkness. The blue police light striped across his back and reflected off Sonya's windshield. Through the utter surprise in her faintly visible eyes, Walker saw a similar relief to what shone in his.

When she jerked her head from him to her left, he followed her gaze. The silhouette of a man with a short woman in his arms stood beside a late model, unmarked white van with its side door open. As if her body went limp, the woman's posture faltered, and the man steadied her.

Like a Mack semi-truck hitting him at highway speed, he felt the impact of a realization that made his head explode in thought. After the last Moralist killing, a final card was found the next day at the scene. The serial killer had returned after the police withdrew and left a note specifically for *Michaels*. It simply read, "Better luck next time, Walk."

When his sergeant used the unwelcome nickname, his mind hadn't assembled the clues into a conclusion. Four years ago, it was written on the Moralist's note. Allen Rawlings was the second person ever to call him 'Walk.' Or the first person, using the nickname a second time. He had him! If not Sandy's killer, his longtime nemesis.

A glance back toward Sonya found something terrifying behind the windshield. When the blue orb raced over her, it reflected off a long, shiny object underlining her chin.

Plagued by an impossible decision, Michaels watched Allen Rawlings, the Moralist, drop his next victim inside the van and slide the side door shut. He had seconds to apprehend the notorious serial killer. To save the next girl's life. Faster than Doc Holliday in a draw, he had his weapon out and aimed at the windshield of the not-quite-white Prius.

"Drop the knife!" Michaels heard a commotion by the van but kept his eyes sharp and his aim true. "I said drop the knife, *Peter*. Let her go."

As the blue light raced by again and again, Michaels tried to see more than Sonya's face and the deadly blade at her throat. Jones' muffled voice shouted something in the distance. Sonya's door cracked open, and the blade pulled left. The pop rang in Michaels' ear.

BRANDON
JONES

Connor's diluted shouting and the glow of a message alert pulled Jones' attention to the passenger side floorboard. A text from Sonya Rawlings on Michaels' phone.

It's him! Allen is the Moralist! He's behind Jonny's Pizza on Dallas Hwy. Come quick.

Logic congealed the scene in the young detective's mind. The Action Board, the revelations from the M.E., interviews with the Rawlings and members of their church, and Allen Rawlings' outrageous and violent behavior now added up. In that split second, it all came together.

Rawlings had killed those eleven young women and taken a hiatus as he delt with his own daughter passing through the same turbulent and immoral world as a teenager. A new killer, a copycat, had taken the reins. Peter Miller was at large, but with a statewide All Points Bulletin on him, he'd soon be in custody. Jones could not yet see why he'd started with his best friend's daughter.

Michaels stood like a statue, not running after the serial killer he had pursued for seven years. Hidden by the line of parked cars between him and the white van, Jones hurried through the grass median. Rawlings was seconds from turning this into a highspeed chase. Academy training flashed through his mind. If the Moralist took off in the van before Jones got him, he'd be no match for the Tesla and Jones' pursuit-driving skills.

The sliding door slammed, and Rawlings moved around the van.

Crouched and moving quickly while trying to keep the noise of his approach from the killer's ears, Jones advanced to the front of the vehicle.

"Freeze, scumbag."

Startled, Rawlings threw a wild punch. Using the momentum, Jones twisted Allen's arm around his back and slammed him face-first into the side of the van. The rapid *thip* of the zip tie clicks as Jones cinched Allen's wrists brought him deep satisfaction.

Thoughts racing through his mind centered not on his career. Nor on the accolades catching the man who gave every teenage girl in Cobb County horrifying nightmares would bring him. The death of his daughter had resurrected the Moralist in Allen Rawlings, and the killings were about to start again. His next victim lay drugged inside the van. Alive.

Jones and Michaels had acted to save countless young lives from a delusional zealot. A madman. In that moment, that fact gave him victory. As he again slammed Allen into the side of the van, he realized that was the validation of his work and what truly mattered.

The echo of a gunshot scorched the air.

WALKER
MICHAELS

T he tiny hole in the windshield etched a spiderweb through the glass, catching the passing blue light like lightning, igniting its jagged cracks. Had he hit Peter? Had the knife already done its damage? For the second time this evening, Walker inched forward, step by hesitant step, to find the dead body of Sonya Rawlings. Time slowed to a crawl as the driver's side door pulled away from the car.

Expectantly, he looked at the door full of dings and scratches and noticed the missing sideview mirror. He imagined Sonya's limp, lifeless corpse falling to the ground. Instead, a shaky foot in a white tennis shoe descended and steadied itself on the pavement.

* * *

A saturation of blue lights chased each other around the small parking lot. An officer directed cars leaving the plaza to use the other exit onto Dallas Highway. Handcuffed—Michaels knew they used zip ties but still said *handcuffs*—and being walked to a squad car, Allen Rawlings watched as his wife ran into another man's arms. Never had reading anyone their rights brought the immense satisfaction mirandizing the Moralist infused into Detective Michaels. That Jones had done it didn't diminish his sense of victory—and immense relief.

In leaving the pursuit of the now identified copycat to the uniforms to go protect Sonya, Michaels had closed the case that haunted his dreams and taunted his waking hours. The Moralist, Allen Rawlings, had been apprehended.

In those final moments, Sonya understood it all. Her text to Walker identified her husband as more than an unfaithful cheat and the impassioned killer of a sick little man in a trailer home. She'd gone to catch him in the act of infidelity and found the Moralist. In his honor, following his pattern, another psychotic murderer had taken her daughter and almost killed Sonya.

Walker explained the conclusion that ran him out of her home with a passion in his eyes to catch a killer. Peter Miller, among others at the church, had expressed concerns about Sandy's moral corruption. Peter, however, showed more than a friendly interest in Sonya Rawlings and had been a newly appointed deacon, looking up to Allen Rawlings as a mentor. Assuming he had learned of Allen's alter ego, Michaels concluded he'd continue the work his tutor had begun.

It shocked Michaels to find Mary Miller bleeding in the passenger seat of Sonya's car. The knife lay on the driver's side floorboard and Mary clutched her shoulder with a hand covered in warm crimson blood. She had only nicked the skin on Sonya's neck before taking the bullet from Michaels' gun.

Several questions remained regarding the four-year lapse in killings. Allen had not killed his daughter, but her death, mimicking his own modus operandi, had driven him out of retirement. Mary Miller's motives for killing Sandy Rawlings took longer to ascertain. As did understanding if she had planned to strike again.

Pieces came together in his mind but didn't tell him if Peter was involved or if Mary Miller had acted alone. An A.P.B. went out to Cobb and surrounding counties for Peter Miller—last seen leaving his in-laws after his wife ran out in a hurry. It wasn't needed. The officers at his home found him pulling in, driving a 2025 Dark Gray Dodge Durango.

Michaels had Jones and Bell debrief Mitsy Davis, the young lady who would have been the true Moralist's next victim. Officer Bell showed remarkable potential to make detective and Michaels thought a female officer would make it easier on the terrified young lady on what could have been her last night alive.

Mitsy Davis now sat with her feet dangling out of the back of the Ambulance. When Michaels went to meet her, Sonya tagged along. Hoping an EMT would look at her neck wound, he allowed it. The woman who had lost her own daughter to a psychotic killer who copied her husband's horrific methods leaned in, wrapped the young lady in a firm embrace, and cried over her. Walker knew the tears were as much for Sandy's passing as for the spared life of Mitsy Davis.

A life Sonya had saved.

SONYA
RAWLINGS

S team escaped and hissed as she prepared the third and fourth espressos. On an elegant cassia wood serving tray, she placed the sugar bowl and four espresso cups on saucers holding tiny spoons. Sonya carefully walked to the table, set the tray down, and handed her parents and Walker their coffees. Knowing his sweet tooth when it came to coffee, she set the sugar bowl in front of the detective.

As she sat, took the fourth cup, and sipped her espresso, Connor came running down the stairs. He flung the refrigerator open and pulled out a bottle of Coke. After kissing his mother's cheek and the top of his grandmother's head, he took a seat next to his grandfather.

"Thank you for coming here, Walker. I dreaded going to the police station, and I'm sorry to say, I don't much care for Starbucks. Not since our trip to Italy, anyway."

"It's no bother. I can only imagine what these last few days have been like for you, all of you. And last night was a late and difficult night. I know it's not likely, but I hope y'all got some sleep."

"I did," Connor declared before guzzling his Coke.

Beyond exhausted from the trip and staying up late into the night, Sonya knew her parents had slept. Her father wouldn't have made it down before Walker arrived if she hadn't sent Connor to wake him.

"Before you start, I'm sure there are things you'll say you cannot tell us. So…" She looked at her parents and then focused her gaze on her son. "No questions. Let's hear what the detective has to say."

Walker dumped two heaping demitasse spoonfuls of sugar into his cup, ruining his espresso. He stirred longer and more vigorously than the fine crystals needed to dissolve, set the tiny spoon on the saucer, and sipped.

In greater detail than Sonya expected, the detective expounded the case against Mary Miller first. She had shocked him by "singing like a canary," as he described it, during her interrogation this morning. The detective said he sensed pride in her confession. Last night, when Peter glanced at his phone to see a routine *Ring* doorbell alert, his eyes bulged. He showed Mary his phone, the police at their front door. She knew "the jig was up," as Walker expressed it, and called Sonya when Allen didn't answer his phone or reply to her messages.

Looking at Sonya, Walker said, "As you were leaving, she received your text."

"I replied by text, explaining I was going to find Allen. Of course, I had no idea of Mary's motivation at the time. As I pulled out of the driveway, Mary phoned again."

"And you almost hit our black and white outside."

Sonya shrugged. "She said she had called to check on me. When I texted that I had gone to find Allen, she was concerned about me going after him alone."

Connor crushed the empty plastic bottle in his hand. "How'd she end up in your car?"

"I don't know why, but I told her where I was... still driving. I was shocked when she told me she suspected he and Charlotte were back together and that I shouldn't go alone. I was so embarrassed anyone else knew about Allen's..." With reddened cheeks, Sonya cleared her throat. "Infidelity. Someone from our church, no less. It was so humiliating. But I guess I liked the idea of having someone with me. Of course, I didn't tell her Allen had killed someone."

"And she met you somewhere?" Connor asked.

"I told her I followed the AirTag in Allen's car, and it looked like we were headed to the old church."

Walker finished his espresso and set the cup down as if afraid to break it. "Miller said she figured out Allen was the Moralist some time back. Toward the end, I mean, of those last killings. Her husband had told her he was with Allen working on the old church van. She didn't buy the alibi." Folding his hands together, he continued, "Said she knew Peter had gone to check on *you* since you had told her Allen had been out of town on business."

"He often did that. I thought it a kindness. I had no idea it bothered Mary."

"She told me she hated how he's always looked at you, ever since you set her up with him. And she said he claimed he was just looking out for a friend's family. While it upset her, she knew you would never be unfaithful to your husband."

"Excuse me, Detective," Sonya's mother politely said. "Is that church van the vehicle Allen used to… do those things?"

"Yes, ma'am. On the night of the last killing, Missus Miller went to the old church to debunk Peter's story. As she pulled up, she spotted the van leaving and followed it to Oregon Park. She watched as a man pulled a large black object from the van. When she followed, she saw someone laying out the body. Mary trailed him back to the parking lot. As the van was pulling away, thanks to a streetlamp, she saw Allen's face clearly." Walker sat back in his chair and smiled. "On top of all the other evidence we've been able to gather, we've got an eyewitness that cements this case."

Sonya remembered the article she read about that last murder. "Do you believe Mary Miller is the person you saw at that scene?"

"She was. Being tall and stocky, we assumed she was a man."

"Wait," Connor said with a grimace. "If Mary Miller is telling all this, and she's a witness now in my dad's case, does that mean she's making some plea deal? She killed my sister!"

Sonya reached for his hand, but the table was too long. "She may get some lenience for her cooperation. But she's helping them convict a serial killer who murdered eleven young women."

"Yeah, my father. And I hope he gets all he deserves for what he did. If *he* hadn't... Sandy..."

"I know, sweetheart," she said in a consoling voice.

"Detective, will my granddaughter's killer get off lightly?"

Walker set his eyes upon Sonya's father. "She won't get much leniency, if any. Mary Miller started volunteering information without any offer from us. It's possible she might ask for something in exchange for testifying in court, once she lawyers up. Her husband is standing by her, and they have money."

With unblinking eyes, Sonya asked, "She just volunteered this information about Allen?"

"Yes. See, she believes what your husband did was the Lord's work, and she was following the example of a loyal disciple. I saw no guilt, no shame in her for what she had done. In fact, she seemed happy that Allen was resuming his cleansing work because of her."

Connor said, "If she respected my father... then why... why my sister?"

"In her twisted way, that *is* why. Mary believed your father stopped his cleansing work, the killings, when his own daughter became a teenager and was in jeopardy from the immoral world. After saying something about Abraham, from the Bible, she said she knew a father couldn't do what was needed to save his daughter's soul. So, *she* did it for him."

"Dear God, this is madness." Her mother looked faint, so Sonya got her some water.

"If this is too much..." Walker looked at Sonya reflectively. "I can stop. I know it's a lot."

She nodded for him to continue.

EPILOGUE

I t had been a long time since such a mouthwatering aroma filled his kitchen. Eating lunch out most days at work, he never went out to dinner and rarely ordered takeout. Walker Michaels' culinary skills left much to be desired, but he always managed to feed himself. Never would he have attempted the meal he could not wait to dig into now.

As he placed the good plates on the table, he blew out a deep breath. It had been four months since his labored exhalations had come from dread and exhaustion, working the resurfaced case that had nearly ruined his marriage and his relationship with his daughter. Now he sighed with joyful expectation.

Looking at the ancient grandfather clock in the dining room, he set the forks and knives—he had been shown the proper way to do it— at each of the four plates and hoped she wouldn't be late. The clank of the latch on the chain-link fence and the squeak of the gate opening chased away the momentary worry.

The rhythmic pounding of his *grandkids'* paws traveled along the side of the house and into the backyard. When the bell rang, he was already opening the door. Bonnie smiled, reached up to wrap her arms around his neck, and kissed his cheek.

"Smells amazing." Though he never asked, she removed her shoes.

Mike entered behind her and did the same. "Sir."

His son-in-law was the only one he allowed to call him 'sir.' 'Walker' was too awkward. 'Michaels' too formal. And 'Dad' didn't feel right to either of them. A good man, Mike made his daughter happy, so he was all right as far as Michaels was concerned. When they were first engaged, he teased his daughter over the Freudian irony of Bonnie Michaels marrying a guy named Michael. For love or fear, he hadn't mentioned it since. After taking their coats, he led them into the dining room.

"Dad, I can tell from the aroma *you* didn't cook." She studied the table. "And there are four *properly arranged* place settings."

The evening's chef came from the kitchen holding a serving tray with a perfectly cooked crust over a glorious Beef Wellington and said, "Hello."

"Sweetheart, I'd very much like you to meet Sonya."

THANK YOU!

I hope you enjoyed this crime thriller. No matter how good a story is, we engage with it when we care about the characters, can relate to their struggles, challenges, growth, and change. Do you know others who would enjoy this novel?

A brief review helps readers find this story and takes only a few seconds. Thank you so much for your support and opinion. Use the direct link to post your review or scan the QR code.

https://link.glassauthor.com/moralist

OTHER BOOKS BY THE AUTHOR

To Gaze Upon a Darkened Cloud

Blending heart-pounding suspense with profound questions about faith, family, and the future of humanity, To Gaze Upon a Darkened Cloud is a visionary tale of survival and transcendence. Will humanity cling to the world it knows, or embrace the unknown beckoning from within the storm? The answer lies in the heart of the tempest.

Finding Idyllium: Earth's Stolen Future

Earth is dying. His daughter is dying. The parallel world of Idyllium is her only hope. Marc must make her end justify his means. A covert mission to save Earth's billions clashes with the fate of a pristine parallel world. From politician to soldier to civilian, ethical lines blur. Loyalties are challenged. The order to assassinate Idyllium's key political leader forces Marc to take desperate turns, dividing members of his team.

Sci-Fi Shorts: Speculative Fiction, Alternative History, UFO Throwback Satire

1 – A desperate time jumper must find a way to bend the laws of physics to avoid being torn from the family he irresponsibly created.

2 – President Kennedy survives his assassination attempt, only to discover that fate itself is now his greatest enemy, and the price of his life is being paid by others.

3 – In a satirical homage to a cult classic, discover the backup plans to "Plan 9 from Outer Space" and find out just how badly an alien intervention can go.

Overlap: The Lives of a Former Time Jumper

What if you had the power to redo your life, and it only made things worse? Marcus repeatedly relives his life when he discovers the overlap. In "normal time" he lives alone, grief and regret his constant companions. Now, Marcus unveils the dark secrets of time jumping to a reporter who holds revelations of her own that could shatter his understanding of reality—again.

The New Europa trilogy

Gift Ojo is relentlessly optimistic. As gnawing doubts are stirred by conspiracy theories and whispers grow into a deafening din, discontent sprouts sabotage, threatening New Europa. When the world expands into something Gift and her friends never imagined, with the marvels come new and horrific tests of their humanity. Gift's journey brings her to the brink of all-out war. Will she have what it takes to stand against her people and find her choice?

books.glassauthor.com

ABOUT THE AUTHOR

Reading is a passion. Writing is an obsession.

B orn and raised in Brooklyn, NY, I live and write in Milan, Italy. As an independent author, I invest in my writing by working with coaches, using beta readers, polishing every manuscript with professional human editors, and finishing with a proofreader. Added to my passion for crafting stories, this offers you quality books that are enjoyable reading and often provide a thought-provoking experience.

I love to expound stories that are driven by relatable characters on meaningful journeys. Drawing from personal experience enriches the writing process and leaves readers feeling like they know the characters they spend time with immersed in a story. That human connection between my characters, readers, and myself, fuels my drive as an author.

Optimistic views of the future through art always interest me, as I believe ours will be bright.

glassauthor.com